- REVIEWS FOR BOOKS BY TROY TAYLOR -

"Troy Taylor's Season of the Witch is the best and most thorough examination of one of America's most famous and colorful hauntings... an engrossing, entertaining and informative read that you won't find anywhere else!"
ROSEMARY ELLEN GUILEY, Ph.D., AUTHOR OF THE ENCYCLOPEDIA OF GHOSTS & SPIRITS

"Season of the Witch is not a book for the faint of heart! Through his tireless research and mastery of the art of storytelling, Troy Taylor transports the reader back in time and into the frightening world of the creature known as the Bell Witch ... it's a legend that only Troy Taylor can bring to life!"
DAVID GOODWIN, AUTHOR OF "GHOSTS OF JEFFERSON BARRACKS"

"Season of the Witch packs a supernatural wallop from page one to the witchingly intriguing ending! Tennessee's most famous case is brought to light in a frightening accurate manner by one of America's foremost paranormal authors. The book is a well written and researched journey into the unknown!"
ROBERT & ANNE WLODARSKI, AUTHORS OF "HAUNTED ALCATRAZ" & "CALIFORNIA HAUNTSPITALITY"

"Season of the Witch is the best documented and most definitive work of the Bell Witch to date! Mr. Taylor has outdone himself in researching and collecting the material necessary to thoroughly examined and address this most mysterious tale ... I highly recommend this book to anyone interested in the full story of the Bell Witch!"
DALE KACZMAREK, AUTHOR OF "WINDY CITY GHOSTS"

Ghost Books by Troy Taylor

HAUNTED ILLINOIS (1999 / 2001)
SPIRITS OF THE CIVIL WAR (1999)
THE GHOST HUNTER'S GUIDEBOOK (1999 / 2001)
SEASON OF THE WITCH (1999/ 2002)
HAUNTED ALTON (2000)
HAUNTED NEW ORLEANS (2000)
BEYOND THE GRAVE (2001)
NO REST FOR THE WICKED (2001)
HAUNTED ST. LOUIS (2002)

THE HISTORY & HAUNTINGS SERIES
I. THE HAUNTING OF AMERICA (2001)
II. INTO THE SHADOWS (2002)

HAUNTED DECATUR (ILLINOIS) SERIES
HAUNTED DECATUR (1995)
MORE HAUNTED DECATUR (1996)
GHOSTS OF MILLIKIN (1996 / 2001)
WHERE THE DEAD WALK (1997 / 2002)
DARK HARVEST (1997)
HAUNTED DECATUR REVISITED (2000)
FLICKERING IMAGES (2001)
VAUDEVILLE, MOVING PICTURES & GHOSTS (2002)

GHOSTS OF SPRINGFIELD (1997)
GHOST HUNTER'S HANDBOOK (1997 / 1998)
GHOSTS OF LITTLE EGYPT (1998)

SEASON OF THE WITCH

HISTORY & HAUNTINGS OF THE BELL WITCH OF TENNESSEE
BY TROY TAYLOR

- A WHITECHAPEL PRODUCTIONS PRESS PUBLICATION -

This book could not have been written without the friendship and support of the Kirby Family of Adams, Tennessee. This book is dedicated to Chris, Walter and Candy with special thanks for the way they opened their home and property to me and welcomed me into the strange and mysterious world of the Bell Witch. Special thanks also goes to Bob Schott, Pat Fitzhugh and to Richard Winer, who first introduced me to this distinctly American haunting.
And of course, thanks and much love to my wonderful wife, Amy, who continues to make not only books like this one possible - but everything else as well. And finally to my daughter, Margaret, who I hope will someday be as fascinated by the Bell Witch as I am!

Original Art & Photography by Troy & Amy Taylor

All other photographs and Illustrations are credited to the Owner in the Text, including illustrations from the book *Authenticated History of the Bell Witch* by M.V. Ingram (1894)

Original Cover Artwork Designed by

Michael Schwab, M & S Graphics & Troy Taylor
Visit M & S Graphics at www.msgrfx.com
Back Cover Photograph by Michael Schwab

This Book is Published by
~ Whitechapel Productions Press ~

A Division of the History & Hauntings Book Co.
515 East Third Street - Alton, Illinois -62002
(618) 465-1086 / 1-888-GHOSTLY
Visit us on the Internet at www.prairieghosts.com

First Printing of Second Edition - July 2002
ISBN: 1-892523-05-1

Printed in the United States of America

In some cases, poltergeists have revealed a conscious intelligence behind their activities... the Bell Witch is a prime example of this type of ghostly activity. For a period of four years, it tortured and persecuted the Bell family of Tennessee with unrelenting fury... even General Andrew Jackson came to see if the unpleasant tales he had heard about the Bell Witch were true. They were.

SUSY SMITH IN PROMINENT AMERICAN GHOSTS

Although the story of the Bell Witch is considered by some to be no more than a legend, many folks in Robertson County and elsewhere in Tennessee, not only believe that the Bell Witch did exist, but that she, or it, still roams, haunts and terrorizes the countryside.

RICHARD WINER IN HAUNTED HOUSES

Whether the hauntings take place in Sumatra, South Africa, or New York, the behavior patterns of ghosts are monotonously similar. There are, however, a few exceptional occurrences and among the most bizarre is the story of the Bell Witch who exerted malignant power in Tennessee during the nineteenth century. The tale has been called by Dr. Nandor Fodor "America's greatest ghost story"....

ROBERT SOMERLOTT IN HERE, MR. SPLITFOOT

It should be obvious that the conception of the poltergeist as a fun-loving prankster is an erroneous one. The intelligence that directs the phenomena is motivate more often by malice than by mischief. Although physical violence toward a certain member of the family is characteristic of several poltergeist cases, there is only one recorded instance where the poltergeist was actually responsible for murder.
On December 19, 1820, John Bell was poisoned by the "witch" that had inhabited their home for four years.

BRAD STEIGER IN STRANGE GUESTS

As he and his company neared the house.. the wagon suddenly stopped fast in its tracks. The driver lashed the horses, but not an inch they would move. General Jackson ordered the men to put their shoulders to the wheel.. but they could not budge the wagon. After awhile, General Jackson threw up his hands and said: "By the Eternal, it's the witch!"
Then a voice came from the bushes beside the road, saying: "All right, General, let the wagon move on. I will see you again to-night."
General Jackson said: "By the Eternal, boys, this is worse than fighting the British."

IDA CLYDE CLARKE IN ANDREW JACKSON GOES GHOST HUNTING
FROM THE BOOK MEN WHO WOULDN'T STAY DEAD

- TABLE OF CONTENTS -

THE JOHN BELL HOUSE

THE JOHN BELL HOMESTEAD AS IT LOOKED AROUND 1817. THE COMING OF THE WITCH, AND THE YEARS OF HORROR THAT FOLLOWED, WERE ONLY MONTHS AWAY.

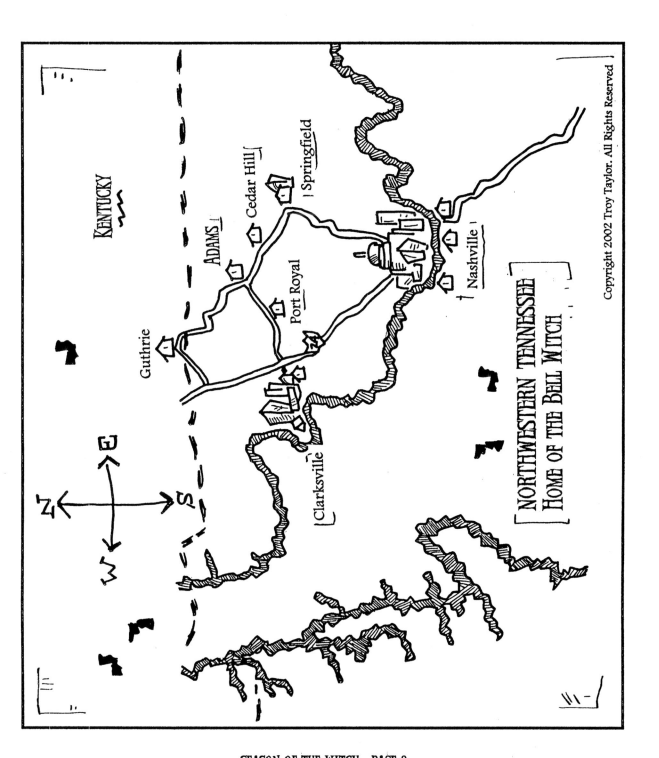

NORTHWESTERN TENNESSEE
HOME OF THE BELL WITCH

- INTRODUCTION -

- BELL WITCH -

To the north was the farm of John Bell, an early prominent settler from North Carolina. According to legend, his family was harried during the early 19th century by the famous Bell Witch. She kept the household in turmoil, assaulted Bell, and drove off Betsy Bell's suitor. Even Andrew Jackson, who came to investigate, retreated to Nashville after his coach wheels stopped mysteriously. Many visitors to the house saw the furniture crash about them and heard her shriek, sing and curse.

THE TEXT OF SIGN PLACED IN FRONT OF THE BELL SCHOOL ON HIGHWAY 41 IN ADAMS, TENNESSEE. IT WAS PLACED BY THE TENNESSEE HISTORICAL COMMISSION.

Neither this book, nor the original first edition of it, were the first books to be written about the spirit known as the Bell Witch of Tennessee. Most likely, they will not the last books to be written either. Over the years, dozens of authors have tried their hand at telling the strange events that occurred on the Bell family farm in the early 1800's, often with both mixed and fascinating results.

Unfortunately, because such a long period of time has passed since the mysterious happenings took place, authors and researcher like myself have had to depend on earlier books and articles for information about the haunting. It's true that some of the accounts of the "witch" were penned by members of the Bell family, and that many of those whose words were set to paper were actual witnesses to the horrifying events, but even so - the first complete book to ever appear about the haunting came as late as 1894.

This was not the first account of the Bell Witch to appear in writing though. That honor goes to a brief record that appeared in the *Goodspeed History of Tennessee* in 1886. However, this account has been attributed by some to have been the writing of Martin Van Buren Ingram, who published the first book on the case in 1894. Although a very obscure title at the time it appeared, Ingram's book has been considered the best account of the events at the Bell farm. He completed the book in 1893 but had not received permission to publish a diary that is contained in it until the death of Joel Egbert Bell, the last surviving Bell child, in 1890.

The book, which was called *An Authenticated History of the Famous Bell Witch, the Wonder of the 19th Century, and Unexplained Phenomenon of the Christian Era. The Mysterious Talking Goblin that Terrorized the West End of Robertson County, Tennessee, Tormenting John Bell to his Death. The Story of Betsy Bell, Her Lover and the Haunting Sphinx* (we'll refer to this as the *Authenticated History* for short!), was published in February 1894. A few thousand copies of the book were printed in Chicago and the illustrations were all engraved in St. Louis. Ingram sold the books through subscriptions, which was a common practice in the book business of the time.

The book is considered the best accounting of the case because it contains the diary of Richard Williams Bell, who titled his own account, *Our Family Troubles*. Richard was only six years old at the time when the haunting began, ten years old by the time it ended and eighteen when the spirit returned a second time in 1828. The events apparently left a vivid impression upon him for they were considered to be accurate by living witnesses that Ingram managed to interview for his own portions of the book.

But how accurate was the rest of the book? Despite the numerous subtitles of the book, which catered to the lurid sensationalism of a time when Spiritualism was at the height of its popularity, Ingram enjoyed an excellent reputation as a newspaper editor and upstanding citizen. He was intimately acquainted with the story and went to the trouble of tracking down as many witnesses as he could.

Ingram had been born in Montgomery County in 1832 but grew up in and around Robertson County, where the wife and children of John Bell were still living at the time. He often heard of the story and later in life married a woman who was directly related to the Bell family. His friendship with the family, especially Joel Egbert Bell (the youngest son of John Bell) and State Representative James Allen Bell (John's grandson), gained him access to the diary written by Richard Williams Bell (James Allen Bell's father) in 1846. Technically, this is the first written account of the Bell Witch, although it was never seen outside of the family until it was given to Ingram. He applied as early as 1867 for permission to print the diary but this was refused until the death of Joel Bell in 1890.

The reason for this was simple - the family wanted the story to be told accurately, but not until after the last of the characters in the drama were gone. James Allen Bell wrote to Ingram and told him that his father had always wanted the story of the "family troubles" to be preserved and to be told accurately in later years. "So many painfully abhorrent misrepresentations had gone out concerning the mystery that he [Richard Williams Bell] desired the writing should be preserved, that the truth might be known in after years, should the erroneous views which had found lodgment concerning the origin of the distress continue to live on through traditions, handed down to an enlightened generation under a version so disparaging."

Bell's letter refers to accusations of fraud that were directed toward Betsy Bell, around whom most of the strange events revolved. In 1849, an exposure story had appeared in the *Saturday Evening Post* and while the editors later retracted the article, the accusations were apparently hurtful enough to cause Richard Bell to put away his diary and to preserve it so "that the truth might be known in after years".

Ingram continued his association with the Bell family and his interest in the story as his status in the community began to grow. In 1866, he founded the *Robertson Register* newspaper and although he had no experience in the printing business, the paper became quite successful. He was convinced by some local merchants to move his operation to Clarksville and he borrowed enough money to start the *Clarksville Tobacco Leaf* in 1869. Ingram remained with the business through health problems and the great Clarksville Fire in 1878 to finally sell his interest in the paper in 1880. His poor health was further complicated by the premature deaths of several of his children but despite this, he continued to dabble in publishing, producing a special interest newspaper and of course, his *Authenticated History* in 1894. Ingram died on October 9, 1909 at the age of 77. At the time of his passing, *Clarksville Leaf Chronicle* editor, W.W. Barksdale, dedicated the front page and editorial section in Ingram's memory. Such a bold step (which broke all of the rules of newspaper publishing) further enhances Ingram's credibility as an author, journalist and upstanding citizen. Barksdale wrote that Ingram was "a man of true mold, he despised all deceit and trickery, and littleness, and with a courage which nothing could daunt, he laid on the journalistic lash unsparingly whenever he thought the occasion required."

What better sort of person could we ask for to have penned the account of a story that can only be described as incredible, inexplicable and frankly, hard to believe? Ingram's reputation was above question and if he could be convinced by the events of the Bell haunting, then we are forced to put aside some of our own doubts and to approach the events that unfolded with an open mind!

A writer of this caliber would not have, and simply could not have, merely concocted a story like that of the Bell Witch. Not only did Ingram enjoy a solid reputation in the community as a respected journalist, Baptist and Freemason, but official records in Tennessee bear out the accuracy of the names, dates and events that are written about in his book. All of the people that he interviewed confirmed that the people in the story were real and were living in Robertson County at the time of the haunting. For this reason, Ingram's *Authenticated History* remains the most historically significant of the books about the Bell Witch haunting.

The next record of the Bell Witch was a pamphlet that was published in 1930 by Harriet Parks Miller and entitled *The Bell Witch of Middle Tennessee*. Truthfully, this small booklet would likely be forgotten today if not for the fact that it was later reprinted in a single volume with an account by Dr. Charles Bailey Bell. The reprinting was done in

1972 by Charles Elder and the two accounts were given the single title of *The Bell Witch of Tennessee*. This black bound volume is one of the most commonly found Bell Witch books in existence today.

Miller's 1930 pamphlet (as well as Bell's 1934 book) was published in response to the legend that the Bell Witch would return to Robertson County in 107 years, or at some point in the middle 1930's. A number of stories and newspaper articles appeared throughout the south during this time, despite the fact that no credible witnesses ever came forward to say that the spirit had returned. Miller's pamphlet offers little more than anecdotes of the Bell Witch and within its few pages, she devotes an entire chapter to a similar poltergeist case that occurred in Surrency, Georgia in 1870. It's an odd little booklet and while it offers little new information about the haunting, it would be remiss of me not to mention it while recounting the early Bell Witch material.

In 1934, another official record of the case was published by Dr. Charles Bailey Bell, which was entitled *The Bell Witch: A Mysterious Spirit*. Bell was a well-known doctor in the 1920's and 1930's, having been an instructor on the brain and nervous system at the Medical Department of the University of Nashville and a staff member of the Nashville City Hospital. He was also a member of the Tennessee State Medical Association and other medical organizations, making him (like M.V. Ingram) another upstanding citizen with much to lose if it was ever considered likely that he was engaged in some sort of trickery or a hoax. The difference with Dr. Bell however is that he was removed from the story much further than Ingram was, even though he was a member of the Bell family. He did not interview those who saw the events in the case first hand but rather passes along second-hand stories through his father, who received the stories from his own father. The only exception to this is his interview with Elizabeth Bell, which took place when she was quite elderly, but which makes the book a rare treasure.

There are both worthwhile points and drawbacks to Dr. Bell's book. First, it should be noted that this is really the first official Bell accounting of the case. Dr. Bell notes in his preface that his father and other members of the family protested vigorously against the publication of Ingram's book, not believing that 1894 was the right time for any account to appear about the family's past troubles. Dr. Bell tells the story of the haunting through recollections that were passed on to him by his father, Dr. Joel Thomas Bell, who in turn received his information from his father, John Bell Jr., one of the important principals in the story.

Joel Thomas Bell was the oldest son of John Jr., having been born in Robertson County in 1831. He later studied medicine at the University of Nashville and then opened a practice in Robertson County, just a few hundred yards away from the old Bell farm. He cared for the people of Adams and the surrounding area for more than 50 years and passed away in 1910. He was highly respected by his patients and friends and the younger Dr. Bell noted that he was remembered by people in Robertson County with "genuine pleasure." Joel Thomas Bell was not known for being a superstitious man, which is carefully noted in the book, and he never really told anyone what he thought of the stories that plagued his family. He expressed the hope to a few close friends, and to his son, that someday the haunting would finally be understood though. He also told his son that he believed Richard Williams Bell's manuscript to be true and accurate, based on his own father's accounting of the strange events.

John Bell Jr. was 24 years-old at the time when the haunting began and would have made an excellent witness if he had written a journal or had provided some other form of direct testimony for Dr. Bell's book. Unfortunately, we only have his testimony as given through that of his son, Joel Thomas Bell, but it is compelling nonetheless and it does provide another side to the events and one that has to be studied closer by anyone who searches for a better understanding of the haunting.

But one thing that Dr. Bell's book can boast and that can be found in no other, is direct testimony from Elizabeth Bell, the target of most of the spirit's wrath. Betsy lived to a ripe old age and was interviewed by the author when he was only 19 and she was in her eighties. She gives a graphic first hand account of the spirit's activities and tells of a visit to the farm by General Andrew Jackson, a part of the story omitted by Richard Bell's account but recalled by witnesses that were interviewed by Martin Ingram. Some have disputed whether or not this visit took place but if not, why was it recalled so vividly by Betsy Bell?

Her account jives well with the accounts of others who were living at the time of Ingram's research and goes a long way in establishing the reality of the mysterious visitation by the Bell Witch. The essential facts in the story stand out equally well in the accounts of the local witnesses too, especially concerning places, dates and of course, the horrible death of John Bell. On this basis alone, we have to concede that the various writings of the time are accurate as to the existence of something that defied explanation on the Bell farm.

What was it though? Unfortunately, that is a question that no writings of the past (or the present) can provide a definitive answer for.

Since 1934, many years have passed and there have been numerous books written that have been, in whole or in part, about the Bell Witch. There have been many theories and ideas espoused about who the Bell Witch actually was and why the spirit may have done the things that it did. Some of them have been thought provoking, some of them entertaining and some of them just plain ridiculous. In some cases, the books have been novels that have posed as true accounts, creating confusion and misinformation and have managed to double the work of researchers who delve into the truth of the events. In other cases, we have been given "debunkings" of the haunting by researchers and "experts" who live a continent away or who have never even set foot in the state of Tennessee.

Of course, that isn't to say there have not been some very good modern books that have been written on the subject, including those by Charles Edwin Price and Pat Fitzhugh. However, these well written and well researched titles are not the books that concern me. The books in question fall under the previously mentioned category of "debunkings", written by doctors and paranormalists who believe they have all of the answers when it comes to the Bell Witch.

Such authors simply shake their heads sadly at the gullibility of the local folks and how foolish they have been to ever believe that the Bell Witch could have existed. Or they say that ghosts simply do not behave in the manner that the Bell Witch reportedly did and so they state that poor Betsy Bell must have been responsible for all of the events. And worse yet, they are amazed and dumbfounded by the belief that the Bell Witch may have never left Robertson County and that something strange and mysterious still walks the forests and hills of the region.

These self-proclaimed experts refuse to believe - but why?

The reason for their lack of belief is simple. They have never walked the land where it all took place for themselves. They have never been amazed and disconcerted by the shadowy woods and hollows of Robertson County. They have never traveled the quiet back roads at night, wondering what lies beyond the roadway in the darkness. They have never thrilled to the thunder of the Red River after a heavy rain.

And they have certainly never walked into the gloom of the ominous Bell Witch Cave - because if they had, it's likely they would not have remained unbelievers for long!

And that is what makes this book different that many of the other books that have come before. I have walked the same ground where the Bell family once walked. I have stood on the land where there bodies are now buried. I have seen things on that same land that I cannot fully explain - and I have spoken with many others who have also encountered the lingering echoes of the spirit that has been called the Bell Witch.

However, I must add that I do not have *all* of the answers about the Bell Witch. The case remains an enigma to me, although I do have some ideas to present about what this strange spirit may have been and where it may have come from. To get to that point though, I won't try to convince you that the Bell Witch was not real or that the events that occurred on the Bell farm were the products of a young girl's mind. I will leave that to the debunkers and to those who have never come to Adams, Tennessee and who feel that they *do* have *all* of the answers.

I want to do something different with this account of the story and introduce the reader to what may be an alternate explanation for the haunting. Unless you read the previous edition of this book, you likely will not have been offered this explanation before. I will warn you by saying that it is a controversial theory and one that is perhaps as strange as the story itself. In spite of that, I do believe that it is backed up the facts in the original case.

And I also believe that it just may answer the question as to why supernatural events continue to occur in Robertson County, in Adams and most especially, on the land where the Bell farm once rested. Could a door have been opened in the early 1800's that still remains open, at least partially, today? Think about that question as you begin this book and try to read it with an open mind. I will do my best to present the evidence and then you can reach your own conclusions about what you want to believe.

In the pages ahead, we will go on a journey together back in time, spanning nearly 180 years and traveling to another time and place. Together, we will revisit the haunted history of the Bell Witch, from its first appearance in 1817 and on through the years to the modern era.

As time has passed, the actual events of the case have become a bit hazy with the telling and the re-telling but I hope to perhaps sharpen things up a little bit by reaching back into the earliest accounts of the case. By examining some of the events that occurred on the Bell farm that have been largely forgotten, or have been ignored, we may be able to discover just what the spirit was doing here - and perhaps why it remains! You see, when the Bell Witch departed for the last time in 1828, its time on earth was far from over. For the first time, this book will uncover a number of strange events that seem to show that the legacy of the Bell Witch continues today!

So, take my hand, if you dare, and discover a place where the next world exists just below the surface of this one - and let me introduce you to the terrifying spirit known as the Bell Witch of Tennessee...

Troy Taylor
July 2002

- CHAPTER ONE -
THE DARK & BLOODY GROUND

High on a bluff overlooking the Red River is land that once belonged to a man named John Bell. It is land that is very haunted, even today, by one of the most famous spirits in the history of America, the Bell Witch. Many believe this old story is merely a legend, but to the people of Robertson County, the witch was, and is, very real.
GHOSTS OF THE PRAIRIE

Just across the Tennessee border from Kentucky is the sleepy little town of Adams, Tennessee. This small village has been here for many years and once served as a busy way station for travelers who journeyed on to the larger city of Nashville. Today though, the town is largely forgotten, lying far off the interstate and with only a narrow, curving two-lane highway to connect it to the outside world.

Adams has made its mark in history though, and in a way that few small towns can boast, or likely would care to. This Tennessee town was once the home of one of the most famous ghosts in American history. It was here in the early decades of the 1800's, that the infamous Bell Witch took up residence ~ and many believe has never left.

When the John Bell family came to Tennessee, Robertson County was still very much a frontier region. The settlers lived in rough-hewn cabins and the acres of farmland that exist today were still thick stands of forest. Most considered the area to be wild and dangerous, as Indian attacks were still a not so distant memory and the Red River, a branch of the Cumberland, was much deeper and more frantic than in these modern times.

And while much has changed in this area, some things remain as mysterious as they were years ago. Over 150 caverns, carved by water from Tennessee limestone, have been surveyed in Robertson County, including the enigmatic Bell Witch Cave. Despite this large number, there are hundreds that remain unexplored and many others that still wait to be discovered.

In addition to these natural mysteries, there are also the unnatural mysteries of the region's first inhabitants, the so-called Mound Builders. These curious inhabitants vanished from this land centuries ago, leaving behind only their ruins and their burial sites. One such burial site was located on the land of John Bell, just above the entrance to the cave where the land's mysterious spirit is believed to lurk.

There have been tales of ghosts, hauntings, curses and the dark forces of the supernatural at work in Tennessee for many generations. But what it is about this land that seems to attract such strangeness? Many would say that Tennessee did not gain its fearsome reputation with the arrival of the first settlers, but rather that its dark and tainted character was present long before their coming.

When these first settlers came over the mountains from the east, they found Tennessee to be a rich and wondrous place. This good feeling was in sharp contrast to the beliefs of the Native Americans who arrived here first. They considered the entire region to be cursed. Except for a small part of southeastern Tennessee and parts of Georgia and North Carolina where the Cherokee lived, and portions of Mississippi and southwestern Tennessee that were claimed by the Chickasaw, the entire region of woods, fields, mountains and valleys was virtually empty. The Native Americas simply refused to live here, following a long held custom that this land should be left barren and empty. But why?

The riddle remains unanswered, but some believe that it may have been because of stories that had been passed down through the generations of the ancient tribes that once lived in and hunted the lands. The Mound Builders had established a mighty civilization across the region, only to vanish without a trace, leaving behind the remnants of their culture in the remains of earthen pyramids and massive burial mounds. Why had they left and why had they abandoned their homes and cities, settlements that rivaled those of cities found in Europe at the time? No one knew but the sinister reputation of the land was more than enough to keep it abandoned and unoccupied. Only the white settlers who came were foolish enough to try and occupy the region!

During the early days of the American colonies, the British crown forbid the colonists to settle west of the Appalachian Mountains. By the 1770's though, the colonists were finally daring to go against the laws set forth by their rulers and a large tract of wilderness was purchased from the Native Americans. In 1775, the colonists and the Indians met at Sycamore Shoals, which is now a part of East Tennessee, to exchange the land for a bounty of trade goods. The Cherokee sold an enormous piece of land, most of what is now the Middle South, for blankets, iron goods, whiskey and other items.

However, not all of the Indians agreed to the sale. During the several days of discussion and argument that preceded the settlement, each of the chiefs was given his turn to speak. Most of them were agreeable to selling the white men the empty land but one chief was violently opposed to the sale. His name was Dragging Canoe and he was the nephew of the great leader of the Cherokees, Attakullakulla. This younger man did not share his uncle's desire for peace with the white men and he came to the meeting to condemn their greed and their relentless desire for more and more land. Dragging Canoe stated that the land was sacred and that it would now be defiled by the white man's plow and ax.

"This is the dark and bloody ground!" he shouted and then repeated his words, hoping to impress their meaning upon the other chiefs who were gathered around the fire. Then, he turned and without saying another word, he vanished into the darkness. Murmurs followed him into the shadows and the bewildered white men questioned the Indians as to the meaning of his words. Was it a prophecy, a curse, or a threat? The Indians refused to explain but they were undoubtedly words of doom.

A year later, the great chief Attakullakulla was dead and the very men who sat down around the council fire were at war with one another. The Native Americans and the white settlers were engaged in bloody battle, as the Indians sided with the British troops during the War for Independence. The end of the war did not stop the bloodshed either because over the course of the next 20 years, the Indians fought against the white man's westward expansion through Tennessee. Cabins were burned and women and children were slaughtered and in return, villages were torched and whole tribes were wiped out. The new land to the west had indeed become a "dark and bloody ground".

But even violence and death could not stop the white men from coming west and many of the settlers who came to Tennessee found a rich area in the northwestern part of the state, a piece of land that would come to be called Robertson County.

ROBERTSON COUNTY - BORN IN BLOOD

Located along the edge of the Kentucky border is Robertson County, a fertile section of land that is broken by heavy forests and immense croppings of limestone. The land is crossed by the Red River and Sulphur Fork, both of which empty into the Cumberland River. These ribbons of water, along with Miller's Creek and Buzzard's Creek, have provided local residents with water for tobacco crops and whiskey distilling for generations.

The first settlers came to Robertson County in the late 1700's, after several years of hostilities between the pioneers and the Native Americans in the eastern portions of the region. Following the purchase of the first western lands from the Cherokee Indians, a war broke out as the white settlers began moving into areas where the Indians still held claim. Many of the Indians began to try and take back the lands by force and raids and massacres began taking place all along the frontier. Soon, the Continental Congress placed a bounty on each Indian scalp and frontiersmen and soldiers began attacking and burning the Indian villages. The Cherokee eventually asked for peace.

Some time after the initial land deeds from the Cherokee, in 1778, an explorer named James Robertson led a group of eight men into the wilderness of Tennessee. Their idea was to form a settlement in an area known as French Lick, along the Cumberland River. When they arrived, they established a settlement and Robertson then traveled to the region where Carter County is located today. Here, he recruited families to come to French Lick and by summer's end, there were small settlements scattered up and down the Cumberland River. A fort was built for protection and was called "Nashboro". In 1783, it was renamed as Nashville. In 1796, when Tennessee became a state, the area known as Tennessee County was divided into two portions. One portion would be called Montgomery County and the other would be Robertson County, in honor of James Robertson.

The first settlement in Robertson County was founded by Thomas Kilgore on the Red River, just west of Cross Plains. It was standing about eight months before Robertson arrived at the Cumberland. Kilgore had come west from North Carolina in the spring of 1778, bringing with him little more than ammunition, salt, and a supply of corn. He traveled on foot through the eastern part of Tennessee, meeting no other white men until he reached a place called Bledsoe's Lick. Here, he found a small settlement of six or eight families. He stayed with them for a few days and then continued on for another 25 miles or so. Here, along the Red River, he found a small cave that he believed would make a secure hiding place from any marauding Indians. The mouth of the cave had a small stream running into it from the Middle Fork of the Red River and Kilgore found that he could wade into the cave without leaving a trail behind.

To be able to claim title to the land that he settled, the law stated that Kilgore had to plant a crop here and remain with it until it matured. Soon after taking up residence in his cave, he planted a few hills of corn. He then spent the summer with his crop, having no food or supplies, other than what he could hunt for or forage for in the woods. In the fall, he gathered several ears of the corn that he had grown and he returned to North Carolina, where he gained the legal title to the land.

Kilgore returned to Tennessee in 1779, leading several other families to the area. They established a settlement and a stockaded fort called Kilgore's Station, which remained a landmark in the area for some years to come.

Around 1780 or 1781, another settlement, called Maulding's Station, was built in the vicinity. It was located about four miles west of the Kilgore settlement but came under such constant attack by Indians that it was abandoned and the residents came to live at Kilgore's Station. The first Indian massacres began in 1781 and hostilities escalated throughout the following year, leading to the deaths of a number of settlers in the area.

One notable series of incidents took place that same year when two young men from the fort were watching for deer at Clay Lick and saw a party of Indians approaching. The settlers opened fire and killed two of the Indians, then fled to the fort. During the night, the Indians somehow managed to steal all the horses from the stockade. Pursuit was immediately made, and the settlers followed a trail that led across Sulphur Fork, and up one of its smaller tributaries toward a ridge. Around noon, the pursuers caught up to the thieves on the banks of the stream, fired on them and then stampeded and recovered the horses. Soon, they were on their way back to the fort and stopped at Colgin's Spring for water. Unknown to them, their Indian adversaries had doubled back and they ambushed the white men at the spring. One of the settlers was killed and another fatally wounded.

The hostilities continued and Kilgore's Station was constantly under attack. In fact, conditions became so bad that even this once secure fort was abandoned and the residents joined another nearby settlement. They remained there until 1783.

The following year, the fort was occupied once again, as the number of settlers was bolstered by new arrivals. It remained a safe harbor on the frontier for several more years, until the Indian attacks finally ceased and an uneasy truce was reached. At this point, the population of Kilgore's Station began to dwindle and the pioneers went in many separate directions, forming their own independent settlements.

Thomas Kilgore, the founder of the fort, and one of Tennessee's first adventurers, lived to be 108 years old. He lived just long enough to see his wild frontier become the most western territory of the fledgling United States.

Prior to this, the Indian troubles in Robertson County continued until around 1794. The forts in the area had become the havens around which all settlements were built. There were a number of them constructed, extending west from Kilgore's Station to an area that is now Clarksville. More settlers came and a one man, Ezekiel Polk, grandfather of President Polk, built a home on Sulphur Fork, about three miles south of what would become Adams Station. He was the first to settle the area near the present-day site of Adams. The Indians were so hostile that he remained only about a year.

In 1788, Samuel Crockett built a small fort in the region that came to serve as a strategic defensive position during the Indian troubles. There were a number of settlers in the area and during the hostilities, the women and children were sent away to larger forts while the men stayed at the Crockett block-house to guard the crops and livestock. Even with these precautions though, a young woman and one of the men, Patrick Martin, were killed by the Indians.

In the same year that Crockett came to the area, the Fort family started a settlement on the north side of Red River, near where Adams is now located. Others who came to live in the area over the next few years are men whose names will be recalled again during our accounting of the "Bell Witch" saga. They include John and James Johnston, Thomas and James Gunn, Corbin Hall, Jesse Gardner, Isaac Menees and, of course, John Bell.

Commerce in the area began with the many local streams, which provided ample water-power and invited the construction of mills. The first was probably built by Thomas Kilgore on the middle fork of the Red River, just northwest from Cross Plains. It was constructed some time between 1785 and 1790. At a little later date, another mill was erected by Thomas Woodard on Beaver Dam Creek. It is also recorded that Major Charles Miles erected a water-mill on Sulphur Fork as early as 1793.

During the first 50 years after the settlement of the county, cotton was a crop of some importance. Nearly every farmer raised enough to clothe his own household, and after the invention of the cotton gin, larger quantities were produced and shipped to areas in the north. About 1830 however, the cultivation of cotton began to decline, and it was not long until its production practically ceased. It would soon be replaced by tobacco, which is a common crop in the area today.

The manufacturing of whiskey was always an important industry in Robertson County as well. In the early days, small home distilleries could be found in almost every hollow. These small operations never produced more than 30-40 gallons at one time and manufactured whiskey by what is known as the sour-mash process. This type of whiskey has since become famous and that which is distilled in Tennessee is considered the best in the nation.

While the early days of the area were certainly filled with violence, bloodshed and danger, there were also events that occurred that were often too mysterious for the settlers to understand. One such event was the terrifying coming of the Bell Witch. However, before our journey through the history of Robertson County comes to an end, it should also be noted that the Bell Witch was not the only ghost who was said to linger on the dark side of the region.

In 1799, a man named Elisha Cheek came to Robertson County. He settled along the Red River, near the Sumner County line. Cheek was an "octoroon" meaning that he was a portion African-American, although he had a white wife and had brought with him a number of slaves from Virginia.

He purchased about 400 acres of land near the river, where he built a mill and distillery. His land happened to be in a prime location on the road between Louisville and Nashville, so he also constructed a hotel that he called "Cheek's Stand". The hotel became a welcoming haven for the many travelers and traders who journeyed north from New Orleans each week. Many of them, weighted down with the Spanish coins that made up the proceeds of the their sales, returned from New Orleans by the overland route. Not surprisingly, as they traveled along a route that was perilous with thieves and bandits, many of these traders did not make it home alive.

Located on Cheek's land was a large cave, which was not only unexplored, but was thought to be very deep and treacherous as well. One night, all of the dogs in the neighborhood began barking and howling and the next morning were found gathered around Cheek's cavern. The locals attempted to drive them away, but met with no success. Occasionally, the animals would return home for food, but always came right back to the mouth of the cave. One of the men who tried to send the dogs away noticed that there was a strange animal among the pack that he had never seen before. This dog refused to leave the cave entrance. The neighborhood dogs remained outside the cave for twelve days before they finally returned to their homes. Only one dog remained behind - the strange animal that no one recognized. Eventually, the dog had died from hunger.

What was the mystery behind the cave? What was inside that so interested the dogs? None of the local men dared to venture into the cavern, but they all had their own ideas as to the mystery. It was rumored that Cheek had murdered one of the wealthy traders who had stayed the night at his hotel and that his body had been dropped into the cave to conceal the crime. It was said that a man riding a horse, with a dog following him, had been seen near the hotel on the same night when the disturbance with the dogs began. The mysterious rider was not seen again after that evening.

From that point on, the residents of the area regarded the cavern with wonder and fear and many claimed the ghost of the murdered man was often seen in the vicinity. They reported seeing the wretched spirit wandering about near the mouth of the cave. Rumors about Elisha Creek spread through the region and soon business at his hotel dropped off as travelers began to speak of ghosts, murder and death.

Cheek died a few years later and it is interesting to note that in the years following the incident with the pack of dogs, the hotel owner never ventured near the old cavern on his property again. And he was never seen outside of his house after darkness had fallen either ~ perhaps fearing that vengeance might be visited upon him by the man who was slain years before.

And while tales of murdered travelers and haunted caves were certainly fodder for camp fire ghost stories in Robertson County in the early 1800's, they could do little to prepare the residents of the area for the events that were to come a few years later. The year 1817 would become known as the "year the witch came" to Robertson County and the region would never be the same again!

- CHAPTER TWO -
THE COMING OF
THE WITCH

"A remarkable occurrence, which attracted wide-spread interest, was connected with the family of John Bell, who settled near what is now Adams Station about 1804. So great was the excitement that people came from hundreds of miles around to witness the manifestations of what was popularly known as the "Bell Witch." A volume might be written concerning the performances of this wonderful being, as they are now described by contemporaries and their descendants. That all this actually occurred will not be disputed, nor will a rational explanation be attempted. It is merely introduced as an example of superstition, strong in the minds of all but a few in those times, and not yet wholly extinct."
GOODSPEED'S HISTORY OF TENNESSEE, 1886

John Bell was born in Halifax County, North Carolina in 1750. He was a descendant of Scottish immigrants who first landed in New England and then came south to North Carolina, taking advantage of land grants being offered by England. John's grandfather, Arthur, and his father, William, established themselves as planters in Halifax, Nash and Edgecombe Counties. John was considered to be a hard-working young man and was apprenticed in the cooper (barrel-making) business as a boy, but chose to become a farmer instead.

In 1782, Bell married Lucy Williams, the daughter of a prosperous businessman named John Williams, of Edgecombe County. Lucy was described as being a very "handsome, winsome lady, possessing those higher qualities of mind and heart which go to make up that lovely female character she developed all through life." Lucy's father apparently approved of the marriage and he presented the couple with two slaves as a wedding gift, a maid named Chloe and her child, Aberdean. This young man, later known simply as "Dean", would become the most valuable slave on the Bell farm.

Shortly after the wedding, using money that he had saved, Bell purchased a small farm in Edgecombe County and he and his wife settled down to raise a family. Most of the Bell land holdings were centered around Tarboro, a settlement located along the Tar River. Here, the Bell family lived for the next 22 years and Lucy Bell bore her husband six children. In addition, Chloe had given birth to eight children of her own, all of whom became servants of the Bell family.

The Bell's began to prosper in the community and John improved his local standing by joining the Union Baptist Church. This church, and other congregations, were supported by the Tar River Association, a religious advancement group that was of great importance to the Baptists. Its likely that Bell made his decision to move to Tennessee based on the relocation of many of his friends from the church, including the Fort family, who had moved to Robertson County and who became influential in the Red River Baptist Church.

In 1804, Bell decided to pull up stakes and move west to the new frontier of Tennessee. Undoubtedly, he was attracted by the promise of cheap, fertile land in this region, as it was being widely advertised by land speculators in the newspapers and reading material of the day. Not only that, many of Bell's friend and acquaintance had already moved west and the family now decided to join them. John Bell was 54 years-old when he and his family came to Robertson County.

At this point, it would be wise to clear up one of the misconceptions about the reasons behind Bell's move from North Carolina to Tennessee. A story that has been told states that Bell left North Carolina either to escape prosecution for the murder of a cruel slave overseer or because his luck turned sour after the man's death. Supposedly, the overseer abused the Bell slaves and also took a liking to the Bell's oldest daughter, Esther. Bell and the overseer had many arguments and one day, their dislike for one another turned violent and Bell accidentally killed the man. According to the legend, the Bell's fortunes turned after the murder and John Bell was soon broke. He then moved to Tennessee to start over again.

Obviously, this story is ridiculous as there is no record of it and it's doubtful that a man of Bell's standing could have escaped legal proceedings by simply moving out of the area. One version of this same story stated that Bell was acquitted of murder charges after pleading self-defense but that the man's ghost was responsible for not only his bad luck in North Carolina - but was the Bell Witch as well! It should be mentioned that Bell was quite well off when he arrived in Tennessee and had the funds to purchase a home and many acres of land.

This legend likely got started because of legal action taken by Bell in May 1820 against a planter named John H. Arnold, who rented a slave from Bell. Arnold had beaten Bell's most valuable slave, Dean, and had wounded his head so badly that he almost died. The affair was eventually settled out of court to Bell's satisfaction. As a humorous aside to this grim incident, it should be noted that Dean told some pretty incredible stories later in life about how the scar on his head had been put there by the Bell Witch!

After arriving in Tennessee, Bell purchased 1000 acres of land on the Red River, about 40 miles north of Nashville and near the settlement that would later be called Adams Station. Although it is not known for sure who previously owned the property that Bell purchased when he came to Robertson County, it was recorded that a home was already located on the land. It's likely that he bought the land from some of his friends from North Carolina, as the property of William Fort and William Johnston were located very close to the Bell farm. The home that later became the focal point of the haunting was purchased by Bell, partially improved, and included out buildings, barns and an orchard. The house itself was a double, one and a half story log cabin and Bell and his sons probably added a number of improvements to it after taking up residence.

The local settlement was a prosperous community at the time and was composed principally of the following families: the Reverends James and Thomas Gunn, who were Methodist ministers; William Johnston and James Johnston, and his two sons, John and Calvin; the Batts, Porter, and Long families; and the Byrn, Gardner, Bartlett, Darden, Gooch, Pitman, Ruffin, Matthews, Morris, Miles, Justice, and Chester families. On the other side of the Red River was the Fort settlement which included families by the name of McGowen; Bourne; Royster; Waters; Gorham; Herring; and others.

According to accounts, there seemed to be little conflict among the early settlers of the region. They established schools and churches together and seemed content in their existence. The only real problems reported were the difficulties in keeping good horses. Apparently, a ring of horse thieves was preying on the region and no legal authorities existed to deal with the situation. So, a man named Nicholas Darning, along with several other area residents, quietly organized a vigilante committee to deal with the thieves. It wasn't long before they had discovered the ring leaders of the operation and found them to be two men of respected families, one of which lived on the Red River below Port Royal and the other a well-known citizen of Kentucky. The regulators took the two men into the dense forest, tied them to tree limbs and then proceeded to whip them with switches. They were then set free but warned that if they were seen again in the area, they would be hanged. Not surprisingly, both men vacated the region at once and started new lives in Louisiana, where they became respected cotton planters and led honorable lives.

The Bell family settled quite comfortably into life in the community. By 1817, they had nine children, seven sons and two daughters, named Jesse, John Jr., Drewry, Benjamin, Esther, Zadok, Elizabeth, Richard Williams and Joel Egbert. Sadly, Benjamin died very young and while Zadok became a brilliant lawyer in Alabama, he passed away at a very early age.

As a few years passed, the family became well known in the area. Nothing but kind words were ever expressed about Lucy Bell, who was loved by everyone. Her home was always open to travelers and the house was a frequent location for social gatherings. John Bell also became a well-liked and much respected man of the community. He was admired by his neighbors and friends and his opinions were often sought out by the men of the area. The wealthy farmer had become one of the leading pillars of the community, but his life was not without personal and financial conflicts.

During the time when the Bell's and other families were settling into the area, several major events occurred that affected the lives of these settlers. In December 1811, a massive earthquake rocked the New Madrid fault and became one of the greatest quakes in American history. A number of towns and communities in the Midwest were destroyed and for a time, the Mississippi River even ran backward. The earthquake had such a physical effect on Tennessee that several lakes were formed during the rumbling that had not existed before. Not long after, tensions with the British erupted again and escalated into the War of 1812. John Bell's oldest sons were called into service with the 2nd Tennessee Regiment under Andrew Jackson to help battle the British in New Orleans.

While these events certainly affected the Bell family, and America as a whole, several events also occurred within the immediate community that had a startling impact on a settlement that was so involved with, and dedicated to, church activities.

After prospering in the community for several years, John Bell became an elder at the Red River Baptist Church, which was presided over by the respected minister and family friend, Sugg Fort. During this period, many religious issues were being discussed that created disharmony within the community. Although this is all difficult for us to understand today, the lives of most of these early settlers were completely centered around the church and it was a major part of their lives. Problems and tensions among the congregation could have an impact on both the personal and social lives of everyone involved.

Many of these issues involved the doctrines of the Red River Baptist Church, which was strictly Calvinist at the time. This principle espoused that God would only save a chosen few for entry into heaven and was generally accepted at this church and many others. However, around 1810, a great debate erupted over the belief system of the church and a new doctrine, known as the Arminian Movement, began to gain in popularity. This movement came from the belief that all men were sinners and that any person could achieve salvation by approaching God and asking forgiveness for his sins. This refuted the ideals of Calvinism and was thought to be blasphemous by older members of the church.

The year that saw the coming of the witch also saw a visit from a minister named Rueben Ross, who came to preach a funeral service at the Red River Baptist Church in July 1817. His sermon had a galvanizing effect on the community and helped to change the views of the local Baptists toward the Arminian Movement. The idea of such a change had troubled local church members for years, despite the fact that Reverend Fort and many other members saw the logic behind it and the conviction of Reverend Ross and others like him. More problems soon arose however as the son of the minister, Josiah Fort, became embroiled with John Bell, and the church, in disputes involving church doctrine, legal and personal matters. The rift between the church and Josiah Fort took many years to heal, although he and John Bell quickly settled their arguments and remained friends.

Bell's problems at this time were not limited to issues concerning church doctrine and personal disagreements though. Just a few months before his problems with Josiah Fort, Bell was accused by the church of usury (charging of excessive interest) involving a slave sale with another local farmer, Benjamin Batts (his sister-in-law was Kate Batts, who we will most assuredly hear more of later!). Although the church cleared Bell of any wrong-doing, the state of Tennessee, represented by William Fort, had already brought suit against Bell in the district court of Robertson County. He was convicted by a jury in August 1817.

And this was not the end of the case. In November, the church reversed its earlier decision and decided that since Bell was convicted of the charge in court, then he should pay a penalty with the church as well. In January 1818, at around the same time the Bell family haunting was becoming known to select members of the community, John Bell was officially excommunicated by the church. Although such charges seem inconsequential to us today, they were taken seriously during that period and it was an extraordinary measure for an elder or deacon to be barred from the church. One can only imagine the additional stress that it must have created in the Bell household, especially at a time when some very frightening events were beginning to occur.

In October 1819, during the height of the haunting, John Bell requested that the church reconsider the charges against him. A committee from five other churches formed a panel to look into the case and eventually ruled that Bell should be allowed back into the congregation. In spite of their findings though, the local members postponed looking into the matter for an entire year. By December 1820 though, it was too late - John Bell was already dead.

The horrific events began in 1817. It was a time that became known to future generations of Bell's as the beginning of "our family troubles."

The first mysterious occurrence took place when John Bell saw a strange-looking animal on his property. He was walking across one of his corn fields when he saw the creature squatting between the rows. Modern accounts mistake this animal for a dog (probably due to a slave's later encounter with a large black dog) but Bell actually described it as "a strange animal, unlike any he had ever seen". He concluded that it was "probably a dog", and having his gun with him, he fired at the animal. The creature quickly turned and ran away. Bell would state that he had no idea if his bullet hit the animal or not.

The second odd sighting took place a few days later. It was late afternoon and Drew Bell spotted a very large bird, which he assumed was a wild turkey, sitting on a fence row. He hurried into the house to fetch his gun but when he got within shooting distance of the bird, it spread its wings and flew off. At that point, Drew realized that it had not been a turkey at all, but what has been an called "an unknown bird of extraordinary size". He shot at the bird anyway and it appeared to fall to the ground. When he ran over to look at the carcass, the creature had vanished.

Then, one evening, a short time after this, Betsy Bell walked out with the children toward the edge of the forest. There, among the trees, she saw something which she described as "a pretty little girl in a green dress", dangling from the limbs of a tall oak tree. When she approached the girl, the apparition abruptly vanished.

It would be just a few nights later that Dean, John Bell's most trusted servant, would come to his master with his own bizarre tale to tell. According to Dean, a large, black dog has begun appearing to him every night. Dean always took a certain trail home from where he visited with his wife, Kate, who was owned by Alex Gunn. At the same point on the trail each evening, the dog appeared and began to follow him. The beast trailed Dean to the slave's cabin, where it then disappeared.

As strange as these events seem to us today, they did not make much of an impression on the Bell family, and would not be connected to the events that followed until some time later. Perhaps living on the edge of the frontier as they did, they were used to strange and inexplicable incidents like these, we'll never know. Regardless, the "coming of the witch" was not realized until the odd events began to be centered on the Bell house itself.

At the time of the haunting, there were five children still living in the Bell house, Betsy, John Jr., Drewry, Joel and Richard. Esther had married Alex Bennett Porter in July 1817 and Jesse, the eldest son, had married Martha Gunn, the daughter of Reverend Thomas Gunn, a few months later. Both of the couples still resided in the area. Zadok had left for Alabama by this time and Benjamin had passed away some time before.

The haunting began at the house in early 1818 with a series of sounds around the exterior of the house. They began as booming, vibrating shakes that first made the family think they might be caused by an earthquake. The terrible earthquake along the New Madrid fault in 1811 had rocked Tennessee and the Bell family feared that another massive quake might be coming.

A fear of an impending earthquake was replaced by a darker fear as knockings began to sound on the front door of the house. When a family member would go to let the caller in, they would find that no one was present. The knockings and rappings were soon followed by hideous scratching sounds. It sounded as though the wood was being peeled from the outside walls, although no cause could be discovered for the noises.

Before long, the frightening sounds moved inside. Richard Williams Bell would later recall that his parents had a room on the first floor of the house, while Betsy had a room above. The four boys occupied a room together, also on the second floor, with John and Drewry sharing a bed and Joel and Richard in another.

"As I remember, it was on a Sunday night, just after the family had retired," Richard wrote, "a noise commenced in our room like a rat gnawing vigorously on the bed post."

John and Drew jumped out of bed to kill the rodent, but as soon as they did, the noise stopped. They lit a candle and examined the bedpost, but found no signs of a rat. They climbed back into bed and the noise started again and continued until after midnight. All four of the boys claimed to get out of bed more than a dozen times and all searched the entire room for the offending animal. They found nothing and to their dismay, the incident became a nightly occurrence that lasted for weeks.

Then, a new wrinkle was added. Each time the boys would rise from their beds, the sound would cease in their room and would begin to be heard in Betsy's room instead. From there, it would travel to John and Lucy's bed chamber, finally rousing the whole household. The irritating sound would continue from room to room, stopping when everyone was awake and starting again when they all went back to bed.

The sounds continued and began to change. The sound of the scratching rat was joined by a noise that sounded like a large dog, pawing at the wooden floor. The tapping and clicking of its large claws could plainly be heard on the floorboards and yet no animal was present. Other noises were described as sounding like two large animals dragging trace chains through the house. Richard Bell also recalled a sound that was like "heavy stones falling" and like "chairs falling over".

The crashing and scratching sounds were frightening, but not as terrifying as the noises that followed. It was not uncommon for the Bell's to be awakened in the darkness by a noise like the smacking of lips, gulping sounds and eerie gurgling and choking sounds seemingly made by a human throat, although no living person was could be seen. The nerves of the Bell family were beginning to unravel as the sounds became a nightly occurrence. Richard Bell stated that "there was no such thing as sleep to be thought of until the noise ceased, which was generally between one and three o'clock in the morning".

The inhuman sounds were followed by the unseen hands that began to plague the household, troubling Betsy more than anyone else. Lamps were knocked to the floor, personal items thrown about, cooking utensils clattered and banged and those belongings not attached in some way to a solid object were launched into the air. Items all over the house were broken and bed clothing and blankets were pulled from the beds. "The phenomena was pulling the cover off the beds as fast as we could replace it," Bell stated.

The hands also did more than trouble inanimate objects. Hair was pulled and the children were slapped and poked, causing them to cry in pain. The shocking blows seemed to come from nowhere. No hands, fingers or fists could be seen and yet they pummeled the family, especially Betsy, as though made from flesh and blood. Betsy was once slapped so hard that her cheeks stayed a bright red color for hours. No warning proceeded the slaps and pinches and they made them all the more frightening.

"I had just fallen into a sweet doze, when I felt my hair beginning to twist, and then a sudden jerk, which raised me. I felt like the top of my head had been taken off," Bell later recalled. "Immediately, Joel yelled out in great fright, and next Elizabeth was screaming in her room. Ever after that, something was continually pulling at her hair after she retired to bed. This transaction frightened us so badly that father and mother remained up nearly all night."

Whatever the cause of this unseen force, the violence of it seemed to be especially directed at Betsy Bell. She would often run screaming from her room in terror as the unseen hands prodded, pinched and poked her. Strangely, it would be noticed later that the force became even more cruel to Betsy after she entertained her young suitor, Joshua Gardner, at the house. For some reason, the spirit seemed to want to punish her whenever Joshua would call.

One has to wonder how these strange and terrifying happenings were perceived by John Bell, a no-nonsense farmer and businessman and a man who had an abiding belief in God and the church. At the time the haunting began, Bell must have been struggling with matters of faith, as he had been recently ousted from his religious congregation, and perhaps even wondering if the events plaguing the house were either divine retribution or some sort of demonic punishment. The stalwart planter must have searched diligently for some clue as to what was causing the noises in the beginning, suggesting rodents, small animals and even tree branches scratching on the outer walls. But as the sounds took a stranger turn and when invisible hands began to slap and beat his children, he realized that what was occurring was something out of the realm of natural events. Night after night of abuse and spectral manifestations soon had Bell living in fear, although he dared not let his family know just how frightened he was. If he allowed his own terror to show, Bell believed that his family might just fall apart.

In addition to dealing with what must have been a mind-numbing sense of fear, John Bell had also begun to develop a nervous condition that affected his tongue, his throat and his jaw muscles. This unknown affliction often made it impossible for him to eat and to chew. On many mornings, he could take nothing more than water for breakfast and his supper would consist of broth or thin soup. He consulted his doctor but the medicines he prescribed did not ease the problem, nor did the folk cures mixed up by the slaves. Finally, Bell began to accept the idea that the illness was somehow caused by the force that had invaded his home. Desperately seeking answers, he realized that he needed to appeal to someone outside of the family for assistance.

One of Bell's closest friends and neighbors was James Johnston and Bell decided to try and enlist his help with the matter. Up until this time, the mysterious events were still a family secret and Johnston would be the first person to whom they were revealed.

One afternoon, Bell sent one of the boys over to the Johnston's home to ask them to come to dinner and to spend the night at the Bell farm. The message carried no warning of what strange events were occurring but John quickly explained things to his friend when he and his wife arrived. We can only speculate as to how the news affected James Johnston but it's likely that his friendship with John Bell prevented him from passing judgment on Bell's possible mental state or from being too skeptical about the events that were described to him. Bell urged his friend to help him conduct an investigation that might lead to the bottom of the weird happenings.

That night, as everyone prepared to go to bed, Johnston took out his Bible and read a chapter from it aloud. He prayed fervently for the family to be delivered from the frightful disturbances, or at least for their origins to be revealed.

Almost as soon as the candles in the house were extinguished, the strange sounds began as usual, although this time they were even more violent, as though to show

Johnston just what the force was capable of. The gnawing, knocking and scratching sounds began immediately and the disturbances continued to escalate as chairs overturned, blankets flew from the beds, and objects flew from one side of the room to the other. As before, as soon as a light would appear in the room where the occurrences were taking place, they would come to a halt and start up again somewhere else.

James Johnston listened attentively to all of the sounds that he heard and closely observed the other incidents that were taking place. He apparently did not frighten easily! He realized, from the sounds of teeth grinding and the smacking of lips, that an intelligent force seemed to be at work. He was determined to try and communicate with it and finally called out. "In the name of the Lord, what or who are you?" he cried, "What do you want and why are you here?"

As though shocked, the disturbances suddenly halted and the house remained quiet for some time. Unfortunately, it didn't last and the violence began again with the ripping of the covers from one of the beds. The disturbances moved from room to room, settling in for an attack against Betsy Bell. The young girl was slapped and pummeled mercilessly. Richard Bell wrote that "her cheeks were frequently crimsoned as by a hard blow with an open hand". The observers cringed as her hair was pulled so hard that she fell to the floor, screaming in pain. The unseen hands pulled her down into a kneeling position and twisted her head so that her face was against the wooden floorboards. The others in the room could only cry out in terror and sympathy, unable to lift Betsy back up again and unable to strike back against the invisible force that was holding her.

As with the previous nights, the events of this evening finally came to a halt, leaving everyone quivering with nervousness and exhausted. Lucy Bell and the children, along with Johnston's wife, retired to bed, hoping to find at least some restless sleep. We must remember that the entire family was functioning on little more than a few hours of sleep each night, battling with the force in the house until the early morning hours. When daylight came, they were still expected to go about their daily tasks of tending the farm, cooking, cleaning, sewing and attending school. After weeks of the nightly abuse, we have to assume that they were close to collapse.

After everyone else retired, John Bell and James Johnston sat up late into the early morning hours, huddled around a candle in the front room. They whispered back and forth as Johnston tried to make some sense of what he had witnessed that night. He had arrived at the conclusion that the phenomena was definitely "beyond his comprehension". He did believe, however, that it possessed an uncanny intelligence, based on the fact that it had ceased action when spoken to. By this, Johnston deduced that it could understand language.

He advised Bell to invite their other friends into the investigation and Bell took his advice, speaking privately to his closest friends and neighbors and asking them for help. Several of them formed a committee to investigate whatever was going on in the house. These men were described by Charles Bailey Bell as being "a number of courageous and determined men, good friends of John Bell, who were almost constantly at his home from that time on until the spirit left." John Bell had chosen these men with care and had apparently chosen well, as each one of them stayed at his side until the very end.

Regardless of the diligence of the committee though, the household was soon in chaos. Word began to spread of the strange events and friends, and even strangers, came to the farm to see what was happening. Dozens of people heard the clear banging and rapping sounds, inexplicable lights were reported in the yard and chunks of rock and wood were thrown at the curious guests. From all over southern Kentucky and western Tennessee came exorcists and witch-finders, all of them claiming they could expel the evil force from the Bell house. Their efforts were all in vain as the disturbances soon had them fleeing from the premises!

The committee formed by Bell, Johnston and their friends continued to search for answers. They set up experiments, trying to communicate with the force, and they kept a close eye on all of the events that took place. They set up watches that lasted throughout the night, but it did no good and, if anything, the attacks increased in their violence. It was almost as if the force resented being investigated and so it decided to punish those present with even greater hostility.

The attacks on Betsy Bell intensified and she began to be treated even more brutally. She began to experience sensations of having the breath sucked out of her body and fainting spells that would leave her unconscious, or in a hypnotic state, for minutes at a time. In addition to the violence directed against her by the unseen hands and fists, she was also being scratched and her skin was being pierced by invisible pins and needles. The stunned witnesses watched in horror as long marks would appear on her hands and arms and as blood would well up and seep from the open wounds. Betsy could do nothing but flinch and cry out in pain.

Unbelievably, the torture began to come more often and Betsy was being so severely punished that her parents feared for her safety when she was alone. Because of this, neighboring girls came almost every night to keep her company. Two of the girls, Theny Thorn and Rebecca Porter, came most often and witnessed much of the reported phenomena. It was also suggested that Betsy should spend some of her nights away from home. It was thought that she might remain unscathed if she could get away from the Bell farm.

The Bell's neighbors, who Richard Bell described as "touched with generous sympathy and were unremitting in their efforts to alleviate our distress", came every night to sit with the troubled family. They were also quick to offer a bed for Betsy Bell so that she could get away from her own house. She went to different homes but it made no difference. The disturbances followed her wherever she went and the events on the Bell farm were repeated in the homes of James Johnston, John Johnston, Jesse Bell, Bennett Porter and others. In addition to the events that occurred wherever Betsy Bell went, they also continued at the Bell home as well.

"This gave rise to suspicion in the mind of some persons", wrote Richard Williams Bell, "that the mystery was some device or stratagem originated by my sister, from the fact that it appeared wherever she went, and this clue was followed to a logical demonstration of the mistake, satisfying all who entered into the investigation."

Meanwhile, James Johnston continued with his investigations and theories of the force being controlled by an intelligent being of some sort. He, along with other members of the committee began speaking to the "witch" (as they had begun calling the force), asking it to speak and tell them what it wanted. They noted that when the force was spoken to, the disturbances would stop for a time and then increase. This went on to confirm Johnson's theories and the investigators persisted in badgering the witch.

We can only guess as to why the investigators began referring to the spirit, or force, in the house as a "witch". It should be noted that while Charles Bailey Bell referred to the Bell Witch as a "mysterious spirit", Richard Williams Bell frequently called it the "witch" in his 1846 manuscript about the case. The term "witch" would seem to imply to the modern reader that there was some sort of witchcraft involved in the haunting, but this was not the case. The spirit itself would later state that it was the "witch" of Kate Batts, a local woman, implying that it was a creation or manifestation of Mrs. Batts, who was suspected of being a witch herself. That is as close as the story comes to involving witchcraft though and we have to assume that the term was applied to the spirit because it was a familiar sort of supernatural being during this period. Most of the settlers of the region were first and second generation immigrants, coming from Scotland, Britain and Ireland, where tales of witches were common. Why they chose to use this term, rather than ghost or spirit, is unknown, although later versions of the case often avoided the use of "witch". For our purposes here, the reader can expect a mixture of different terms in reference to the haunting, as I have tried to remain as close to the original writings of the case as I can.

As the investigations continued, so did the visits to the Bell farm by friends and neighbors. The mystery had continued to gain wide notoriety and people came from all over to crowd into the house and yard each night and to witness the bizarre demonstrations. The visitors called out for the witch to talk, or at the very least, to rap on the walls or smack its lips in reply to their queries. The phenomenon continued to develop and there was soon little doubt, even to the casual curiosity-seeker, that there was an intelligence behind the force.

The committee continued to try and provoke responses from the entity, peppering it with questions that required "yes" or "no" answers, or which could be answered with numbers. Replies were returned to the questions in knocks or raps, as if an invisible fist was tapping on the wall.

Such a method of communication was astounding at the time, as the investigators had nothing to base such methods on. More than 30 years later, in March 1848, similar communications with an alleged spirit in Hydesville, New York would go on to create the Spiritualist movement. These communications, later dubbed the "Hydesville Rappings", occurred in the home of the Fox family when John Fox, his wife and his daughters began trying to determine the source of a ghostly presence that was haunting their home. The events became quite famous and known all over the world but were not the first such communications to occur in American history, as the reader can plainly see. However, the 1848 communications may have been the first attempts to contact the spirit of a deceased person though ~ as will be shown in later chapters!

The knocking and tapping in the Bell household went on for some time but the committee members continued to harass the witch with questions, daring the presence to speak.

Soon, it began to whistle in reply to the questions. It was not the whistling that one associates with trying to produce a musical melody though, but a whistling, rasping sound ~ as if someone was trying very hard to speak! The whistling progressed and developed until it became a weak, indistinct whisper. Words were being formed but they could not be understood, at least at first.

"I do not remember the first intelligent utterance, which, however, was of no significance," wrote Richard Bell, "but the voice soon developed sufficient strength to be distinctly heard by every one in the room."

The scratchings, rappings and whispers had become a voice. The spirit that had wreaked havoc in the Bell house was now beginning to talk. The problem was, once the so-called witch began to speak ~ it seemed that she would never be silent again!

- CHAPTER THREE -
THE WITCH FINDS HER VOICE
THE SEASON OF THE WITCH IN ROBERTSON COUNTY, TENNESSEE

The close-throated whistling noises soon turned into faint, indistinct words and the voice of the witch began to gain strength. Not surprisingly, the word spread quickly about this new wrinkle to the mystery. Soon, members of John Bell's investigative committee, and other interested parties, descended on the harassed household, increasing their efforts to get the witch to talk. Their goal was to try and get the witch to disclose its reasons for being at the Bell house - although little did they know that their efforts would be rewarded with literally months of lies, trickery and verbal abuse!

One of the first real statements the witch made after gaining the ability to speak was the answer to what it really was and why it was there. It would be a very ambiguous answer, but it would be one of the only completely honest answers it would ever give as to why the haunting was taking place.

"Who are you and what do you want?" one of the committee members demanded of the witch.

"I am a spirit," came the reply, "I was once very happy but have been disturbed."

This utterance was given in a feeble voice, but Richard Williams Bell stated that it was clearly heard and understood by everyone who was present. These were the only words the witch spoke for several days and although the committee members tried to obtain more information, this was the only explanation given at the time. Later, as the reader will soon discover, the witch would reveal many other identities and a score of reasons why she was haunting the Bell family. Thanks to the confusion created by the spirit's ongoing deceptions, the identity of the witch would never be completely resolved.

The next occasion when the voice of the spirit was heard was on a Sunday night, not long after its initial contact with the investigators. By this time, the voice of the witch was much stronger and on this night occurred the spirit's first intrusion into the matters of the Bell family.

The family was seated in the front room of the house, discussing an impending trip that was to be made by the younger John Bell. He was going to North Carolina to tie up some business dealings that his father still maintained there. He was planning to leave by horseback at dawn the following morning. The trip was of great interest to the rest of the family, especially the younger children, and there was much talk about the long journey ahead of him, how long he would be away, the best route to take and of course, talk of the business matters themselves. As was usual during this time period, a number of friends were also at the house. They too were giving John some good-natured advice about his trip, but then came some advice from an unexpected source!

From nowhere came the voice of the witch. "Do not leave on your journey," the witch said to him, and then went on to make the first of what would become a number of eerily accurate predictions. She informed John that he would have a hard and tiresome trip, which would be plagued with bad luck. The estate that he was to close for his father would instead not be completed for some time and John would return from the arduous journey empty-handed. In addition, the spirit also told him of a young woman from Virginia who was coming to Robertson County to visit some friends and would arrive the following afternoon. Not only was this woman beautiful, but she was wealthy as well, and if John stayed in Tennessee, he would be able to win this young lady's heart.

John laughed at the revelations of the witch and left the following morning for North Carolina, just as he had planned. The trip turned out to be a particularly miserable one and he was not able to return home for more than six months. When he did come back to Tennessee, he brought no money with him. To make matters worse, just a few hours after John's departure, a very attractive young lady from Virginia arrived in the community. She visited her friends for several months and then departed just before John's return. Just as the witch predicted - the two of them never met.

Over the course of the next few weeks, the voice of the witch began to be heard more and more often. The committee members continued to visit the house and pressed the spirit with questions. They had succeeded in getting the witch to admit that she was a disturbed spirit, but now the most urgent questions were how the spirit had been disturbed - and what could be done to remedy the situation.

"I am the spirit of a person who was buried in the woods nearby," the witch told the investigators, "and my grave has been disturbed.. my bones disinterred and scattered... and one of my teeth was lost under this house. I am here looking for that tooth."

While this statement seems rather strange, it actually stirred a memory for the Bell family. It recalled an incident that had taken place years before and by now had been entirely forgotten. Several seasons earlier, the farm hands had been clearing some land and had stumbled upon a large mound, which John Bell had guessed to be an Indian grave. The slaves had worked around the mound, careful not to disturb it.

A few days later, a local boy named Corban Hall had visited the farm and Drew had told him about the discovery of the Indian grave. The two boys decided to open up the grave and see if they could find any relics with which the Indians buried their dead. They set to digging and although they found no relics, they did find a collection on ancient bones, which were promptly scattered. For some reason (which only those readers who were once young boys will understand), Hall carried an old jawbone with him back to the Bell house. While he and Drew were examining it, the jawbone fell to the floor and a tooth was dislodged and fell through a crack in the floor.

Moments later, John Bell caught the boys with the jawbone and gave them both a severe scolding (and most likely, a switch to the backside). He called one of the slaves to the house and instructed him to return the bone to the Indian grave. The jawbone was taken back to the burial mound and put back under the earth, along with the other bones the boys had disinterred.

It is interesting to note that no member of the Bell family, nor any of the investigators, connected the opening of the burial mound to the coming of the witch, which occurred a disturbingly short time later.

Regardless, the comment made by the witch reminded Bell of these earlier events and he decided to take up a portion of the floor and search for the missing tooth. John and the boys took axes and saws and began tearing up the portion of the floorboards where they remembered the tooth having been lost. Once the boards were removed, they began digging in the dirt below. "The dirt beneath was raked up, sifted and thoroughly examined", wrote Richard Williams Bell, "but the tooth was not found. The witch then laughed at father, declaring that it was all a joke to fool 'Old Jack'."

But what happened to the tooth? Whether the witch's tale was true or not, the family distinctly recalled the fact that it had indeed fallen into the crack in the floor. Had the witch taken it for some reason? And why use this incident to torment John Bell?

The excitement in the community grew as word spread of the witch's increasing number of communications. People came from around the area, and from the far-flung regions, to hear the unexplained voice. The stories attracted the believers in the unknown who credited the spirit as being the ghost of an Indian, an evil spirit, and even the result of genuine witchcraft. The accounts also brought the debunkers, who came to the Bell farm intent on exposing the haunting as a hoax. Most of them ended up leaving in a state of puzzlement, while others expressed their opinions about the witch. Some charged that the voice was a sort of trickery being worked by the Bell family in order to draw crowds to the farm and make money off of them.

Unfortunately (at least for John Bell's pocketbook), this was not the case. The crowds who came to the farm paid no admission and the Bell's allowed them to stay as long as they wished. Most were fed, along with their horses, and many stayed the night in a warm bed. No one ever left the farm hungry and while many offered to pay for their meals, Bell refused to accept their money. Even his friends tried to convince him to accept the donations, insisting that he could not afford to keep entertaining the large crowds. Through all of it though, Bell refused to take the money. He never considered the witch a "wonder" or an object of delight. He thought of the creature as "an affliction" and its presence in the house as "a calamity" of a most dire nature. His sense of honor did not allow him to accept money so that visitors could witness something so terrible.

The witch had now gained an audience for her new voice and as the crowds came to the farm, the spirit seemed to bask in the attention. The witch now claimed to be able to leave the Bell farm and witness events that were taking place in other parts of the community - and it reported these events, no matter how bad, in great detail. No personal life in the community was safe from scrutiny by the witch and Charles Bailey Bell wrote that the witch was "indeed a great tattler and made mischief in the community... Nothing of moment occurred in the country, or in any family, that was not reported by the witch at night. The development of this characteristic led the people to inquire after the news and converse with the witch as they would with a person, very often inquiring what was transpiring then at a certain place or house in the neighborhood. Sometimes the answer would be: "I don't know; wait a minute and I will go and see', and in less than five minutes it would report and the report was generally verified."

The witch gave evidence to this ability one evening when Lucy Bell came into the house and asked if anyone knew if Jesse had returned home from a trip. Jesse Bell, who lived about a mile away from the Bell homestead, had been away for several days at this time. The family members replied that they didn't know and their answers were followed by the sudden voice of the witch. "Wait a minute, Luce, and I will go see for you," it reportedly spoke. In less than a minute, the voice came again and claimed that not only was Jesse at home but that he was sitting at a table and reading by the light of a candle.

The following morning, Jesse stopped by the house for a visit and when he was told what had happened, he verified the story of the witch. In fact, he had been reading (as the witch described) when a knocking came at the front door. Before he could answer it, the door had opened and closed immediately.

"What was that?" his wife had asked, coming in from another room.

Jesse shrugged. "I reckon it was the witch," he told her.

In addition to meddling in personal affairs, the spirit also seemed to possess a great knowledge of the Bible and religious matters - or at least was adept at mocking and imitating what it heard. It was said that the witch could "sing any song in the hymn books of that time and quote any passage of scripture in the Bible". Richard Williams Bell reported that the witch delighted in taking issue on religious subjects. She would often enter into theological discussions with visitors or with the Reverends James and Thomas Gunn, Reverend Sugg Fort and most especially James Johnston, a lay minister, who the witch actually seemed to admire and had nicknamed "Old Sugar Mouth".

Nearly every Sunday evening, the witch would entertain the occupants of the Bell house with every nuance of the Sabbath services that had taken place in the community. It would tell which hymns were played and what the minister preached about, followed by a fiery criticism of the sermon. One night the witch even gave a word for word repetition of one of Reverend James Gunn's sermons, so duplicating the words and the voice of Gunn that it was almost as if the man was present! Several of those who were in the house, and who had attended the service that day, attested to the fact that it was the same sermon.

On one occasion a short time later, Reverend Gunn preached a sermon at Bethel Methodist Church, which lay about six miles away from the community. On that same morning, the Reverend Sugg Fort preached at Drake's Pond Baptist Church, which lay seven miles in the opposite direction. Both ministers came to the Bell house that evening and after supper, the witch began to direct its conversation toward Reverend Gunn, discussing various points of his sermon from that day.

"How do you know what I preached about?" Gunn asked the spirit.

"I was present and I heard you", stated the witch. The spirit then proceeded to begin quoting the text of the sermon just as Gunn had presented it.

While Reverend Fort agreed that this was astounding, he also noted that the witch had not been able to hear his own sermon that morning, which had been taught 13 miles distant from the church where Gunn had been preaching. The witch would not be able to comment on the subject of his service, he said.

"Yes, I can," replied the eerie voice. "I was there." It then went on to mock Fort's words and voice, uncannily imitating him. There was no one else present who could have heard both sermons, but both ministers admitted that the words presented by the witch were accurate.

How the witch could have achieved the remarkable displays of reporting the events of the neighborhood and reciting Sunday services is unknown. Aside from us simply shrugging and admitting that the spirit was a supernatural creature, we have no solid answers. The Bell Witch is unlike any other entity in paranormal history. It was very much a strange mixture of what we expect from the unknown. It was a being that called itself a witch and yet was apparently some sort of spirit. However, despite being a spirit, it seemed to know nothing of other departed spirits, of human survival after death or of communication with the dead. But even ignorant of these things, the spirit was able to duplicate, and very much surpass, the range of phenomena that is usually associated with traditional ghosts.

While the spirit seemed to possess the power to be in many places at once and to have a supernatural ability of passing on information about the living, it seemed incapable of communicating with the dead. There was never an instance in the record of the haunting where the witch claimed to have such a power. In fact, John Jr. is told much later (when he inquired of the witch for news of his deceased father) that while it could imitate John Bell's voice to perfection, it had no desire to deceive John Jr. in thinking that his father's spirit had returned. The witch seemed to be quite positive that who died did not talk to those left behind.

The implication of the witch's denial of communication with the dead is that the witch was not a spirit who survived bodily death. It seemed to be an entity that defied the usual explanations and even in its own testimony would speak of the deceased John Bell as being "not of this world". The witch simply considered itself to be part of the earthly plane and not of a spiritual one.

To some, this would seem to mean that the witch was nothing more than a fragment of a living personality that had broken free, in some mysterious way, to wreak havoc on the Bell Family. Or that the witch was somehow conjured up from the subconscious of one of the principals in the case, carrying out the unconscious desires of this person in violent and seemingly magical ways.

The problems with such theories are many however. While the witch was admittedly ignorant to the ways of the spirit world and certainly never behaved like a typical ghost, it does not possess the characteristics of a human agent directed "poltergeist" either (as we will discuss in a later chapter). There is never any indication that the witch was conscious of a dependence on a living person or that it was in any way connected to only one person, as later theories regarding Betsy Bell would claim.

Because of this, we have to consider the idea that the Bell Witch was something far stranger than anything we have ever considered before. As the coming pages will show, there has never been another haunting like that of the Bell Witch!

While the witch's amazing pronouncements were occurring, the work of the Bell Committee investigators was continuing. They had never stopped trying to learn more about the witch and to discover the source of the voice. They also continued to puzzle over the bizarre force by which the spirit caused the physical effects in the house to take place. During the time when the voice of the witch was growing stronger, the movement of furniture, the scratching and rapping noises and, of course, the attacks on Betsy Bell were still going on.

The investigators interrogated the witch about its personality and character and about the reasons for the haunting. They received no new replies until one day, a question from James Gunn prompted a previously unheard response. It was almost as if the witch had grown weary of their constant asking.

"I am the spirit of an early emigrant," it told them, "who brought a large sum of money and buried my treasure for safe keeping until needed. In the meanwhile I died without divulging the secret, and I have returned in spirit for the purpose of making known the hiding place, and I want Betsy Bell to have the money."

Strangely, the investigators eagerly swallowed this new story. I am uncertain as to why they would have believed that the witch, who spent most of its time viciously attacking poor Betsy, would suddenly want to bestow a treasure upon her! For some reason though, they believed it and began urging the spirit to reveal the hiding place. At first, the witch still refused to tell and then relented, but only under certain conditions.

The spirit stated that the hiding place would only be given out under the condition that Drew Bell and Bennett Porter (Esther Bell's husband) agree to dig for the loot and that every dollar exhumed would be given to Betsy. The witch also made them promise that "Old Sugar Mouth" (James Johnston) would go with them to make sure that the agreement was carried out to the letter. He would be in charge of counting the money and then handling it for Betsy.

The boys quickly agreed to do the work and Johnston consented to handle the treasure and keep it in trust for Betsy until she was older. With these arrangements agreed upon, the spirit announced that the money was hidden under a large flat rock at the mouth of a spring on the southwest corner of the farm. The site overlooked the nearby Red River and the description the witch gave was so detailed, they had no trouble finding it. All of those present that night were familiar with the spring, having frequented it on occasion, but none of them could have described it as carefully as the witch did, which assured them ever further that what the spirit was telling them was the truth. The witch also instructed them to begin work early the next morning, in case word got out about the location and someone else beat them to the money.

Shortly after sunrise, Johnson, Drew and Bennett Porter assembled at the spring. They found the familiar site just as the witch had described and set to work. They first cut poles and made levers to move the rock, digging out around it so as to get the wooden poles beneath it. This task took them half of the day to complete and as those who have ever spent a summer in Tennessee can tell you, it was a hot and tiring job. Finally though, the rock was upended and moved - but no money was found.

As the reader can imagine, this was cause for some concern. After discussing the matter, the three men decided that perhaps the treasure had sunk down below the earth, or had originally been buried at some depth. So, they decided to start digging. Drew began loosening the dirt and Porter began shoveling it out. After a good part of the afternoon, they had succeeded in opening a hole that was about six feet across and just as deep. Still, no treasure was discovered.

At this point, they decided that enough was enough and realized there was no treasure to be found. The group had not stopped to wonder how, if it had taken all three of them to lever and move the rock, a single man had managed to do move it, hide a treasure and then move the stone back into place. They were now feeling a little silly about believing the witch's story about an "early emigrant".

Tired and hungry, they returned to the Bell house toward evening to wash up and get something to eat. Not long after they sat down with heaping plates of food, courteously provided by Lucy Bell, the witch made its customary appearance.

The sound of the spirit's laughter filled the house and she began taunting the three men for their gullibility. She mocked them for being so easily duped and went on to give (what was to everyone else) a very entertaining account of the treasure hunting folly. According to Richard Williams Bell, "the description of the affair kept the house in an uproar of laughter, and it was repeated with equal zest to all new comers for a month".

Somehow, I doubt that Drew, Johnston and Porter found the incident quite so amusing.

In spite of the "hilarious" antics of the witch, the reader should be aware that none of the incidents previously described as taking place in the Bell house had come to an end.

In fact, objects still moved about the house at will, strange noises still awakened the family at night, sheets and blankets were still pulled from the beds, pillows continued to be jerked out from beneath the heads of sleepers and much more. New happenings were added to the witch's repertoire as well, including items that would appear and disappear at will and the sound of "large stones" or "cannon balls" that would rumble down the staircase from the upper floor, never seen by anyone who was witness to the thundering noise.

Of all of the witch's manifestations though, most disturbing were, or course, the continued attacks on Betsy Bell and the physical ailments that plagued John Bell.

Oddly, the witch would sometimes regard Betsy with tenderness, only to attack her with terrible force later that same day. As mentioned previously, these attacks were especially severe after a visit by young Joshua Gardner. She was also subject to fainting spells and moments when her breath seemed to be sucked from her body. These incidents would leave her utterly exhausted and lifeless and she would black out for up to 30 or 40 minutes at time. Once she awoke however, she would be completely restored and would have no memory of what had occurred.

Although the Bell family admitted there was no proof these incidents were caused by the witch (and she never took credit for them), it was believed they were. Prior to the coming of the spirit, Betsy had always been very healthy and outside of childhood sickness, had never been seriously ill. The strange spells she began experiencing came on in the evenings, just at the time when the witch usually appeared. During the time that Betsy lay unconscious, no sound would come from the spirit, then when the girl awakened, the witch would begin to speak.

Some writers have suggested that these spells are proof that Betsy Bell was somehow responsible for the visitation by the witch. It has been said that since the witch did not speak or move objects about while Betsy was in the midst of a trance, then she must have somehow been controlling the force, albeit unconsciously, when awake. Others have also pinned the blame on poor Betsy, comparing her seizures to the sort of trance into which Spiritualistic mediums descend into when communicating with the dead. This theory does not explain the reason that the witch remained silent during the seizures though, for if we compare them to a medium's trance, it would be more likely that the spirit would communicate at this time, rather than remain quiet. However, it does seem more plausible to assume that the spirit was a separate entity, rather than assuming that it was a split-off part of Betsy's own personality. Could the witch have been using Betsy as a channel, or as a medium, through which it could make contact? This certainly seems possible, although once again, such a theory cannot explain how the witch managed to make itself known when Betsy was not present, as would often prove to be the case.

Betsy's catatonic spells were of great concern to the family, but of no lesser concern were the ailments being experienced by John Bell himself. During the first year of the haunting, Bell began to complain of a curious numbness in his mouth that caused his tongue to become stiff and to swell. In fact, his tongue and throat became so swollen that he would be unable to eat for days at time. He even had difficulty swallowing and drinking water, which added to his discomfort.

As the haunting progressed, he began to come down with other unexplainable symptoms as well. Most notable were the bizarre facial tics and twitches that he suffered. Once these "fits" would seize his face, he would be unable to talk or eat and they would sometimes cause him to lose consciousness as well. These odd seizures would last anywhere from a few hours to as long as a week. However, once they passed, he would be in good health until the next attack came along.

The spells gradually increased, both in length and in severity, and undoubtedly carried the man to his grave. The opposite was the case for Betsy Bell. It seemed that as her father's troubles increased, her symptoms began to go away. Eventually, her afflictions stopped completely and she never suffered another symptom of any kind.

But why John Bell?

We'll probably never really know but from the very beginning the witch had made it clear that it was going to get "Old Jack Bell" and would torment him until the end of his life. In addition to his illness, Bell was also physically abused by the witch and many witnesses would recall him being slapped by unseen hands or crying out in pain as he was prodded and stabbed with invisible pins. Whenever Bell's name was mentioned in the presence of the spirit, it would begin screaming and would call Bell every vile and offensive name it could muster up. It was obvious that the spirit violently hated him and his torment would only end with his death. Bell's doctor, George Hopson of Port Royal, was helpless when it came to finding a cure for the seizures and ailments. The witch laughed at his efforts and declared that it was the cause of John Bell's problems and no medicine existed that could cure him.

Apparently, the witch was determined to get John Bell any way it could and yet after all of this time, it had never explained why it hated him so much. What had Bell done to cause the spirit to despise him so greatly? And why had the Bell house been singled out for the haunting?

Then, one night, the answer was revealed by the witch. The reply came to a question posed to the witch by the Reverend James Gunn. He asked once again just who the spirit was and why it was tormenting the Bell family. According to the spirit, it was unable to lie to a direct question given to her by the man of God.

Of course, the reader must realize that, despite this pious sounding statement, lying to a man of God had never stopped the Bell Witch before. In the past, it had already claimed to be many things, including, an Indian spirit which was hunting a lost tooth, a spirit that had returned because of a lost treasure, the spirit of a child buried in North Carolina, it claimed to John Johnston that it was the spirit of his step-mother and there were others. As you can see, there was no reason to believe in this last incarnation more than any of the others.

The spirit spoke up and announced to Reverend Gunn that it was the "witch" of a local woman named Kate Batts. To his credit, Gunn did not believe this story but many of the people in the community certainly did and the word spread quickly. This was something that the local people could understand and they clung to the belief that the spirit had somehow been directed against Bell and his family. The belief that the witch could spring from the evil influences of Kate Batts created an answer to the riddle. The idea of some unknown spirit haunting the house for an unknown reason was utterly foreign to them, but now the spirit seemed to have a purpose. Kate Batts' connection to the spirit became so complete in many people's minds that they began referring to the spirit as "Kate", a nickname that has endured after all this time.

But who was Kate Batts? Later in the book, we'll look more closely at the various identities that have been given to the witch since the time of the actual events, but briefly, she was a local, eccentric woman who had no love for John Bell.

Curiously, the strange events at the Bell house had begun a short time after a ill-fated business deal between John Bell and Benjamin Batts, Kate's brother-in-law. Apparently, Bell had sold Batts a slave and had charged excessive interest in the matter, which led to harsh words between he and the Batts family. As mentioned already, Batts was not the only person to think the deal was disreputable. Bell had been accused by leaders of his own church of dishonesty in the matter and although acquitted by the church, was convicted in August 1817 by the state of Tennessee. This caused the church to reconsider their decision and in January 1818, Bell was expelled from the congregation. A few local wags were quick to point out Bell's expulsion when the strange events first began to occur at his house and then once the witch actually claimed to be in league with Kate Batts, they were quick to speak of the connection.

As mentioned already, Kate Batts was a rather strange and eccentric woman and counted few friends in the neighborhood. Her husband was an invalid and so she was forced to handle most of their business interests. She had a reputation for being hard to deal with and after her family's business deal with John Bell soured, Mrs. Batts spent a lot of time maligning his character in Robertson County. Many people were afraid of her and feared incurring her wrath, so she was largely avoided. As has been the case throughout history, women like this have often been regarded with suspicion when it comes to witchcraft and the supernatural.

Over the years, there have been many stories that have sprung up about John Bell and his relationship with Kate Batts. Perhaps the oddest story claims that Bell was actually engaged to Kate Batts while living in North Carolina. Not long after being betrothed to her, he learned what an angry and disagreeable woman she was and tried to call the wedding off. Needless to say, she refused to allow it. Then one day, she fell down on his farm and struck her head, knocking herself unconscious. Bell thought she was dead and dragged her body into the root cellar and locked the door. Kate awoke the next night and began moaning and calling for help, but Bell ignored her and she died two days later. Bell then deposited her body on her own farm and allowed a neighbor to discover her and assume she had met with an accident. Bell later married another woman and moved to Nashville but Kate Batts' ghost came back to haunt him as the Bell Witch.

In addition, Bell has also been said to have killed Kate Batts over the slave deal and it has also been claimed that he starved her to death by locking her in his smokehouse.

Obviously, such stories were untrue as Kate Batts was alive and well during the haunting, and for some years after. In fact, when she learned that the spirit was now calling itself "Kate" and claimed to be her "witch", she demanded that charges be pressed against John Bell, as she was sure that this was his way of trying to discredit her in the community.

While it was obvious that she hated the man nearly as much as the spirit did, it is unlikely that she had anything at all to do with the haunting - or at least that she knew of. However, the folklore of the case still makes Kate Batts to blame and that is perhaps because it has been so hard to separate the living woman from the spirit who took on her name. The problem seems to lie in the fact that people have a natural need to find some sort of blame, or reason, as to why the witch would so persecute the Bell family. Just as the local residents were quick to seize on the idea that the spirit was somehow connected to the living Kate Batts, more modern readers are quick to believe that her ghost revenged herself on John Bell for some horrible wrongdoing. People just seem to have a tendency to look for a reason why such things would occur. In other words, what terrible sin did John Bell commit to be punished in such a horrific way? It's easy to believe that he must have taken the life of the real Kate Batts, but this was not the case. And there are no simple answers in the story of the Bell Witch!

Shortly after the announcement to Reverend Gunn though, the witch began to be called "Kate" by the local folks and she was quick to answer to that name. So, as Richard Williams Bell said, "for convenience sake, I shall hereafter call the witch Kate, though not out of any disregard for the memory of Mrs. Batts".

As the name "Kate" began to be attached to the presence of the spirit, a new development occurred in the haunting. It was a series of events that were so frightening they managed to even scare off most of the curiosity-seekers who had been hanging around the Bell farm for weeks.

A few days after Reverend Gunn had coaxed his latest revelation from the witch, four distinctly different personalities took up residence in the Bell House, each claiming to be a separate "witch". Prior to this, Kate (except when angry) had been a soft, delicate woman's voice, other than when she was imitating someone. But these new voices were different and used constantly vile language and uttered horrible threats of pain and death against the Bell family and the visitors. The four creatures called themselves Blackdog, Mathematics, Cypocryphy and Jerusalem. Who these spirits were, why they made themselves known and what purpose they actually served are questions that remain some of the most puzzling aspects of this already mysterious case. These new presences seemed to be separate from that of Kate and seemed to dash any theories that the haunting could have been the unknowing work of Betsy Bell. For this reason, the incidents regarding the four separate spirits are largely ignored by those who want to dismiss the haunting as nothing more than the product of a troubled mind.

The spirit that called itself Blackdog claimed to be the leader of this eerie group and spoke with a harsh feminine voice. The voices that belonged to Mathematics and Cypocryphy were different but yet still seemed to be female, while that of Jerusalem sounded like the voice of a boy.

Unlike Kate's frightening, and yet expected, presence in the house, the visitations by these additional spirits were downright terrifying. They would arrive with much noise and bring with them a whirlwind display of moving objects and horrifying sounds. It got to be so bad that, for the first time, John Bell began to speak of leaving the property and abandoning the farm - but it was no use. The family was quickly informed that should they leave, the creatures would follow them to the ends of the earth.

These new developments succeeded in frightening away most of the spectators and unfortunately, most of the neighbors as well. However, those families, like the Gunn's, the Johnston's, the Fort's, and men like Frank Miles and William Porter, drew even closer to the Bell family, realizing that they were in more need than ever of friends and allies.

During the visitation by the group of spirits, the nights grew even longer. The creatures filled the dark hours with shouts and screams, the singing of bawdy songs and noises like drunken men fighting. The spirits also quarreled fiercely among themselves, using obscene language and what witnesses described as "blasphemous oaths". Once the sessions would deteriorate to this point, the voice of Blackdog would override the others and begin threatening and denouncing them until the fighting stopped. This spirit continued to act as the leader and sent the others off for various errands each night. One or two of them always remained behind however and would create disturbances in different parts of the house.

On one strange occasion, all four of the creatures seemed to be very drunk. Their words slurred badly and they filled the house with the rank smell of whiskey. The spirits claimed to get the whiskey at a still belonging to John Gardner, which lay some four miles away. At other times, the visits were not so nightmarish and the family and their guests would be treated to rich feminine voices that would sing any hymns that were requested of them. These sessions did not last for long though and soon the creatures were back to their usual antics.

Not long after the incident with Gardner's whiskey, the four spirits departed the house and did not return. However, there was one other strange incident, connected to this visitation, which may mark one of the few times the witch (or creatures connected to her) ever put in an actual appearance.

One evening Betsy went over to visit her sister, Esther, who was married to Bennett Porter. The two young women were walking across the road to the barn to gather eggs when they spotted a lady walking up the lane to the house. Bennett Porter was not at home but was working at Fort's mill, which was under construction at the time.

Esther was just past the yard when she thought she recognized the woman on the road as one of her neighbors. She spoke to her in greeting, but the woman did not reply. She repeated it but the woman still did not answer. As she walked, the woman took off her bonnet and allowed her long hair to spill down over her shoulders. She began combing it, her eyes focused on some distant point.

Esther approached her but the woman did not seem to notice. She appeared to be deeply absorbed in thought and Esther invited the lady into the house, repeating the offer several times, to which the woman paid no attention. Finally, Esther threw up her hands and walked off, convinced that the woman had something wrong with her or that she had offended her in some way.

She walked over to the barn, where Betsy was already gathering eggs, and called her attention to the woman, who was still standing by the gate, combing her hair. They stood and watched as she climbed onto the fence rail and sat for several minutes before tucking her hair back into the bonnet and climbing down. She then proceeded across the road and entered the stable lot, where she would have realistically had no reason to go. The lot enclosed about three acres of ground and a stand of young trees. The only focal point in the area was a large, knotty log, which lay on the ground in the center of the stand of saplings.

The woman walked slowly across the lot and was just passing by the old log when she was joined by three other persons, two young girls and a boy. Each of them bent down one of the saplings, sat down on them and began riding up and down on them as if they were springs.

Needless to say, Esther and Betsy were a bit surprised by these events, as was Porter, who returned home while all of this was going on. The problem was that he was unable to see the strange figures who were riding the bent-over trees - he could only see the saplings as they waved up and down. His first thought was that these apparitions (which still only his wife and sister could see) were somehow connected to the witch. Angry and perhaps a bit frightened, he fetched his gun from the house. While Porter was getting his gun, the figures jumped down from the saplings and ducked behind the log. Each would occasionally show their head from behind the barricade.

When he returned, he handed the gun to Esther and directed her to shoot one of the figures. She handed it back to him however and directed him to shoot at a large knot on the log, where one of the heads had appeared. He took aim and fired off a shot. The bullet took a large chunk out of the fallen tree but there was no sign of the odd figures. The three of them waited for several minutes, but the trespassers appeared to be gone. Porter would later state that they could not have escaped from the lot without being seen.

Porter, Esther and Betsy walked over and searched the lot for the apparitions. Other than the bent saplings, and the mark of the bullet on the log though, there was no sign that they had ever been there at all.

And who were these strange figures? Some sort of spirits, eerie doubles for real people, or even the witch incarnate? We'll never know - but later that night, during the visitation by the spirits, it was announced to the company present that Bennett Porter had shot at Jerusalem and had broken his arm with a bullet!

- CHAPTER FOUR -
ANDREW JACKSON &
THE BELL WITCH
OR, "OLD HICKORY" GOES GHOST HUNTING

When the witch had a hatred for something, she was quick to inform anyone who would take notice of it. Not only did she beat and torture Betsy Bell, especially when she entertained Joshua Gardner, and made life horrible for John Bell, but she also had a strong aversion to the Bell's slaves. "I despise the smell of a nigger," she reportedly said, "the scent makes me sick."

It is certain that no one would ever accuse the witch of being polite but the reader has to understand that, unfortunate as it is, the terminology used to describe the Bell slaves was in common use at that time. Still, Kate had an uncommon dislike for them. For this reason, she often chose to taunt and bother them, although she never did so at their own cabins. Their own homes seemed to be safe from the presence of the witch but the slaves claimed to encounter her many times on the property, usually in the darkness and away from lights of the main house.

Not surprisingly, the Bell slaves were very frightened of the spirit, especially since she frequently complained about them. Their fear was heightened further by John Bell's most loyal servant, Dean, who had come from North Carolina with the family. Dean would often tell stories to the other slaves about his own encounters with the witch, including the previously mentioned incident with the black dog that followed him through the woods. While Dean was sometimes known for spinning some pretty tall tales, he had a genuine fear of the witch. Regardless, I have not recounted most of the incidents recalled by Dean as he was not the most reliable witness in the case. For instance, one night, he returned to the Bell farm from visiting his wife with a bloody wound on his head that he claimed had been caused by the witch. Records were later revealed to show that the wound had been suffered at the hands of a man who had rented Dean for a time, John Arnold. The wound had been so grievous that John Bell sued Arnold over it and the matter was settled out of court.

But not all of the slaves were known as being as fanciful as Dean, who constantly spun his chilling stories. Harry, one of the house slaves, had his own reasons for believing there was some truth to the tales. One of Harry's jobs was to make sure that a fire was lit in the hearth each morning. As the presence of the witch became stronger at the house, he became fearful of working inside and neglectful of the fire. John Bell scolded him several times and on each occasion, the boy promised to do better.

One morning, when Harry was once again late, Kate's voice rang out in the house and told Bell not to fret over the servant - that she would be sure that he wouldn't be late again.

A few days later, Harry was even later than usual and Bell began to scold him once again. "Hold on, Jack," came Kate's voice, "didn't I tell you that I would attend to this?"

Harry had just laid the kindling down and was on his knees blowing the coals in the hearth to a blaze when an unseen force seized the boy by the back of the neck and then began whipping him on the backside. Harry yelled and begged to be let go and the witch answered him by threatening to repeat the punishment if the boy was ever late again. John Bell would later state that he had heard the blows that Kate inflicted on the boy and they sounded like someone being paddled with a strip of wood. He couldn't see anything other than the boy being held down onto the floor though, although he was sure that the boy would not be late with his duties again!

Thanks to Kate's rather venomous statements against the slaves, Lucy Bell invented a plan that she believed just might keep the witch out of their house, at least for one evening. The spirit had frequently railed against the sight, sound and especially the smell of the Bell slaves and Lucy was well aware that perhaps for this reason, the witch had never bothered the slaves in their own quarters. This is quite interesting in that we would not expect a ghost to actually have a nose (or the equivalent of one) but for some reason, the witch claimed to sense a certain smell about the slaves that she could not tolerate. Lucy surmised that perhaps by keeping one of the slaves in the Bell house for the night, she might be able to use its prejudices against the creature and cause the witch to stay away from the main house as she did the slave cabins.

One afternoon, Lucy began to put her plan into action. She craftily recruited one of the slaves, a young girl named Anky, and told her that she wanted her to sleep in the Bell house that night. Lucy told no one of her actual plans, knowing that if she spoke them aloud, the witch was sure to overhear. She merely explained to Anky that she wanted the girl to sleep in her room for the evening. The girl expressed some misgivings about the arrangement, fearing not only the witch, but the other slaves as well because Anky had previously been confined to outdoor work. A position within the household was a coveted one by the slaves and the girl feared that she might incur the wrath of the others due to her apparent promotion in status.

Lucy quickly soothed her fears and told the girl to say nothing to the other slaves. She also assured her that Kate would be too busy entertaining the company in the main room to be bothered by Anky's presence in the bedroom.

So, that evening after supper, Anky quietly slipped into Lucy's room and laid a pallet on the floor beneath the bed. The high bedstead had a white, fringed counterpane that hung all the way to the floor and hid the girl completely. No one would have any idea she was there. She soon settled herself to await the coming of the witch and the talking that would follow.

Soon, the main room was filled with visitors who talked quietly and waited for Kate for to arrive. As for Lucy, she waited anxiously to see what would happened with her scheme.

A short time later, the voice of the witch rang out over the buzz of the conversation in the room. "There is a damn nigger in the house!", Kate's voice thundered, "I can smell her under the bed and she's got to get out."

A moment later, a noise was heard from beneath the bed that sounded like someone choking and trying to clear his or her throat, hawking and spitting. Anky came rolling out from where she had been hidden, her face literally covered with what appeared to be white spittle and flecks of foam. It was as if the witch was coughing the contents of a phlegm-filled throat onto the poor girl's face! Anky scrambled to her feet and wiping desperately at the foul liquid, she ran from the house in tears.

Now, the witch's wrath was turned toward the other occupants of the house. Her voice flared again. "Luce, did you bring that nigger in here?" she demanded.

"Yes, I did," Lucy replied calmly. "I told Anky she might go under my bed, where she would be out of the way, to hear you talk and sing."

Immediately upon Lucy's admission of guilt over the incident, Kate's anger cooled. " I thought so," she replied calmly, "nobody but you, Luce, would have thought of such a smart trick as that - and if anybody else would have done it, I would have killed the damn nigger."

As the reader has been able to plainly see, when Kate had a hatred for something, she was sure to let everyone within earshot know about it. This was also said to be true when it came to the things that Kate liked. Throughout the haunting, she made it clear that she held great respect for the reverends among the Bell's friends, even though she would tease and berate them about their sermons. When she did this, she often played the "devil's advocate" with them, provoking them into religious conversations. She also had a fondness for James Johnston, whom she referred to as "Old Sugar Mouth".

But above all, the witch dearly loved Lucy Bell. It has never been clear just why this was, or what had happened to make her shower affection on the woman, but it was clear that she cared deeply for her. Perhaps she had great sympathy for Lucy as she was saddled with Kate's arch-enemy, John Bell, but who knows? What we do know is that as much as the witch abused John and Betsy Bell, she held a special place in her spectral heart for Lucy. From the very beginning, Kate manifested a high regard for Lucy. "Old

Luce is a good woman," the witch often said.

"This was very gratifying to the family," wrote Richard Williams Bell, "we were all much devoted to her, and this earnest expression of tender respect for her, so often repeated, was to a great extent an assurance that whatever might befall other members of the family, mother would be spared personal affliction."

Of course, this certainly did not mean that Lucy was not afraid of the creature. She did everything she could to exercise a gentle nature toward Kate and by doing this, she appeased the witch in many circumstances and turned Kate's wrath away from the rest of the family. This didn't always work though, because even when Lucy was able to temper the anger the witch had toward Betsy, the hatred toward John Bell continued to be beyond control.

Around the middle part of September 1820, the kindness the witch felt toward Lucy reached its peak. Just a short time before, Lucy was taken ill with pleurisy and was put to bed. Her condition worsened as time wore on and soon, she was gravely ill. No one was more upset by this turn of events than Kate. She made frequent appearances at Lucy's bedside, her voice seemingly choked and tearful. "Luce, poor Luce," she would cry, "I am so sorry you are sick. What can I do for you, Luce?"

These and many other expressions of sympathy came from Kate, day in and day out. The voice remained there in Lucy's sick room, prattling on throughout the day and evening, only pausing while Lucy slept and becoming more cheerful when it seemed the sick woman might be growing stronger. "The persistent jabbering and disquietude was enough to craze a well person," recalled Richard Williams Bell, "but mother bore it all patiently, frequently replying to questions."

At some moments, Kate was too much for even Lucy to bear and she would state that she was much too sick to talk. The voice would then hush for some time unless something was called for or needed that might ease Lucy's suffering. At that point, the witch would order this item to be brought and would announce its exact location. And so Kate remained by Lucy's bedside and while no visitor could claim to know from where the voice of the witch was coming from, they could not deny that she was there, keeping watch over her beloved Lucy.

Some days later, Lucy awoke feeling somewhat better than she had. She had rested well during the night and the morning found her in better spirits. Kate offered to sing a song for her, which was something everyone agreed that the witch excelled at.

"Yes, Kate, sing something sweet," Lucy answered.

The voice of the witch filled the room and soon there was not a dry eye in the house. The visitors to the sick room wept openly and Lucy's eyes filled with tears and trickled down her cheeks. "Thank you, Kate," Lucy told the spirit in a choked voice but soon descended into even greater depths of illness.

Lucy gradually grew worse, the disease reaching a serious and nearly fatal stage. The smell of decaying flesh filled Lucy's bedroom and she was scarcely conscious for more than a few moments at a time. The doctor held out little hope for her recovery. An illness such as this was common on the Tennessee frontier and few survived it.

During Lucy's most lucid moments, her family and friends urged her to try and eat something. Her appetite had failed entirely, which distressed Kate even more than the others. The neighbors brought Lucy many tempting things to eat, believing that getting some food into her system might help her to recover.

Soon, the witch seized upon her own ideas about getting Lucy to eat something. The first items to appear were the hazelnuts, which were ripening in the bottoms and woods of the farm. Lucy had always been fond of them and Kate believed the appearance of some fresh nuts might get her to eat. Kate's voice again came from nowhere. "Luce, poor Luce, how do you feel now? Hold out your hands, Luce, and I will give you something."

Lucy held her hands weakly out in front of her and suddenly a cluster of hazelnuts appeared out of thin air above the bed and rained down into her hands. This event was witnessed by several ladies who had come to call on her and needless to say, they were more than a little surprised.

"Say, Luce, why don't you eat the hazelnuts?" Kate's voice called again and Lucy answered her by saying that she didn't have the strength to crack them open.

"Well, I'll crack them for you!" the presence stated and with that, the sound of cracking was heard and the nuts in Lucy's hands split themselves open and fell onto the blankets of the bed.

The appearance of the nuts (and later, other objects) was among the greatest wonders achieved by the Bell Witch. Not only did this seem to show that the spirit had a dual nature of both benevolence and anger, but the fact that these mysterious appearances usually occurred before the startled eyes of many witnesses gives the true facts behind the haunting even more credibility.

The unexplained appearance of physical objects is called an "apport", meaning that the objects seemingly appear from thin air. Prior to Lucy's illness, there had been many objects that would disappear from the Bell household, only to reappear later in places where they should not have been. This was unusual enough, however, these disappearances and appearances were committed out of sight of witnesses. Once the witch began to "conjure up" food to help Lucy through her illness, she no longer transported items to the house in secret.

At a later occasion, Lucy was entertaining a group of neighbor ladies at the house for a Bible study class when the witch decided that she would provide the refreshments. A wide variety of fruits simply appeared out of the air and dropped onto plates, or into laps, with the witch's spoken invitation to eat them. Like Lucy's hazelnuts, the fruit was very fresh and edible.

One afternoon, during a birthday party for Betsy Bell, the witch suddenly called out that she had a surprise for the friends and family who had gathered together. A large basket suddenly appeared on the table, containing oranges, bananas, grapes and nuts. The spirit called out that she had brought the fruit from the West Indies - but offered no explanation as to how it had accomplished this.

No explanation was offered either as to how the fruit was brought to Lucy's sick room, although the witch never claimed to go to the West Indies to retrieve it. On the same day that she bought the hazelnuts, Kate returned again to Lucy's bed and brought with her a large cluster of grapes that she had obtained somewhere in the forest. She prodded at Lucy to eat them and so the sick woman ate as many as her stomach could hold. She remarked to her friends at how wonderful they tasted.

And apparently, the fresh fruit and nuts were just what she needed for Lucy began to slowly improve. She had been near death for more than 20 days and no one was happier to see her get well than Kate. The witch was heard singing joyfully and told everyone who came to the house that Lucy's cure was owed to Dr. Hopson, the Bell's family physician. Strangely, in this case, Kate was hesitant to claim the credit for something that she most likely had accomplished herself. Despite the aspersions which have been cast on the Bell Witch over the years, it cannot be denied that she saved the life of Lucy Bell.

It seems that Kate's new found skill at apporting physical objects into the house did not end with Lucy's illness, as mentioned already. . A little while later, when Lucy was still gaining her strength back but was able to entertain visitors, the witch repeated her performance.

"Who wants some grapes?" she loudly asked a room full of visitors and family members. Before anyone could answer, a large bunch of wild grapes dropped out of the air and fell into Betsy's lap. "The bunch was passed around and all tasted of the fruit," Richard Bell wrote, "and were satisfied that it was no illusion."

I have attempted, within the pages that have gone before, to get across the idea that the witch was known for her harassment of other people in the community and not for her terrorizing of the Bell family alone. Of course, this statement should be altered to say that all of those who were visited, or who encountered, the witch were friends and intimates of the Bell's and not merely passing strangers. For those skeptics, of both that time and this one, it should be noted that all of these people readily attested to the visitation and the existence of the witch. They certainly regarded the spirit as an outside force and not as a hoax, or manifestation of the family. Kate was definitely a creature to be reckoned with!

Two of those who testified to the existence of the witch were the Johnston brothers, John and Calvin. These two men were frequent visitors to the Bell farm and held many long and intimate conversations with Kate. They were regarded in the community as honorable and honest men, although were markedly different in personality. Calvin was thought of as a plain and forthright fellow, with little use for deception or dishonesty, while John was seen as quite the opposite. He was still well thought of and spoken of a good man, but was much more shrewd than his brother. He was well known for making use of any legitimate means at hand to accomplish a purpose, a skill he plied against Kate.

The witch was very fond of talking and John took every opportunity that he could to engage her in conversation, hoping that he could extract some clue from her as to the mystery of the haunting. While John may have been a skilled trickster, Kate was even more devious and it seems that she was well aware of what he was attempting to do.

One night, the question arose as to the how the witch managed to slap someone in the face when she technically had no hands. Despite the spirit being an invisible force, those who were struck by her certainly noticed the blows! The slaps felt as though they had come from an open hand and at times, the blows would even leave marks like the print of fingers on the unlucky person's cheek.

Calvin Johnston came up with the idea of asking the witch to shake hands with him. After much persuasion, Kate agreed. She did have one condition though, that Calvin would not try to grasp or hold onto the hand that would be placed into his. He agreed and stretched his hand out in front of him. Immediately, he felt the press of a small, cool hand against his. Calvin would later swear that the hand he felt was small and delicate, just like the hand of a lady's, and no one ever doubted him.

John Johnston then began to beg the witch to touch his hand as well. He stated that he was just as good a friend of the witch as his brother was and he deserved to feel her hand as well. Not surprisingly, Kate refused. "I know you, Jack Johnston, you are only looking for a way to catch me!" she said, although John swore this was not the case. "You're a grand rascal, and I won't trust you".

Kate refused to give into him and John Johnson was never able to trick the witch into shaking his hand, although she reportedly shook hands with several other people. Only a few people ever testified to the soft caress of the Bell Witch - but a much greater number told of the sting of her open hand!

One of those who felt the witch's less kindly touch was Nancy Ayres, the daughter of John Johnston and his wife, Patsy. Nancy was born in 1819, during the midst of the haunting and was often brought along with her parents when they went to visit the Bell home. She was interviewed by M.V. Ingram in the 1890's, as he was compiling his *Authenticated History,* and she told him of many stories that her father recalled about the Bell Witch. One such story involved her being spanked by the witch when she was a baby!

At that time, Betsy Bell frequently stayed the night with the Johnston's so that she could stay away from home and hopefully get some rest out of reach of the witch. Unfortunately, the witch often followed her to the Johnston house but John Johnston invited and urged her to come anyway, hoping to offer her some respite if he could and also to follow up on every clue and line of investigation that might offer a solution to the mystery of the haunting. He felt that if he could study Betsy more closely, more information might be revealed. He had been dismayed by the fact that several people who had been trying to detect the cause of the haunting had failed and so they created their own theories as to what was occurring on the Bell farm. In their opinion, Betsy was making the strange events occur, using a remarkable sort of ventriloquism, and working in collusion with another person. Johnston feared that such stories would reach the ears of the Bell's and so he hoped to prove this could not be the case, if possible. We have to remember though that John was a shrewd and clever man and its likely that he might also have suspected that foul play was occurring, despite his friendship for the Bell family. Perhaps he believed that he stood a better chance at determining what was taking place if Betsy were to spend a few nights alone at the Johnston house.

While the witch did not always accompany Betsy to the house, on the occasion in question, she did - talking, scratching, knocking over chairs, pulling the blankets from beds and causing such a disturbance that it was impossible to sleep.

The commotion was especially a problem for little Nancy, who was only an infant at the time. The baby was frequently frightened by the loud sounds and spent much of the night crying. She later stated that she was "fretful and worried mother a great deal, she having to get up frequently to rock my cradle."

Finally, the crying of the baby began to even have an effect on Kate. She spoke up sharply over the sound of the baby's wails, "Patsy, why don't you slap that child and make it behave itself"" she questioned Mrs. Johnston, adding "... and if you don't, I will!"

Moments later, John and Patsy heard what appeared to be a hand connecting with skin and Nancy began to scream! The Johnston's sprang out of bed and put a match to one of the lamps, urgently searching the room to see if anyone else (especially Betsy) had entered it. As Patsy held the baby, John looked everywhere, only to find the room was otherwise empty. Whoever had slapped the baby was nowhere to be found and there was no way that anyone could have gotten in or out of the room without detection.

But, as Nancy Ayres told Martin Ingram several decades later, the cruel spanking did serve somewhat of a purpose. "They said that I behaved like a little lady for the balance of the night," she said.

William Porter was another friend of the Bell family and was a very prominent citizen of Robertson County. He also would later speak of his own encounters with the Bell Witch. He spent many nights at the besieged Bell farm and took his turn entertaining Kate so that others could get some rest. He was also a member of John Bell's investigating committee and took every opportunity to pester and bother Kate about her reasons for haunting the house. Despite his antagonizing her though, Kate took a shine to Will Porter and spoke of him with fondness - and perhaps she even had other ideas in mind for the eligible young bachelor.

At the time of the haunting, Porter lived alone in a log cabin a few miles from the Bell house. The house was fairly large and had been divided into two rooms. At one end of the house was a large fireplace and opposite it, through a door in the dividing wall, was the bedroom.

One cold night, as Porter was preparing to go to bed, he built up a large fire to burn down and keep him warm throughout the dark hours. As soon as he got into bed, he heard a familiar thumping and scratching sound along the wall. That sounds like one of Kate's tricks, he thought to himself, and he was right.

The covers on the bed drew back and Porter heard a soft voice, which was unmistakably Kate's, whisper into his ear. "Billy, I have come to sleep with you and keep you warm," she murmured.

Porter, although frightened, managed to remain calm. "Well, Kate, if you are going to sleep with me," he replied, "you must behave yourself."

He nervously pulled the blankets tighter to him as he felt the covers being lifted on the opposite side of the bed. Then, a solid form slipped beneath them. Porter recalled that the figure that crawled into the bed seemed to give off a chilling sensation. It washed across him in icy cold waves. The blankets continued to slip from his hands, despite his tight grip on them, as if Kate were rolling herself up in them.

When Porter could stand it no more, he jumped out of the bed. When he looked back, he saw a human-like figure, about the size of a woman, twisted beneath the covers. He could see nothing of her face or form, only the shape of a small body wrapped up in the heavy covers.

Porter suddenly had an idea that would end the haunting of the Bell house for good! He sprang forward and grabbed the shape under the covers, scooping it up into his arms, blankets and all. He would throw the entire bundle into the blazing fire and be rid of the witch once and for all!

He turned and started for the fireplace and all at once, the bundle in his arms began to grow supernaturally heavy. Not only did Kate's weight seem to increase, but the bundle began to give off a noxious, overpowering odor. Porter was halfway across the room when she became so heavy, and the smell so bad, that he was forced to drop her. The bundle hit the floor and Porter began to gag and retch from the sickening stench that emitted from it. He stumbled to the front door and threw it open, sucking in breaths of cold, clean air from outdoors.

"After being refreshed," Porter remembered (as he told the story often), "I returned to the room and gathered up the roll of bed clothing and shook them out. Kate had departed, and there was no unusual weight or offensive odor remaining - and this is just how near I came to catching the witch."

Another friend of the Bell family, and John Bell Jr.'s best friend, was a man named Frank Miles. He was very large and powerful man and most regarded him as the strongest man in all of Robertson County. Frank was a rough and burly individual and what we might refer to as a "mountain man". He resided in a remote section of the region and spent most of his time outdoors. Miles was one of the few settlers who was on good terms with the Indians that still remained in the area and was often seen as having much in common with their "wild and dangerous" ways. Miles spent much of his time at the Bell farm during the haunting and had come to think of himself as the protector of the family, and most especially of Betsy Bell. He was under the impression that his strength alone would give him some advantage over Kate.

Miles stayed many nights at the Bell farm, taunting the witch to make an appearance. He was convinced that if he could just get his hands on her, he could get rid of her for good. To most of us, this is not exactly a clear way of thinking, but somewhere along the line, Frank Miles got the idea into his head and refused to let go of it.

Kate seemed amused by Franks' taunts and threats and she teased him mercilessly in return. She dared him to attempt to catch her, purposely moving things around very close to him and begging him to try and stop her. She would laugh at him and cajole him into what became legendary fits of anger. Miles would end up losing his temper and would run around the house, clutching at the air, hoping to get his hands on Kate.

Whenever he would lie down to sleep, she would jerk the blankets from the bed. Miles often caught them in flight and tried with all of his strength to keep the witch from pulling them away. In this manner, they would engage in a spirited tug-of-war, which Miles inevitably lost. Even as powerful as Frank Miles was, he was no match for the strength of the witch. Before the fight was over, the bed covers would usually tear in two, leaving Miles sitting on the bed with scraps of the blanket still clutched in his hands.

Kate would torment Miles more by abusing Betsy in his presence. He could hear her being struck and would see the red welts appear, but he could do nothing. This made him crazy but being a simple man, he simply didn't realize that he was causing many of these attacks to occur. He would tell Betsy to sit close to him and that he would protect her. Kate would then begin slapping her and pulling her hair - just to get a reaction from Frank Miles. Of course, Miles would become enraged again and would start yelling and stomping about the room as he always did. This amused Kate to no end.

On one occasion though, Kate apparently got more than her fill of Miles' antics. She suddenly began slapping Miles himself. His head was rocked backward by the blows and Kate told him that if he didn't leave the house, she would continue beating him until he did. Miles got even madder and began cursing the witch and calling her a coward for picking on poor Betsy and for refusing to take form and confront him to his face.

In revenge, Kate launched her attack on Betsy once again, pulling her hair and pinching her so violently that the girl began to scream in agony. Finally, Frank realized that his continued taunts were not helping Betsy, but hurting her instead. From that time on, he treated the witch with quiet respect and learned not to abuse her if he wanted to protect Betsy Bell at all.

The Bell Witch always made it quite clear that she was not going to suffer fools lightly. Throughout the haunting, as has been mentioned already, there were a number of "witch-slayers" and debunkers who came to the Bell farm, intent on either driving out the witch or proving that the entire affair was a hoax. These detectives, wise men, witch doctors and conjurors were all allowed to practice their schemes and magic arts in any way they wished and without fail, each of them left the farm confessing that the strange events were beyond their understanding.

On one occasion, a "witch doctor" arrived and announced that he could cure Betsy Bell of the spirit if she would take the medicine he gave her. The conjurer told her that it would likely make her quite sick but if she swallowed it all, the witch would be gone. While her mother and Betsy's closest friend, Theny Thorn, begged her not to swallow the foul mixture, Betsy replied that she "would take anything that anybody would give her, even if it was poison, to get rid of her excruciating pest."

Betsy took the medicine and within an hour became very sick and soon began to vomit. Incredibly though, the expelled contents of her stomach were found to contain dozens of pins and needles! The witch seemed to find this hilarious and spoke aloud to assure the family that this was the only conjurer to visit the house who had done them any good - he had made Betsy throw up enough pins and needles to supply the entire community!

The conjurer was astounded, believing that his own folk magic had been at work to create the pins and needles, and went on his way, quite satisfied with himself. Theny believed that Kate had somehow dropped the objects into the vomit by mysterious means, as Betsy could not have lived with them in her stomach. She did declare that they had been real brass pins and needles though, wherever they had come from, and that she and her mother had gathered some up and kept them throughout both of their lives.

Another conjurer created quite a controversy on the Bell farm. This particular "witch killer" collected 12 silver dollars from John Bell and then placed them into a bowl of water. He then proceeded to perform a variety of incantations over them. He instructed the family to leave the money in the bowl over night and on the following morning, to have Betsy drink the water and after that, the witch would be gone. However, when daylight came, the witch was still haunting the house - but the silver dollars were gone!

John Bell was furious and blame was placed on one of the slaves. The young man had carried wood into the house during the night and had been near the bowl of water. Bell threatened to whip the man if he did not return the money. Before he could carry out his threats though, Kate's voice was heard by John Bell. It was the only time that she ever came to the defense of one of the slaves, who she vehemently despised. "Hold on, Jack," she said to Bell," that nigger is innocent. I can tell you who got that money." She then went on to whisper the name of the man in Bell's ear and also to tell him that he had gone to Springfield and bought "some nice things with it."

A few evenings later, John Johnston was visiting the house and was entertaining the witch while the family and other visitors slept. After everyone else had gone to bed, Johnston was leaning back in a chair against the wall, waiting for Kate's presence to arrive. He felt something touch him on the shoulder, he later recalled, and then heard the voice of the witch. "Did you hear about the money scrape that we had the other evening?" Kate asked him and Johnston replied that he had.

Kate went on. "It was funny. I saved that nigger from a good whipping by telling old Jack who got the money," she told him and then also told John about the man's trip to Springfield and the purchases that he made with the 12 silver dollars, a considerable sum in those days.

A few days later, Johnston had the occasion to be in Springfield and out of curiosity, he inquired at the store where the witch said the untrustworthy friend had made his purchases. He was surprised to discover that the transactions had taken place just as the witch had said!

(Note: I have been unable to find any record of who this person may have been. This is not surprising though for it's likely that none of those who recorded the case wanted to cast aspersions on anyone, even if that person was dishonest. Such vague reporting is common throughout the story, especially when it comes to gossip and stories that are

passed on by the witch concerning neighbors and friends of the family. I imagine that many lurid things were told that did not appear in the accounts of the case!)

Another conjurer who visited the Bell farm was a man named Dr. Mize, who lived in Simpson County, Kentucky (about 35 miles from the community) and who was known all over the region for being a skilled magician. He was not a stage illusionist, as we think of a magician today, but a man who was renowned for his skill with the folk magic, healing and cures. He was also one of the few such people who came not because of curiosity about the witch, but because he was actually summoned to the house by John Bell. There had been much talk among Bell's friends that Dr. Mize might be just the man to get rid of the bothersome spirit. He had an excellent reputation and so they urged John Bell to send for him.

By this time, Bell was starting to grow quite concerned about his own physical condition. His twitching spells and seizures were growing more frequent and more severe and he began to fear that the witch really was going to carry through with her promise to kill him. Kate's animosity toward him had increased as well and her threats had become more dire, and thus more terrifying.

Finally, Bell consulted with James Johnston about the matter of the wizard. Both men felt they had exhausted every other possibility in dealing with Kate and decided they might as well give Dr. Mize the opportunity to try and get rid of the witch. Johnston offered to accompany Drew Bell on the trip to Kentucky. They would leave later that night, around three o'clock in the morning, when no one else was about and when Kate was usually silent.

The word was spread through the household that Drew was to accompany Johnston on a business trip that would last for two or three days. Otherwise, the entire affair was kept secret. That night, the two men slipped away under the cover of the night and rode off toward Kentucky. They reached Simpson County by the following morning and managed to get directions of where to find the so-called "wizard".

When dawn came at the Bell farm, Kate put in her first appearance of the day and right off, asked about the location of Drew. Everyone in the house answered her queries with ignorance and soon Kate announced that she was leaving. She was not heard from for the rest of the day, but returned that night in good spirits. She laughed and announced that she had discovered the two men's secret plans and went on to add her own strange details about their trip.

"I got on their track and overtook them about 20 miles distant," she told everyone, "and followed along some distance, and when I hopped in the road before them, looking like a poor old sick rabbit, 'Old Sugar Mouth' said 'There is your witch, Drew; take her up and put her in your lap. Don't you see how tired she is?" Kate then continued to gossip and relate details about the journey.

Of course, no one knew for sure just how true the story was until Johnston and Drew returned the following evening and confirmed everything Kate had said. Johnston told them that he didn't really believe the rabbit was the witch when he joked with Drew, but was merely passing the time as they rode.

Regardless, the purpose of the trip had been achieved and they had found Dr. Mize at his home in Franklin, Kentucky. They explained to him why they had come and told of the strange phenomena related to the witch. Mize replied that while the case was a little out of the ordinary as far as most phenomena went, he would gladly come and see what he could do about it. He had no doubt of his ability to "remove the spell" and expose the witchcraft that had brought the calamity upon the Bell's in the first place. He gave them a date, ten days later, when he would come to the house and begin the experiment.

On the promised day. Dr. Mize arrived at the Bell farm. He claimed to be prepared for business and began boasting of his knowledge of the spirit world and his skill at casting out devils. He quickly set to work and stayed at the farm for three days, never hearing a breath from Kate during the entire time. As the witch had often done before, it remained silent, as though observing the meddler who claimed that he was able to rid the farm of the creature.

In the meantime (probably with nothing better to do), Mize discovered an old shotgun in the barn that had not been in working order for some time. He announced to the family that the witch had put a spell on it and that this had caused it not to work. He cleaned the gun, readjusted the lock and trigger, performed some "conjurations" and got the gun working again.

John Bell was not impressed. He had sized up Mize when the man had arrived and had gotten more than his fill already of the man's loudmouth boasts and bragging. He knew the man had worked no magic with the old gun and was ready for him to leave the farm. Still though, he courteously allowed him to stay, knowing that once that Kate did put in an appearance, they would see the true mettle of the man.

After getting the "hexed" gun back in working order, Mize became even more confident of his skills and now announced that the witch had most likely left and would probably not return again. He was certain that she would not show up while he was present at the farm anyway. Witches, he said, were always shy of him.

With those pronouncements, Mize remained at the farm for the next couple of days, generally making a fool of himself as far as the Bell's were concerned. He spent his time working sorcery, making curious mixtures and performing incantations, all to the amusement of the Bell family and their friends.

Finally (when she could probably stand no more), Kate made an appearance. Her first words were demands of Dr. Mize, as to what he was trying to do and why he was at the farm. Mize tried to remain very calm and outwardly, was not bothered by the harsh, disembodied voice. He was very evasive in reply to Kate's questions and answered that she had no business prying into his affairs.

Of course, this had never stopped Kate before and she didn't let it deter her this time either. She continued to harass him with queries then began insulting him, questioning his skills as a magician. She suggested that he had left out some very important ingredients in one of his magic mixtures. Mize demanded to know what they were and Kate craftily answered him, stating that he would know if he was a genuine witch doctor.

"If you were," she told him, "you would know how to aerify that mess, so as to pass into an aeriform state, and see the spirit that talks to you, without asking silly questions."

This statement apparently startled Dr. Mize as he realized that Kate knew the purpose of the concoction that he had been mixing. She soon took to cursing him and calling him a fraud and an old fool. As the shrill voice surrounded the man on all sides, he began to get very frightened and ran for the house. Finally, Kate left him alone.

It wasn't long before Dr. Mize was packing his belongings, planning an early start the next morning. That thing, he told the household, knew much more about witchcraft than he did and for that reason, he could do nothing about it. He would bid the family farewell and be on his way at sunrise.

The next morning, Mize mounted his horse and spurred it towards home - but the animal refused to budge. Suddenly, Kate's voice rang out in the yard. She would get the animal to move and she would also accompany the doctor home! With a snort and a hard kick, the horse jumped and then took off at full speed, leaving Dr. Mize to hold on for dear life.

Kate returned to the Bell house that night, once again in great spirits, describing the trip home with the "old fraud" and the tricks that she played on him along the way. Needless to say, Dr, Mize did not return again to the Bell farm during the haunting - or at any time after that either!

Many of those who came to investigate the case did not do so with the idea that the supernatural might be at work. A great many of them were convinced that some human prankster was involved, or that the Bells themselves had been deceiving their friends for some time.

One such man was a handsome stranger that Richard Williams Bell referred to only as "Mr. Williams". This man was a professional detective who arrived at the Bell farm one day, stating that he had heard much of the witch mystery and wanted to look into it. He told the household that he was interested in things that no one could explain and had considerable experience unraveling tangled affairs and mysteries. Williams had apparently traveled a great distance to come to Tennessee and over the next few hours, he explained that he did not believe in the supernatural, but believed there was a simple explanation for the events taking place. He was also a self-proclaimed expert in detecting sleight-of-hand performances and illusions and if such things were going on at the farm, he would detect them.

John Bell welcomed the detective with open arms. By this time, he was long past believing in a logical explanation for the witch but if this man wanted to satisfy his own curiosity he was welcome to. It is also possible that, deep down in his heart, Bell truly hoped that someone would succeed in solving the mystery and that his family would be able to live in peace.

Williams settled into the Bell house and cheerfully accepted the offers of food and bed for the night. Richard Bell described the man as being quite the talker and guessing from the description he was given in Bell's writings, he began to wear on the family after awhile. Bell wrote: "Mr. Williams was a rather portly, strong-muscled, well-dressed, handsome gentleman. He was no less self-possessed, and wise in his own conceit, full of gab, letting his tongue run continually, detailing to the company his wonderful exploits in the detective business, and was very sure he would bring Kate to grief before leaving."

A day and a night passed with Williams in the house and during this entire period, Kate made no sound other that a little scratching on the walls and some thumping about the room. It was as though she wanted the family to know she was still present, but would make no spectacle for the conceited detective.

Finally, Williams began to grow impatient and irritated. He soon began speaking his mind about the case and spoke to a small group of visitors who had dropped by the house to observe Kate's activities. He unwisely told these men that he believed the Bell family had invented the whole affair in an effort to attract visitors to the farm and to get money from them. Williams also added that he was convinced the actors behind the "witch" were afraid to make any demonstrations while he was present. They knew his business and profession, he said, and knew that he would expose them as charlatans.

Almost as soon as those words left Williams' lips, one of Bell's friends came over to him and repeated the detective's claims and accusations. To say that John Bell was angry would be an understatement and his son, Richard, noted that he was "outraged". He had extended Williams every courtesy and hospitality and had offered any assistance that he could to help the man get to the heart of the matter. Now, without a shred of evidence, he was making bold and disparaging remarks about the Bell family. John Bell rose from his seat and went to find the man - he was determined to remove him bodily from the premises.

As he marched across the yard, he felt the familiar, prickling presence of the witch. "No you don't, old Jack," Kate warned him, "you just let the man stay - I will attend to the gentleman and satisfy him that he is not so smart as he thinks."

Bell said no more and stifled his anger. Below the surface, he simmered, but to Williams' face, he treated the man with the same courtesy that he had shown him before.

That evening, the house was crowded with visitors, all anxious to experience the witch. The night wore on without a sound from Kate and it began to get very late. Williams fussed and fumed and once again, opened his mouth when he shouldn't have. He snorted in derision at the entire affair and announced to several other guests that no so-called "witch" was going to show up while he was there.

Another hour or so passed and the assembled company began to grow tired. Lucy had placed some straw mattresses on the floor for the guests and Williams selected one for himself and stretched out on it. Soon, all of the lights in the house had been extinguished and the family and guests began, one by one, to drift off to sleep.

Williams was just on the verge of drifting off himself when he felt a tremendous pain in his arms and legs! It was as if several large men were holding him down and pinning him to the floor. He was unable to move and he gasped loudly in pain! Soon, solid blows began to rain down upon him and his face twitched back and forth as solid slaps reddened his cheeks. It felt as though he was being beaten by an entire gang of men! The fists and sharp hands seemed to come from everywhere at once, poking and prodding his abdomen and pummeling his chest, his arms and his kidneys. It was all that he could do to cry out even once before the air was punched from his lungs.

One of the guests, shaken awake by the sound of the beating, lit a nearby candle and soon, all were astounded to see the burly detective in the throes of agony. His arms and legs were stretched out and held fast and his body was rocked by stinging blows. Williams began to scream in terror! A mad, cackling laugh sounded in the room and Kate's voice rang out. Which one of the Bell family did the detective believe had a hold of him? she asked him. Was he still so sure that she was a hoax?

Williams was never given a chance to answer before Kate began beating him again. Kate did the all of the talking instead and she spoke a good bit more than the detective cared to hear! By the time she was finished with him, Williams was all done in. "The detective was badly used up," wrote Richard Williams Bell, "and the worst scared man that ever came to our house."

Terrified, the man sat up the rest of the night, perched on the edge of a chair with a bright candle at his elbow. Kate continued to harass him all night long, questioning him as to what members of the family were in on the joke, how much longer he planned to stay and about just what he had learned from his investigations.

As soon as daylight came, Williams fetched his horse and rode off. He could not be convinced to stay long enough to have breakfast.

But not all of the investigators were intent on proving that the witch was not real. In many cases, those who delved into the mystery of the witch were trying to answer the accusations of debunkers who insisted that the family were merely trying to deceive the public with tales of a ghost. Many of these men were friends of the Bell's and while they may not have made their investigations common knowledge to the family, many of them were pursuing possible solutions on their own. They needed to satisfy their own curiosity about a possible hoax (like John Johnston) or wanted to have the ammunition in their arsenal to defend the family against verbal attacks by those who doubted the case.

The most prominent accusations of the time were made by those who insisted that Betsy Bell, or one of the others, was using ventriloquism to create the voice of the witch. I will not bother the reader with the number of reasons why this could not be possible at this time, but suffice it to say, it was a common enough solution offered by the doubters in those days.

One friend of the Bell family, Dr. William Fort, was so distressed by the idea that one of the Bell's could be inventing such a ruse that he traveled all the way from his home in Missouri to investigate the matter. Dr. Fort gained the cooperation of the Bell's and had each of the accused members of the family be seated in a room with him and then he proceeded to silence all of them while the witch was speaking. Not only did he place his hand over their mouths, but he also placed another hand over their throat to feel the possible sensation of their voice box. During the entire experiment, Kate rambled on and on with no change or modulation in the tone of her spectral voice.

Dr. Fort went away convinced of the reality of the haunting, as did John Johnston, who was a good friend of the Bell's but (as mentioned earlier) was concerned about the possibility of deception. Over time, perhaps thanks to the ghostly visitations in his own home, John became totally convinced that Betsy was innocent of the charges of fraud leveled against her. He had been told that the witch never talked when Betsy's mouth was closed, but Johnston proved this was wrong and found that Kate would speak when Betsy had her lips closed together - and even when she was not around at all. He recalled many occasions when the witch would address him directly, even though Betsy was asleep or was staying the night at the home of a friend.

In addition, he also believed that the witch did, knew and said many things about which Betsy could have known nothing. Kate talked and gossiped about happenings around the region and seemed familiar with everyone's business. She also spoke of things that no one who would be present knew about (only to have the information confirmed later) and would often address strangers by name, telling everyone where the stranger was from even before they could introduce themselves. She could also quote huge portions of scripture, had immense knowledge of the Bible and then on the other hand, could curse and swear like a sailor!

Johnston simply did not believe that Betsy Bell, or any other member of the family, could be capable of the things that the spirit had done!

He came to believe that the spirit was an intelligent entity and not a parlor game of some sort. Kate passed on an incredible amount of information to Johnston, which was recalled later, and this was perhaps done because she had taken such a liking to him. According to Johnson, he would often converse with the witch late at night, after everyone else had gone to bed. As stated before, he would entertain Kate so that the Bell family could rest. Years later, he would remember one conversation that he had with her about the reasons behind the haunting.

Johnston always seemed to find that he got the best response from the spirit when he flattered her and made her feel important. He did so on this night and then proceeded to ask her to tell him more about herself, in confidence, with no one else listening.

But Kate refused. "No, I can't tell you all that yet," she replied. "I can't tell you that, but I will before I leave."

"How long before you leave?" Johnston queried.

"I won't tell you that either, but I will not leave as long as Jack Bell lives."

"Have you really come to kill Jack?"

"Yes," the witch snapped at him. "I have told him that often."

"What has Jack done that you want to kill him?"

"Oh nothing particular - I just don't like him."

"But everybody in the country likes him and regards him as a fine gentleman, don't they?" Johnston pressured her into answering.

Kate testily replied. "Yes - and that is the reason he needs killing."

"But Kate, if you kill Jack without giving a better reason than that, people will think hard of you, and then according to the law, you will be hung for murder, won't you?"

Johnston never reveals how he thinks that the spirit can be arrested and charged for murder!

Kate replied cryptically to Johnston's question. "No, it's catching before hanging," she said and seems to mean that no one can hang someone that cannot catch - or even see, in this case.

"Yes, but isn't the maxim 'murder will out' equally true?" Johnston answered, perhaps hoping to imply to the spirit that if John Bell is killed, then those who are angry about the crime might find a way to discover who, or what, Kate is.

The witch was unconvinced by this though. "That may be - but still its catching before hanging!"

Johnston then tried to change the subject and he turned the conversation toward the topic of Betsy Bell. "Well, Kate," he said to the presence, "tell me why you hate Betsy, isn't she a sweet and lovely girl?"

"How do you know that I hate Betsy?"

"Because you are always following her and hurting her."

"Is that any proof that I hate her?" Kate scoffed.

"But you pull her hair, pinch her arms and stick pins in her."

"Well, don't lovers play with each other that way sometimes?"

"No, I never did," Johnston told her. "No man who really loves a girl would serve her as you do Betsy." This part of the conversation is interesting to note because it seemed that Johnston was under the impression, despite the fact that the spirit spoke with a woman's voice and was called "Kate", that the presence was actually a male.

"How do you know that I am a man?"

"Because you get drunk and curse sometimes and say and do thing that no proper woman would."

"But why should I be a woman - may I not be a spirit or something else?"

"No Kate, you are no spirit. A spirit can't pull covers from beds, slap people, pull hair, stick pins, scratch and do such things as you."

The witch seemed to get some amount of delight from Johnston's reply. "Well, I will make you think I am a spirit before you get home!"

"How are you going to do that?"

"I'm going to scare you."

"You can't scare me, Kate. I know that you are too good a friend to do me harm and therefore, I am not afraid of you."

"Well, just wait until you start through the woods home and see if I don't make you hump yourself."

Johnston laughed off the warning and asked Kate once again just who she was and where she lived.

The spirit quickly replied. "I live in the woods, in the air and in the water; in houses with people; I live in heaven and in hell; I am all things and anything that I want to be - now don't you know who I am?"

Johnston pressed the presence for a more straightforward answer but Kate refused to give it. The account states that they talked long into the night and around the time the embers in the fireplace began to burn low, the witch departed and so Johnston decided to start home. He pulled his coat about him and stepped off the front porch and into the night.

He later said that almost as soon as he reached the woods, the trees and bushes around him began to shake and crack as if some huge creature was approaching in the darkness. Sticks and tree branches started to snap and quiver and pieces of wood began to rain down on him as though something that he could not see was towering above him. And while Johnston never admitted, in his tellings of the story, that he ran away, its not hard to imagine that he did. It seems likely that he dashed along that forest trail just as fast as his legs would carry him ~ and it seems just as likely that he never made light of the warnings of the Bell Witch again!

Perhaps the most mysterious investigator of events at the Bell farm was an "Englishman" whose true identity was never revealed ~ not in the writings of the case nor by the witch itself! According to Charles Bailey Bell, this Englishman came and spent several months on the farm, becoming good friends over time with John Bell Jr. He had expressed a determination to solve the mystery of the witch, although like all of the others, he never succeeded. Only John knew who this man actually was because it was expressly understood with all present that his name and residence were not to be known. This was readily agreed to by the Bell family and their friends and even Kate managed to keep his secret, which was not something the witch normally would have done. She made no announcement of the man's identity, but she did, according to Charles Bailey Bell, give "some extra performances, apparently for his enlightenment, telling him that he would have some real tales to write up on his return to England." John never revealed who this man was but only assured everyone that he was a man of high class and of great intelligence. It has been surmised by some that he may have been a member of Britain's royal family, but even this is nothing but guesswork.

Needless to say though, the Englishman was suitably impressed by the works of the witch as even the most skeptical were said to be in awe of the supernatural powers displayed. During his visit, at a Sunday night meeting in the Bell home, the spirit repeated the sermon of Reverend James Gunn, preached at the Bethel Methodist Church, for those who had not been in attendance at the morning service. Reverend Gunn was present on this evening and his voice was imitated so closely that it was thought at first that he had been talking. As before, Gunn was amused by this mimicking and admitted that the sermon text and the prayers offered had been the same as the ones that he had given that morning. The witch then went on to deliver a different sermon by the Reverend Fort, which had been at his own church that morning. The performance was astonishing.

The Englishman was said to have given serious thought as to how something like this could be accomplished and the witch seemed to take note of this. The spirit's voice addressed the man and told him that he was "sensible" to have remained in the house and praised him for not "saying the foolish things that others had." But since he was puzzled by what he had seen, Kate would give him some time to think about things. In two or three hours, she promised him, he would hear from home and she asked him what message he might want to pass along to his family.

During the time of his visit, the witch had often told the Englishman of events that were taking place at his home. He always found out that the information passed along to him was true through the letters that he received in care of the Bell family. However, this was the first time that the witch had ever offered to convey a message in the opposite direction, so the Englishman decided to take advantage of this and also decided to test the true powers of the witch.

He spoke up. "Tell them that in my opinion, never since the world was created have men seen and heard the marvelous things that I have witnessed during the past three months."

About three hours later, the voice of the witch (which had been silent until this time) broke the stillness of the room and repeated in the Englishman's voice the astonished statement that he had given. No sooner were these words spoken when another voice was heard. It exclaimed incredulously: "Why, that is my brother's voice; where are you brother?"

The Englishman told John Bell and John Jr., who were the only other persons present at the time, that the voice he heard was a perfect imitation of his brother back in England. Moments later, it was followed by another voice, a clear woman's voice that was unlike the voice of the spirit itself. This voice spoke: "Tell him not to stay any longer; he has heard and seen enough - and we do not want any more visits like that here!"

The Englishman knew that the second voice was undoubtedly that of his mother but to prove it, he wrote to John Jr. after he returned home and stated that the words of the witch had been correct. His mother and brother had been amazed by the visitation and were hardly able to believe what had happened.

It has often been said that there are three names from Tennessee that are familiar to people all over America - Davy Crockett, Andrew Jackson and the Bell Witch. It might surprise many people to know that two of those personages, Jackson and the Witch, actually crossed paths at one time. In fact, the event was so memorable to Jackson that the future president told anyone who would listen that he "would rather face the whole of the British army than deal with the torment they call the Bell Witch".

Andrew Jackson is remembered by most today as one of the most influential of the pre-Civil War American presidents, but he had a checkered and adventurous career before that. Jackson had been born in Waxhaw, South Carolina in 1767, the son of a poor farm couple who had come to America from Northern Ireland just two years before. Jackson's father died just a few days before his son was born, clearing land on his family's farm. His mother did the best that she could to raise him on her own, but Jackson possessed a frontier lad's thirst for excitement. Elizabeth Jackson hoped her son would become a minister, but Andrew had other plans.

She did however, insure that he received a good education. In those days, men who were able to read were still quite rare and Jackson's knowledge of letters gave him a respected status in the frontier community. Several times each day, he would stand in a public place and read aloud from the latest newspapers. His voice guaranteed a receptive audience and made him quite important in the area, even as a young boy.

Around this same time period, the American Revolution broke out as the colonies had finally gotten their fill of economic exploitation, high taxes and interference in their internal affairs. In 1778, the British launched what turned out to be a poor strategy to retake the colonies by invading the southern regions and moving northward. The Revolution in the south became largely a guerilla conflict with bands of American fighters ambushing British troops and then vanishing into the forests of the Carolinas and Georgia.

The war reached the Jackson family very quickly. Andrew's oldest brother was killed in 1779 and his mother became a nurse. Jackson (then 13 years-old) and his brother, who was three years older, joined the mounted militia and fought bravely. In April 1781, both boys were captured by British troops. While Andrew was imprisoned, one of the British officers ordered Jackson to clean his boots, but the young man refused. The Englishman lashed out with his sword and wounded Jackson's hand and his head. He was then forced to march, along with his brother Robert, to a military prison that lay more than 40 miles away. While incarcerated in the filthy camp, both brothers came down with smallpox. Andrew survived his bout with the disease, but his brother did not. Jackson was later released in a prisoner exchange, arranged by his mother, but the entire affair produced a lifelong hatred for the British. His hatred was further inflamed when his mother also died from smallpox, having contracted it caring for the wounded.

After the war, and after America's successful bid for independence, Jackson lived with relatives and tried his hand at saddle making and teaching. He had a reputation as a troublemaker though ~ riding his horse too fast, drinking and fighting - was feared by most men for he grew quite tall for the period, standing more than six feet.

His destiny changed in 1784, when he left home and took up the study of law in Salisbury, North Carolina. He was admitted to the bar in 1787 and just one year later, he moved to the frontier state of Tennessee. He settled first in Jonesboro and opened a practice, finding that lawyers were much in demand to settle land claims, arrests and bad debts. However, trouble found Jackson right away. An argument with another lawyer in town led to an insult and Jackson, a notoriously good shot, challenged the other man to a duel. At the last minute though, Jackson presented the man with a side of bacon and a joke and the two patched up their differences and went to have a drink.

A few years later, Jackson moved further west to Nashville, which would become his lifetime home. Shortly after his arrival here, he was appointed to the post of Attorney General. Jackson's rugged stubbornness made him the perfect candidate for this job. At that time, Tennessee was filled with rough and tumble settlers and frontiersmen, who often refused to pay their debts and who ignored the laws of the state. Jackson answered their vigor with his own and many of these men found themselves spending time behind bars until their debts were settled.

Around this same time, he met the daughter of one of the city's founders, Rachel Robards. Rachel was considered to be one of the most beautiful women in the region and was also reputed to be the best dancer, best storyteller and an accomplished horsewoman. Jackson immediately fell in love, despite the fact that Rachel was married. She was separated from her husband, but her marriage vows had not yet been severed. Rachel's husband returned to Nashville to try and patch things up with her, but when he found out that she had been seeing Jackson, he filed charges against him. At the trial, Jackson fiddled with a huge knife while he shot murderous glances at his nervous rival. The case was eventually thrown out and Rachel's husband began divorce proceedings right away. Jackson and Rachel married in August 1791, even though her divorce was not yet legally final - a problem that would return to haunt Jackson later on.

Shortly after this, Tennessee became the 16th state in the Union and Jackson was asked to help write the constitution and design its government. Tradition has it that it was Jackson's idea to name the state "Tennessee", after the Cherokee name of the river of the same name in the area. In 1796, Jackson was elected as the first member of the United States House of Representatives from Tennessee but missed Rachel and resigned the seat. Six months later, he took over one of Tennessee's seats in the U.S. Senate for a friend who had been expelled from it for wrongdoing. When the term ended, he spent the next six years as one of the state's three superior court judges.

Soon, Jackson's leadership abilities earned him a position as a Major General in the Tennessee militia, but the appointment did not come without controversy. There were some, and most prominently former governor John Sevier, who opposed Jackson in military command. Jackson's old enemy declared that he was little more than a savage and was unfit to lead troops. In 1803, the two men encountered one another on the steps and the state capitol and the governor made a disparaging comment about Rachel Jackson. Angry words flew, followed by fists and bullets. The two men had to be separated by others and Jackson challenged the other man to a duel. Sevier refused and so Jackson took out an advertisement in the newspaper, calling the older man a coward. The disgraced politician then apparently convinced a wealthy young marksman named Charles Dickinson to insult Rachel's honor and to provoke a duel with Jackson. Andrew responded as he was expected to and met Dickinson's party in a Kentucky field at dawn. Dickinson got off the first shot and his bullet struck Jackson in the chest. Jackson fired just moments after the other man but his bullet found its mark and Dickinson was killed. The bullet in Jackson's chest was so close to his heart that it could not be removed by the surgeons of the time. It remained with him for the rest of his days.

Rachel nursed her husband back to health and from all accounts, she became the center of his life. She was a calming influence on the hardened frontiersman and was known for being generous to friends and strangers alike. Rachel ran the household, which was always swarming with visitors since everyone was welcome, and oversaw the Jackson's 20 slaves. A sad series of miscarriages kept the Jackson's from having any children of their own but in 1810, they adopted the child of a sick relative and their lives settled down until war brought Andrew Jackson back into military service again.

As war was breaking out with the British in 1812, Jackson began looking for a military command. He helped to fund and raise an army of volunteers from Tennessee and hoped to be named their commander. However, military leaders in Washington were wary of Jackson's reputation and ignored his requests. Finally, a friend managed to get him an officer's commission and in 1813, the militia was ordered to New Orleans to reinforce American troops there against British invasion. No sooner did they arrive there than Jackson was ordered to disband his army. Needless to say, the General was more than a little angry. The government had not provided food, clothing or even pay for his men but had expected them to make the march on their own, only to be told to disband when arriving. So, in typical Andrew Jackson style, he refused and turned his men and marched them back to Tennessee. Jackson was nearly ruined financially by his support for the venture but rallied his men anyway. One of them commented that "He's as tough as old hickory" and the nickname stuck. "Old Hickory" returned to Nashville in a dark mood and promptly got into another fight with a rival, a colonel of volunteers named Thomas Hart Benton.

Benton made several remarks about Jackson's integrity and judgment and Jackson came after him at the hotel where he was staying in Nashville. He burst in the door with a gun in his hand and pointed it at Benton. Meanwhile, Benton's brother, Jesse, opened fire on Jackson. The distraction allowed Benton time to fire twice at the general. Jackson fell with a wound in his arm but managed to wing Benton with his own shot. Others soon joined in the fight with guns and daggers and Benton was stabbed five times. He managed to survive the battle to move to St. Louis and there he became a prominent citizen, politician and city leader. Doctors who treated Jackson after the fight ordered that his arm be amputated but Jackson refused and the bullet was left in his arm.

Some weeks later, Creek Indians, who were being supplied and encouraged by the British, killed nearly 400 men, women and children in what is now Alabama. Jackson left his hospital bed to lead 2,000 men in a campaign against them. The militia fought in a terrible battle near Horseshoe Bend on the Tallapoose River in March 1814. Jackson's army wiped out the entire Indian force of 800 warriors, but before the battle, he allowed the women and children of the Indian army to cross the river to safety. Then, known to the Indians as "Sharpknife", Jackson imposed a harsh treaty on the Creeks and required them to surrender 23 million acres of their land. This victory brought Jackson national attention for the first time.

Exhausted and sick, Jackson rode home to a wild welcome in Nashville. He fell into bed for nearly a month, suffering from not only his poorly healed bullet wound but from infections and chronic dysentery. During his recovery, Jackson was promoted to the army's highest rank and was given command of the entire southern theater of war. There was much to do, especially with the British massing in the West Indies for an invasion of New Orleans.

Jackson reached New Orleans with a small advance party on December 2, 1814. The city was a rich and bustling port in those days and the export center for the cotton-growing south. It was also diversely populated by French, Spanish, Creole, Irish, Americans, Africans (both free and slaves) and even pirates. The city was largely in a panic at the threat of the approaching British forces. Although still sick, Jackson unified the various factions in the city, proclaiming martial law and organizing a solid defense.

The defenders of New Orleans were badly outnumbered and had no military training whatsoever. Ammunition was in short supply. Artillery was woefully inadequate. And to make matters worse, the commander was confined to his bed with dysentery and a high fever. In spite of his health though, Jackson still managed to enlisted the aid of every breathing human being who could fire a gun. He accepted the assistance of regiments of free people of color, Kentuckians who came downriver on flatboats, Choctaw Indians and even pirate brigades under the command of Jean Lafitte and his brother, Pierre.

Lafitte had a fleet of more than two dozen ships, hundreds of battle-hardened men on his payroll and a ready supply of cannons hidden away in the local bayous. He asked for a deal from Jackson - his help in exchange for a pardon for his countless crimes. Jackson agreed and Lafitte and his men joined in the battle to save the city.

On December 23, a warship crept near the shore where the British were camped outside of New Orleans and blasted the encampment with cannon fire. Moments later, Jackson's ground troops swept over the British soldiers. The English forces were led by General Pakenham and although fresh from defeating Napoleon, they suffered a severe blow at the hands of ragtag troops made up of Kentuckian Long Rifles, ill-prepared militia men, Indians, Creoles, free men of color and pirates. The fighting raged back and forth for several bitterly cold days between Christmas and New Years Day. The British continued to be reinforced with each passing day until they greatly outnumbered the American forces in New Orleans. Jackson remained awake around the clock, overseeing the free citizens and slaves as they dug earthwork fortifications and manned the cannons that had arrived, thanks to Lafitte and his pirates.

On New Year's Day, the British attacked the city's defenses, only to be driven back. Then, on January 8, the final battle took place on the muddy and mist-covered grounds of Chalmette Plantation. The Americans huddled behind bales of straw and cotton and soon began to hear the ghostly sounds of bagpipes and drums coming from the fog. Long after they heard the sounds of the approach, they were able to see the colors of the Duchess of York's Light Dragoons and the tartans of the 93rd Highlanders. The British troops charged, advancing in tight, efficient lines.

But the combat-hardened troops were no match for the desperate men of New Orleans. The militiamen, the hastily organized regiments and the pirates savagely blasted the British lines without mercy. By later that day, Jackson's army had prevailed, with only 15 men dead and 40 wounded. The British were not so lucky. The carnage on their side consisted of 858 dead and about 2,500 wounded.

Shortly after the battle, news reached the city that the British had signed a peace treaty at Ghent on Christmas Eve, two weeks before the Battle of New Orleans.

Andrew Jackson became the "hero of New Orleans" and this description was remarkably fitting. A man with no formal military training, leading a force that was more rabble than army, had risen from his sickbed, gone 70 hours straight without sleep, and had defeated one of the most feared armies on earth. He made news all over America and rumors began to spread that he might even be president someday!

In 1824, the American presidential election was held to determine who would succeed James Monroe in office. Representing the Democrats, Jackson ran against John Quincy Adams and Henry Clay. In popular votes, Jackson won triple the support of most of the other contenders for the office and nearly twice as many as Adams. However, since no candidate had a majority of the electoral college, the election was sent to the House of Representatives. After political dealings among party leaders, Clay gave his support to Adams and three days later, Adams was named as the new president. He quickly named Henry Clay as his secretary of state. Jackson and his backers were certain that Adams had paid Clay off and accused Adams and Clay of having made a "corrupt bargain" that had denied the people their choice for president. Jackson resigned from the Senate, where he had been serving, and returned to Tennessee. However, he vowed to avenge the "stolen" election and deny Adams a second term. The Tennessee legislature started the election rolling by nominating Jackson for president in October 1825.

The election of 1828 was the first mass-marketed election, complete with fireworks shows, barbecues and rallies - and it was also very nasty. From the beginning, it was personal. Jackson was already convinced that he was the rightful president and Adams' backers were horrified at the thought of the vulgar westerner in the White House. The attacks on Jackson were without mercy. His opponents took out newspaper advertisements claiming that Jackson's mother had been a prostitute and made much of the scandal of Jackson's relationship with Rachel, who had not been divorced when the two of them had originally married. The common people seemed to be outraged and nearly three times as many people came to the polls as had voted in the previous election. Jackson swamped Adams by over 140,000 popular votes and more than twice as many electoral votes. The election results reflected the power of Jackson's personality as a popular hero and also a new era in party politics.

Despite his triumph in the election though, Jackson was to suffer a personal tragedy soon after taking office. The heartbreak of scandal and public attacks wore on Rachel and three days before Christmas 1828, she cried out "I'm fainting" and fell dead. Jackson was utterly shattered by the loss and never stopped blaming his enemies for it. "May God Almighty forgive her murderers, as I know she forgave them. I never can," he said.

One of the most pressing problems of Jackson's presidency was how to remove the Native Americans from their ancestral lands in order for expansion by the United States. Professing concerns for their welfare, he proposed moving them to the distant lands of present-day Oklahoma, west of the Mississippi. The policy turned out to be a disaster. Thousands of Cherokee Indians perished on the "Trail of Tears", a forced march of over 800 miles. Thousands more refused to leave and Jackson (and his successor) used the army to hunt them down throughout the 1830's.

Jackson will also be remembered for taking on the powerful Second Bank of the United States. Jackson hated banks, all banks, but especially the Second Bank, which had been chartered in 1816. He believed that the bank symbolized the greatest corruptions of America, as it was a private institution that was owned by wealthy eastern and European stockholders. The bank influenced interest rates for loans and the rate of inflation in the country. In addition, it was also in charge of issuing paper money that was supposed to be backed by gold. Not surprisingly though, there was much more in the way of paper bank notes than there was in gold. Jackson's fight against the so-called "Monster Bank" won him popular support among the working classes and allowed him to swamp Henry Clay in the election of 1832.

The bank war, Indian removal and other hotly contested issues of the time were somewhat overshadowed by the internal bickering and intrigue in Jackson's administration. From the time that he had first taken office, Jackson had appointed party loyalists to government jobs, claiming that he was merely getting rid of the crooks and long term office holders that had been supporters of John Quincy Adams. He was soundly attacked for this. In addition, he also had problems in his cabinet as vice president John C. Calhoun and secretary of state Martin Van Buren immediately began squabbling over who would take over for Jackson in 1836. All of this was forgotten though in the wake of the "Peggy Eaton Affair" in 1831.

It all began when Margaret O'Neale Timberlake, the beautiful and popular daughter of a Washington tavern owner, married Jackson's close friend, John Eaton, in 1829. "Peggy", as she was known, had been having an open affair with Eaton while she was still married to her first husband. Shortly before Peggy's marriage to Eaton, her husband committed suicide, citing her affair as the cause.

When Jackson appointed Eaton as secretary of war, the refined wives of Jackson's other cabinet members refused to accept Mrs. Eaton as their social equal. Jackson saw the insult to the Eaton's as a replay of the gossip and snobbery that had hurt (and essentially killed) his beloved Rachel. He also viewed the attacks as a conspiracy against his presidency as well and used the scandal to purge his cabinet of all supporters of vice president Calhoun, as his wife had started the gossip about Peggy Eaton. Martin Van Buren then offered his resignation and other cabinet members followed his lead. Jackson did not meet with the remainder of the cabinet for over a year, but he did consult with his unofficial "kitchen cabinet" of non-elected and non-appointed friends, including Van Buren, who succeeded Jackson as president a few years later.

When Jackson finally left office, he found that the White House had taken what was left of his health and his fortune. His old wounds and tuberculosis tortured him but his popularity with the people never waned. On the day of Martin Van Buren's inauguration, Old Hickory was still the main attraction. Thousands of people came to see him and traveled to the train station for one last goodbye. Jackson returned home to Nashville with only ninety dollars to his name.

The old plantation, the Hermitage, was in a state of disrepair and his estate was deeply in debt. He retired from public life but at the president's request, he still continued to advise Van Buren by mail. In 1840, he made the trip to New Orleans to celebrate the 25th anniversary of the great battle and by this time was hobbling with a cane. He passed away just five years later and more than 3,000 people attended his funeral. He is buried today at the Hermitage, just beside his beloved Rachel.

Andrew Jackson is remembered today as the first president to truly be chosen by the people and not the ruling elite. He was known for bringing the common man into the White House and his backwoods, populist style ushered in an era of increased participation in the political process. The grizzled old soldier from Tennessee had changed America forever.

There is no denying that one of the highest points of Jackson's career was the Battle of New Orleans in 1814. One of the men who was part of the volunteer army of Tennessee and who served closely with Jackson during the battle was John Bell Jr. He and Jackson had formed a close friendship and John had served the general as an aide during the campaign. When Jackson received word in Nashville of the strange goings-on at the Bell farm, he decided to go and investigate the stories for himself. One can only imagine what the old soldier must have thought of the bizarre and outlandish tales that were being spread about the countryside and was concerned that his friend, John Bell, was being slandered, as he had been himself in the past. Whatever he believed though, he soon set out for the farm.

Jackson traveled with a party of men from Nashville, who brought along their own provisions and supplies. They departed in the late afternoon with a number of mounted men and a large wagon stocked with gear and pulled by four draft horses. The group traveled up the turnpike to Robertson County and at some point, as they neared the Bell farm, one of the men in the party made a joke about the witch.

Suddenly, almost as soon as the words left the man's lips, the large wagon ground to a halt. The driver cracked the reigns over the horses' backs, but no matter how hard the animals pulled, the wheels of the wagon refused to turn. Jackson and several of the other men, after spouting the appropriate curses, climbed down from their mounts and looked over the wagon. They could find no reason why the vehicle would not move. Puzzled, they urged the horses on and to the animals' credit, they tried with all of their might to get the wagon moving again. However, it stayed completely still.

Jackson cursed again. "It's the witch!", he shouted and I imagine added a few more colorful expletives about the devious creature.

Then from the trees overhead came a disembodied and highly amused voice. "They can go now, General," it said. Jackson spun around and several of his men spread out to look for the speaker. Of course, they found no one. Then, the voice of Kate came again. "I'll see you all later on tonight," she promised.

Jackson was perplexed when his party reached the Bell farm, but matters of the witch were forgotten for a few hours as he visited with the Bell family. John Jr. was unfortunately away during his friend's visit but the rest of the family was delighted to meet the man of whom their son and brother had spoken of so highly and a man who had figured so prominently in the news of the day. The elder Bell was much impressed with their distinguished guest and accommodations were prepared for him, as was a large dinner. The assembled party grew even larger when word spread of the general's visit among the Bell's friend and neighbors.

As dinner was being prepared, Jackson's men unloaded the contents of the wagon while Jackson told of what had occurred on the turnpike. As the men made camp in the yard, the general adjourned inside for a drink and to await the coming of the witch. He sat and talked for several hours with the group about the war, Nashville and about the Indians who once lived in the area.

Soon, the men from Jackson's party also joined them and among the number was a man who fancied himself a "witch tamer". Like so many others who had visited the Bell farm in the past, the man was full of boasts about his power over the supernatural, and Jackson had only consented to bring him along so as to cover every avenue of investigation. Everyone who was present was said to have humored the man, and as mentioned before, the Bell's had already seen more than enough of characters like this one.

This witch tamer, just the others, made a number of claims that boiled down the fact that no witch would dare to make an appearance while he was present. He always carried with him, in situations like this, a pistol that was loaded with a silver bullet. He stated that if the spirit dared to show up, he would send the creature back from whence she came!

As was normal with Kate, when surrounded by loudmouths, she did absolutely nothing. An hour or more passed with no activity and no sound, other than the soft murmur of conversation. After a time, even General Jackson was beginning to grow impatient. Finally, the witch tamer took matters into his own hands. He stood up on a wooden chair and in a loud voice, dared the witch to appear.

These words were followed by a howl of pain! The witch tamer jumped down from his chair and began dancing about as if his back side were on fire. He hollered loudly and grabbed hold of the seat of his pants. "Help me boys!" he called out. "I'm being stuck by a thousand pins!"

Kate laughed loudly. "I'm right in front of you," she cried, "shoot me!"

The witch tamer drew his pistol and tried to take aim at the air in front of him. I imagine that Jackson, the Bell's and the Tennessee men all scrambled for cover themselves! He pulled the trigger on the pistol and only a puff of gunpowder smoke emerged from the barrel ~ the pistol refused to fire! With that, Kate began cackling again.

Still dancing about and holding his back side, the witch tamer began to feel other stinging pains as invisible hands slapped and pinched him. Jackson himself saw the man's head rock back with the force of a slap and saw the red mark appear on his cheek. Then, the man's hands began grasping at his face. "She's pulling my nose off!" he screamed.

The man stumbled forward, looking to the others just as if something was yanking on the end of his nose. Suddenly, he was flung toward the front door, which opened on its own, and was sent sprawling into the dusty front yard. All the while, the witch's voice screeched maniacally, offering obscene advice about how to be a good witch tamer.

Of course, none of this came as any surprise to the Bell family. They had seen many an "exorcist" get what was coming to him at the hands of the witch. As for Jackson, he was not only surprised, but highly entertained by Kate's shenanigans. He roared with laughter at the antics of the spirit and told John Bell that he had never seen anything so funny in his life. I imagine even Bell allowed himself a smile as tears of joy trickled down the crusty general's face.

But Kate was not done with the men from Nashville just yet. "There is another fraud in your party, General", she told Jackson. "I'll get him tomorrow night!"

The men from Nashville began looking at each other very nervously and to a man, refused to spend the night inside of the house. They retired to the camp outside to sleep, but not before urging Jackson to leave the farm at daybreak. At first, the pleas of the men fell on deaf ears. General Jackson was fascinated by the phenomena and besides that, hoped in some way to assist his friend with the family's troubles. Eventually though, the men convinced Jackson that leaving would be in the best interests of all concerned.

They left the next morning at dawn - and none of them ever returned to the Bell farm. In fact, by noon the next day, they were already in Springfield, heading back rather quickly to Nashville.

We will never know what finally convinced Jackson to pack up and leave the farm. He had expressed an interest to John Bell about staying an entire week and Bell had readily agreed that he was welcome to do so. At some point though, the general's nerves got the better of him and he left. Years later, Betsy Bell would recall this visit to Charles Bailey Bell, her young relative, and she told him that her brother visited with Jackson many times in the years after this visit. However, during all of those meetings, Jackson never disclosed to his friend just what had convinced him to leave that morning.

There were some secrets, it was said, that are best not told.

- CHAPTER FIVE -
THE DEATH OF JOHN BELL & THE FATE OF BETSY BELL'S COURTSHIP
THE CURTAIN CALL FOR THE BELL WITCH

After nearly four years of the haunting, John Bell continued to periodically suffer from the same afflictions of the body - the curse that had been visited upon him by the witch. She told him that she would hound him into the grave, and she did.

By late 1820, Bell's physical condition had grown even worse. The jerking and twitching of his face still continued, as did the swelling of his tongue and the seizures that seemed to grip his entire body and which would leave him nearly paralyzed for hours and days at a time. The spells became even more violent and toward the end of his days, Richard Williams Bell accompanied him everywhere he went. The family feared that a seizure would come upon him while working and if no one was with him, he might fall and be injured.

Around the middle of October, Bell once again became ill. This time, the spell lasted for eight days and he was confined to his bed the entire time. During his convalescence, the witch stayed by his side, just as she had when Lucy Bell had gotten sick some time before. Only with John Bell, the witch did not whisper words of kindness nor sing to make him feel better. She raved and cursed in the sick room like a maniac, bothering him so that he could not rest and wishing loudly that he would simply die and leave the world a better place.

But once again, John Bell managed to prevail and he came out of the sickness. It was another week before he was back on his feet again, but after this, he felt much stronger. He called Richard early one morning to go with him to the hog pen, which lay about 300 yards from the house. He wanted to make sure that the hogs that were destined for slaughter were separated from those to be kept as stock.

The two had not walked very far before one of John Bell's shoes was jerked from his foot. The incident occurred so quickly that neither he nor Richard had time to think about what had happened. Richard scratched his head and retrieved the shoe, then bent down and slipped it back on his father's foot. He tied the strings quite tightly into a double knot. Then, the two of them started back up the path again.

They had not gone much further when the other shoe flew off in the same manner. Richard fetched it also and tied it in the same manner as the other one. They found the incident quite strange (apparently not realizing it was the work of the witch at this point) and after much discussion continued up the path. Richard would later note in his writings that the shoes had been tied firmly and fit his father quite closely.

They continued to the hog barn without incident and Bell directed the hands as to how he wished the animals to be separated. Once this was finished, he and Richard started back to the house, intent on breakfast. They had not gone very far before both of John Bell's shoes were once again torn from his feet. Seconds later, he was slapped so hard across the face that he had to lie down beside the dirt path, needing a moment to recover from the blow. This seemed to be something that the witch would do, but the spirit had been strangely silent during the entire episode.

While his father rested, Richard replaced the shoes on his feet. Within seconds, they had flown back off again and then Bell's face began the spasmodic twitching that was so horribly familiar. He started to shake and contort and Richard shrank back in fear.

From the air around them finally came the shrieking voice of Kate, who was cursing and singing - this was undoubtedly her work. As the sudden spell passed, Richard saw tears begin to stream from his father's eyes. Every bit of courage the beleaguered man had left was now gone. He turned to Richard and made what turned out to be a prophetic statement. "Oh my son," he said, "not long will you have a father to wait on so patiently. I cannot much longer survive the persecutions of this terrible thing. It is killing me by slow tortures, and I feel the end is nigh."

That may have been the moment when the inevitable hit Richard as well. "This expression sent a pang to my bosom," he would later write. "Mingled sorrow and terror took possession of me and sent a tremor through my frame that I will never forget."

John Bell took to his bed as soon as they reached the house and while he was up and down over the course of the next few weeks - he would never leave the house again.

Over that period of time, Bell continued to decline and nothing done by his family or friends seemed to ease his suffering. Lucy stayed beside him most of the time, only spelled by John Jr. and the other children. John Bell's friends, and members of the original investigating committee, were as saddened by his decline as the family was. It is not hard to imagine that their despair must have been accompanied by feelings of having failed their friend somehow by not getting to the root of the mystery of the witch.

And all the while, as John Bell writhed in pain or was convulsed with seizures, Kate remained nearby, laughing and cursing at the dying man.

On December 20, 1820, John Bell breathed his last.

On the morning of the 19th, Bell failed to rise as he had every other morning. Even as sick as he was, he never failed to stir and take some sort of sustenance, even if it was only water and bread. On this morning, however, he did not awaken. Lucy went to check on him after rising and it appeared that he was sleeping very soundly. She decided to let him rest and sent John and Drew to attend to the livestock while she prepared breakfast. She decided that she would awaken him once the food was prepared.

A little less than an hour passed before Lucy went back into Bell's sick room. She touched her husband gently on the shoulder, but he did not wake up. She then shook him a little harder, but again, there was no sign that he knew she was there. She realized then that while he was alive, he was in some sort of a stupor.

Lucy called out to the rest of the family and John ran back inside. He had always attended to his father's medicine and he went immediately to the cupboard where it was kept. His father had gone through similar periods before and usually a dose of his medicine would revive him. When John opened the cabinet, he discovered that all of the medicines that had been prescribed to his father had vanished. In place of them was a small, "smoky-looking vial" that was about one-third full of a dark colored liquid. He asked at once if anyone in the house had moved the medicine but all denying touching it, or even knowing what medicine had been there. No one had any idea what may have been in the vial.

Immediately, John sent one of the slaves to Port Royal to fetch the family doctor, George Hopson. A short time before the discovery of the strange vial, several of Bell's friends, John Johnson, Alex Gunn and Frank Miles, had arrived at the house. They were as puzzled by the appearance of the bottle as the family was.

The group gathered around the sick bed and continued to try and raise John Bell. Just then, Kate's voice split the air of the room. The witch laughed loudly. "It's useless to try and relieve Old Jack - I have got him this time," it said. "He'll never get up from that bed again."

Angrily, Frank Miles questioned the spirit about the smoky vial that had been found in the cupboard. Kate admitted that she had put it there and claimed that she had given Bell a large dose of it the night before, "which fixed him," she added.

This was all of the information that Kate would give in regards to the liquid and no one had any idea where it may have come from, or how John Bell had managed to ingest it. Even if Kate had not brought it into the house, it was possible that Bell, roused in the middle of the night and looking for his medicine, may have swallowed it by mistake. Even so, where the bottle had come from was still unexplained.

It was then suggested that the mysterious liquid be tested on something. Alex Gunn disappeared outside and quickly returned with one of the barn cats that could be found on the property. John Jr. dipped a straw into the vial and the drew it through the cat's mouth, wiping the dark liquid on its tongue. The cat jumped out of Gunn's arms as if it had been prodded with a hot poker! It whirled about a few times and then fell to the floor with its legs kicking in the air. The animal was dead in less than a minute.

Whatever was in the bottle - it certainly appeared to be deadly.

Bell lay all day and through the night in a coma and could not be roused to swallow any medicine that might counteract the effects of the drug. Dr. Hopson was sure that he had taken, or had been given, the contents of the bottle as Bell's breath smelled the same as the liquid in the vial. Frank Miles, in the throes of despair, cast the vial and its contents into the fire. When he did so, a blue blaze shot up into the chimney "like a flash of powder."

John Bell never regained consciousness and early on the morning of December 20, he took one last shuddering breath and died. His final moments were met by great joy from the witch. She laughed heartily and expressed the hope that Bell would burn in hell. With those chilling words, she departed and was not heard from again until after the funeral.

Even the most hardened reader will admit that this is a chilling account. It is rare in the annals of the paranormal to hear of a spirit that actually injures a person, let alone takes a person's life! By the witch's own admission though, she had killed John Bell. But how exactly was this accomplished and did she really do it by her own hand? Within this horrific account, many questions remain unanswered.

First of all, there is no question that the witch would have possessed the strength in her spectral hands to merely strangle John Bell, especially in his weakened condition. She had been beating and pummeling nearly the entire family (as well as friends) for four years, although aside from a few slaps, John Bell had been almost completely spared this type of physical abuse. The spirit professed an incredible hatred of the man but could it have been afraid of him as well? It would seem so, as she used the cowardly method of poisoning him when the man was already near the end of his life from the ailments that had plagued him for so long.

It would have also have been helpful to have more information about the contents of the smoky vial. It obviously contained poison but the method by which it was smuggled into the medicine chest, replacing all of the other bottles inside, is very odd. We know that the witch was capable of moving objects about and causing them to appear and disappear at will, but never before had the creature performed in a manner that would have made it possible for her to carefully administer a poison into John Bell's mouth while he was sleeping. It should be noted that it would have had to have been a careful and measured dose to cause the effect that the witch claimed. In the morning, Bell had been sleeping soundly and was left alone until after breakfast. At that time, Lucy found him to be in a stupor. However, the witch claimed that she gave Bell the poison the night before! But if the poison had almost immediately killed the cat, how did Bell manage to take it, sleep through the night and then fall into a stupor (hours later) that would last until he died on the following day? And why was the poison vial deliberately thrown into the fire, utterly destroying the evidence of the murder?

The questions that remain are these: was the witch lying about the time when John Bell was poisoned? Or were the accounts of Bell's death altered slightly to place the blame solely on the witch? I have no doubt that she was guilty of Bell's murder, but was the killing actually carried out by her hand - or by the unwitting hand of another?

Taking into account the size difference between John Bell and the cat, it is conceivable that Bell could have lasted for a longer period of time after having been administered the poison. Regardless though, he would have almost had to have been poisoned during breakfast because shortly after this, he was found to be in a stupor with the smell of the poison on his breath.

But why did the witch go to the trouble of destroying all of the other medicine in the cabinet so that she could leave only the poison behind? I believe that she did so with the deliberate intention of having one of the family members administer the poison to John Bell, believing that it was his medicine. This would be the only sound reason for her to have transported the poison to the house and to replace the medicine with it. What better psychological effect could she achieved than to have one of the family members accidentally kill the head of the household with what they believed was a curative for his ailments?

Whoever had administered the poison must have been someone well known to Bell so that he could have been awakened from a sound sleep in order to take what he and this person believed was medicine. Who this person might have been, be it family member or close friend, will never be known but in spite of possessing the hand that took John Bell's life - the blame for the murder lies squarely on the shoulders of the witch. It was the spirit who had not only caused Bell to fall sick in the first place, but who had deviously switched the medicine bottle with a vial of poison. I feel that the witch knew full well that Bell would be given the poison and that was the reason that she placed the vial in the cabinet, rather than simply dispose of Bell by other means within her power.

I am also of the opinion that the written accounts of the haunting were altered so that no one in the family would be blamed for the John Bell's death. Since the witch was ultimately responsible anyway, it was easier to place the blame solely on the spirit and leave out any mention of accidental poisoning. I believe that this also explains why the poison vial was destroyed as well. It should be noted that the bottle was thrown into the fire by Frank Miles, a man who was the self-professed "protector" of the family.

The Bell's had certainly suffered enough at the hands of the witch by this time and there was no need to punish them any further by allowing word to get out that the witch was unwittingly assisted in her final plans for John Bell.

John Bell's burial took place a few days later and it has been said that the funeral was the largest ever held in Robertson County, before or since. The services were conducted by the Reverends James and Thomas Gunn and by Reverend Sugg Fort, all of whom had stuck by John Bell from the beginning of the strange events. Bell was laid to rest in a small cemetery, a short distance from the Bell house.

After the grave was filled, the mourners began to walk away. As they left the scene, the voice of Kate returned, echoing loudly in the cold morning air. She was singing at the top of her spectral lungs. "Row me up some brandy, O! Row, row, row! Row me up some brandy, O! Row me up some more!" she squalled in a loud voice and could still be heard celebrating the death of John Bell as the last of the family and friends entered the house.

This ended the most terrifying chapter of the haunting and marked the case of the Bell Witch in the annals of supernatural history forever. It became one of the only cases ever recorded in which a spirit was responsible for the death of one of the principles in the story.

But the Bell Witch was not finished - at least not quite yet.

After the funeral, the activities of the witch seemed to decrease, but she was not quite gone. Kate remained with the family throughout the winter and spring of 1821, but she had changed. She was not quite as vicious as she had once been, not even to Betsy Bell, around whom her activities continued to be centered.

During the entire haunting, it was made clear that Betsy would be punished as long as she continued to allow herself to be courted by Joshua Gardner. After the death of John Bell however, Kate's activities were not so violent and Betsy and Gardner began to believe that perhaps the witch might allow them to be together in peace.

As it had been with John Bell himself, the witch had never made it clear just why she disliked Joshua Gardner so much. She simply hated him and never explained why. Kate spent a great amount of time pleading with Betsy to end her relationship with him and also made it clear that she would beat the girl until she did so. The odd thing about it was that Kate acted as if she were punishing the girl for her own good!

There was no doubt that Joshua was in love with Betsy, and that the feeling was mutual. Both of them had attended the local school, which was run by Professor Richard Powell, who was later smitten with Betsy himself. Even if Powell had not been married at the time, everyone agreed that Joshua and Betsy were very well suited for each other.

Everyone but Kate, that is.

Once the violence of the haunting had subsided somewhat, Betsy and Joshua began to renew their relationship, which had previously been cooled thanks to the witch. On Easter Sunday of 1821, the two of them celebrated the holiday by becoming engaged, much to the delight of their families and friends. The following day, the young couple, along with two other couples, Theny Thorn and Alex Gooch and James Long and Rebecca Porter, decided to go fishing and to have a picnic along the Red River.

The couples had settled down along the river bank when Richard Powell appeared. Powell was in the midst of campaigning to represent Robertson County in the Tennessee legislature and had heard about the picnic. As all of them were former students of his, he had an excuse to join them. Likely, Powell had also joined them because he had heard of Betsy's engagement to Joshua Gardner. He asked her if he could speak to her alone for a moment and then confessed his attraction to her. Powell's wife had recently died and he hoped that he might begin to court Betsy. She had little interest in her old professor though and her only reply to him was that she promised him an invitation to the wedding. A short time later, the Powell left.

After lunch, the couple all decided to do a little fishing and Joshua and Betsy sat down on a large rock and cast a line into the water. A few minutes later, the line was seized by what would have been a huge fish - if it had been a fish at all! The line and pole were pulled into the water and vanished downstream. At that same moment, the eerily familiar voice of the witch rang out. "Please, Betsy Bell, do not marry Joshua Gardner," Kate intoned. The plea was repeated two more times and then the voice faded away.

This must have been the breaking point for Betsy. She must have finally realized that the witch was never going to leave her alone as long as she continued to stay with Joshua Gardner. She had seen what the creature had done to her father and she simply cared about Joshua too much to see the same thing happen to him. Kate had already shown what she was capable of and to marry Joshua Gardner would mean risking his life as well.

Thus ended the engagement of Elizabeth Bell and Joshua Gardner. The two of them parted that afternoon and as far as I know, never saw one another again.

After arranging his affairs, Joshua Gardner departed from Robertson County and went to live in western Tennessee at a place called Gardner's Station. He lived a long and successful life, married twice and died in 1887 at the age of 84. Whether or not he ever thought of Betsy Bell again is unknown.

To this day, a legend persists that states that the Bell's and the Gardner's have never intermarried because of the witch's denial of marriage between Betsy and Joshua. However, family records show that there were indeed marriages between the two families. The story likely got started however because of a direct Bell descendant named Charles Willett, who secretly courted a direct descendant of Joshua Gardner. In the small community though, everyone knew about their secret courtship, despite their attempts to conceal their relationship. Unfortunately, the two of them never married and it's likely that this is the reason why the story of no marriages between the two families has continued.

In the early summer of 1821, the remaining members of the Bell family were seated around the fireplace after supper. They were talking quietly when something that looked like a cannonball thundered down the chimney and rolled out into the center of the room. It exploded in a cloud of smoke and heavy mist, accompanied by the familiar voice of the witch.

"I am going," Kate cried out. The witch bid an affectionate farewell to "Luce" and promised that she would return again in seven years to visit the Bell house and every house in the neighborhood.

"This promise was fulfilled as regards to the old homestead," Richard Williams Bell later wrote, "but I do not know that it visited homes in the vicinity. It returned in February 1828."

- SEASON OF THE WITCH -
PHOTOS & ILLUSTRATIONS

(Above) An 1894 illustration of Kate Batts, as she was remembered in the community. This now legendary woman was blamed for the strange manifestations of the Bell Witch and was feared in the community for her eccentricities and harsh tongue. Others also claimed that she was a witch.

(Left) The roadside historical marker on Highway 41 that tells the story of the Bell Witch and the events that took place on the nearby farm. This is one of the only instances where a state government has acknowledged the existence of a ghost!

(Above) The death of John Bell is shown in this 1894 illustration. Here, Bell's friends test the poison from the vial on one of the cats.

(Below) An Illustration of Andrew Jackson and his men on the way to the Bell Farm - just before they encountered the witch!

(Left) Professor Richard Powell, the man Betsy Bell eventually married. (Above) The famous 1894 illustration showing a very harassed looking Betsy Bell.

(Right) An illustration of Betsy Bell's Easter engagement to Joshua Gardner. Unfortunately, the engagement would never last - thanks to the witch

Three of the principle players in the haunting of the Bell Witch.

(Left) Joshua Gardner, Betsy Bell's lover and for a short time, her fiancee.

(Below Left) James Johnston - one of the friends of John Bell and one of the original members of the investigating committee
(Below Right) John Bell Jr.'s close friend, and the "protector" of the family, Frank Miles. Both men are shown as they looked at an older age.

(Above) The John Bell homestead as it looked around the time of the haunting in 1817. This 1894 illustration was drawn from memory. (Below) This current photograph shows the site of the Bell house today. The house is now completely gone and only an old well remains. The land is private property, still owned by Bell descendants.

(Left) An 1984 illustration showing the old Bell family graveyard, which is located in the woods near the former location of the Bell home.

(Below) A current photograph that was taken in this eerie cemetery that shows the replacement headstone for John Bell, after the original was stolen in the 1950's. The cemetery is private property and is not accessible by public road. Trespassing is prohibited.

(Above) This photo shows the entrance to the Bell Witch Cave, an area that has been notoriously hard to photograph over the years. (Below) The iron gate that protects the mouth of the against trespassers.

(Above) A photo taken by one of the owners of the cave that shows a strange energy above a sinkhole on the property. No explanation has been given to reveal the source of the energy, which was not seen when the photo was taken (Courtesy Chris Kirby)
(Below) One of many strange photos taken inside of the cave. This one shows a strange energy to the right of the woman in the photo (Courtesy Nancy Napier)

(Above) This photo by the author shows two strange balls of light that were observed moving through the woods on the property. The match the descriptions of the lights reported by Bill Eden and many others. (Below) A ball of light captured on film during an investigation of the cave. The light was photographed just after a sudden temperature drop. The photo was analyzed by Kodak and other independent labs and it was reported not to be "lens flare" or anything wrong with the film.

- CHAPTER SIX -
THE RETURN OF THE BELL WITCH
THE AFTERMATH OF THE HAUNTING

The Bell Witch finally departed on that summer evening in 1821, although even at that time, she had been a much different creature than the one who had originally plagued the household. It was as though John Bell's death had taken something out of her. Perhaps it had been the hatred, who knows? Regardless, the spirit was of a different nature when she departed ~ and was also a different creature yet when she returned in the promised seven years as well.

One thing that seemed to be sure to the remaining members of the Bell family was that the witch would keep the promise that she made and that she would come back. The spirit had a lasting effect on the family and to say they were traumatized by the events of the preceding four years would be an understatement.

It was said that Drew, for instance, lived his entire life like a haunted man. In fact, he never believed the spirit left at all and family members would later recall that he spent each day wondering if the voice of Kate would be heard in the house. He remained a bachelor his entire life, after seeing how the witch effectively ended the engagement of his sister and Joshua Gardner. He always feared that if he ever married, the witch might interfere with his life as well.

After John Bell's death, Lucy stayed on at the homestead, but eventually the rest of the family married or moved away. By the time the witch returned in 1828, only Richard and Joel remained with their mother at the Bell house.

The return of the witch was marked by the same sort of activity as when the original haunting first began. It started with scratching sounds on the exterior weatherboards of the house, then moved to strange sounds inside of the house. Soon, the blankets were being pulled from the beds and objects were vanishing and then appearing again in other locations.

The three Bell's made a pact amongst themselves. They were determined to ignore the activity and if spoken to by the spirit, they would ignore it. In this way, they hoped the visitation might end quickly. And so it did - the witch departed from the house after a few weeks, never speaking and apparently unconcerned with the remaining members of the family, even its beloved Lucy Bell, toward whom so much care was directed a few years before.

The most active elements of the witch's 1828 visit however took place at the home of John Bell Jr., who had built a house on land that he had inherited from his father. It was a short distance away from the original homestead and in early March, the witch came to visit him there.

The details of the conversations between John and Kate have appeared in Charles Bailey Bell's writings on the witch and strike me as not only quite odd, but rather hard to believe as well. It is possible that the conversations recorded in the book did take place, at least to some degree, but my skepticism comes in regards to the details of such extensive religious conversations being recalled verbatim as they are in the book. Regardless, the witch did spend some amount of time at John's house and many things were discussed, including Kate's prophetic visions of the future.

The witch first appeared one night as John sat reading and the two of them had rather heated words, at least from John's side. It was clear that (understandably) there was some lingering resentment over the senior John Bell's death. The witch returned again the next night, but as the rest of the family had done, John decided to keep the return visit a secret. In fact, Frank Miles was the only person outside of the family who knew the witch had come back.

When Kate returned the following evening, she found John reading about the Battle of New Orleans, in which he had participated under the command of General Jackson. The witch informed John that there would be another battle at New Orleans and that the city would be captured by a man from Tennessee. This man, who in 1828 was an officer in the United States Navy, would be considered an enemy then. This battle would cause John to decide to join in the fight against him, although John would depart from the world before he could do so.

It should be noted that on April 25, 1862, Captain David Farragut of the United States Navy captured New Orleans during the Civil War. Farragut had been born in Knoxville, Tennessee in 1801 and in 1828 had been a junior officer in the Navy. John Bell Jr., although elderly by the time the Civil War began, decided to enlist in the Confederate Army after New Orleans was captured. Before he could do so though, he died from pneumonia.

The witch then went on to make other predictions. She stated that the United States would engage in wars but aside from the war that she had just spoken of, when the slaves would be freed, none of them would be serious until a great war that involved the whole world would occur. We assume that by this prediction, the witch referred to World War I, which had taken place two decades before Charles Bailey Bell's book was published. The witch also stated that the United States would have become a world power by this time.

And she continued on to say that for some time after this great war, there would be threats and signs of another great upheaval, "which if it comes will be far more devastating and fearful in character than the one the world thought too terrible for the mind to grasp." It has been said that this prediction referred to World War II, but I am not convinced that it does. The witch was not stating that a war would actually occur but that it might occur and than if it did, it would be terrible.

Upon re-reading the lengthy sections of Bell's book that tell of the witch's return in 1828, it becomes more clear that the witch is not necessarily speaking of her own return in 1935 (as it has been said she would do after 107 years) but rather the destruction of the world around this time! She did say that she would come back but also that the world would end unless conditions improved.

The spirit spends a lot of time talking about the fact that America is an old country that was once inhabited "millions of years ago" by another civilization that was destroyed. According to the witch, all of the inhabitants of the earth were wiped out at this time by a "quavering and a shaking of the earth, so mighty that were oceans had been, there became dry land; where valleys and beautiful fields had been, there became oceans; a general leveling, upheaval and change of the entire surface of the earth." She told John that if scientists knew where to dig, they would find the remains of the lost civilizations beneath the earth.

The witch warned him that the present civilization of earth was traveling along a perilous path toward its own destruction as well. "Some countries will, within the next century," she told him, "prohibit religion of any kind being taught; will abolish the missionary organizations formed in their country; at that time the world will be near the ultimate finish... there will come a time when the food growing conditions of the world will change... there will be droughts and floods as in the Bible times. The world will be unfortunate in that there will be no man whose prayers for rain will be answered. If men before that time will heed the warnings of nature and no longer destroy the natural growths, they may continue to reap the harvests."

John Bell was much affected by the words of the spirit and later told his son that he believed the world would suffer a great cataclysm around 1935. "I do not believe the spirit will appear as it did in our home... I think the country will have reached a stage in in its history that Spiritual conditions must improve," he explained. If things did not change, the spirit predicted that the world would become to hot for humans to exist on it. The heat would rise so rapidly that it would become uninhabitable for a time and then suddenly, the world would be destroyed by a mighty explosion. As mentioned, Bell believed this would occur around the time of the spirit's promised return in "seven years, to which one hundred will be added."

There has been much made of the doomsday prophecies of the witch but in truth, how accurate (and how genuine) were they really? If we take the 1934 writings word for word, then we have to believe that the witch predicted the Civil War, the freeing of the slaves and World War I. However, it should be noted that all of these events had already occurred prior to the publication of the book in which they appeared. Could Charles Bailey Bell have put his own "spin" on the predictions in an effort to make his own points about the state of the world in 1934? Obviously, it's impossible to say but perhaps Dr. Bell was trying to use the words of the witch to send out a warning about the state of affairs in the world at the time.

Of course, that is only one way to look at it. We also have to consider the idea (if we believe in the story of the Bell Witch at all) that the predictions were real and eerily came to pass just as the witch said they would. I only base this on the unnerving predictions that she made about the end of the world. According to John Bell Jr., he believed that the witch's predictions stated that the world would end in 1935, but did they really? She never specifically said this and only told him that the end would come if the state of the world did not change. Charles Bailey Bell made much of the spiritual and religious problems facing the planet but if the reader looks back over the quotes that were presented on the preceding pages, it can be seen that the spirit spoke more of the natural state of the world than the spiritual one, at least in regards to the destruction of the planet.

The witch spoke of growing conditions, floods, droughts and rising temperatures and insinuated that if man heeded the warnings that nature was giving him, he might avert the disaster that she was warning of. I think that it is impossible for the reader to ignore the fact that scientists have been warning us about these same things for a number of years now. How often do we hear of "global warming" and the dangers of destroying the rain forests. Could the Bell Witch have been right when she warned that the planet was facing terrible events in the future?

Throughout the days of 1828, Kate stayed with John Jr. over several months and as mentioned, engaged him in a number of lengthy, philosophical discussions. On the final night of her visit, she summoned John Jr. and Frank Miles to her and bid the two men farewell. She promised to return once again in 107 years (1935) but there is no record that she ever did so - and thankfully, the world did not end either.

In spite of the witch's failure to return, there are still those who maintain that the spirit of the Bell Witch has never this region at all. But more about that later on....

What became of the Bell family once the haunting came to an end?

ELIZABETH BELL

Some time after Joshua Gardner's departure from the region, Richard Powell came calling at Betsy's door. The young girl had been depressed for some time but eventually succumbed to Powell's attentions and agreed to marry him. The former teacher was a number of years older than Betsy and had been married before (his first wife had died in

1821). However, no one frowned on their marriage, including Kate, who showed her approval by keeping silent. The couple eventually married in 1824.

Professor Richard Rowell Ptolomy Powell was born in Halifax County, North Carolina in December1795, making him a decade or so older than Betsy Bell. He came from an intelligent and well educated family and always desired to make something of himself in public office and in the higher classes of Robertson County. After marrying Betsy, Powell did make it into public office, serving as the Sheriff of Robertson County, an extremely trustworthy position, from 1830 to 1833 and also as a State Representative from 1833 to 1835. In 1837 though, he was handicapped by a massive stroke. In an attempt to put away some money for the future care of his wife and children, Powell invested money in a steamship enterprise that ended disastrously. He lost $10,000 in goods in an accident that occurred during a river launching in Clarksville. This left his family completely bankrupt and even a petition drawn up by more than 80 friends in Robertson County (including Joshua Gardner) to the State Legislature on Powell's behalf failed to win the family any relief. He died in 1848 and Betsy remained a widow for the rest of her years, always maintaining that despite the hardship after her husband's stroke, her marriage had been a happy one.

In recent years, Richard Powell has become something of an enigma in the Bell Witch case and stories have spread (thanks to a fictional novel) that he kept some sort of journal about the Bell Witch haunting, revealing many family secrets within its page. There is no evidence that he kept any such journal and if he had, there would likely be no mention of the witch within its pages. The Bell family did not encourage any discussion of the haunting within the family, or with outsiders. Having married Betsy in 1824, Powell would have certainly honored this family restriction. The only book that Powell ever wrote was titled *Mathematics* and it remains (outside of records of his public service) one of the only sources of information about him. A copy of this book can still be found in the Tennessee State Archives and it contains mathematical problems that Powell kept throughout his life. It is believed that his father was the author of the problems but in places where Powell solved them within the pages of the book, the notations show that he was an extremely intelligent man.

After her marriage to Powell, Betsy cared for their family home and helped her husband with his political career. She also cared for their eight children, which obviously occupied most of her time. Although details of her adult life are mostly unknown, family stories maintain that Betsy would not sleep alone at night and that she would rarely ever discuss the witch with anyone. In fact, the only time that we know of when she talked openly about the terrible events on the farm were to Charles Bailey Bell when he interviewed her late in life.

She was very quiet about the haunting, even though as time passed, the mystery continued to be discussed and rumors were sometimes raised that named Betsy as being responsible for the strange occurrences. As one generation passed into the next and eyewitnesses passed away (who could have refuted such claims), the case achieved the status of legend. In 1849, the *Saturday Evening Post* published a lengthy sketch about the case that was written by a reporter who slanted to story to make it appear that Betsy had been the culprit behind the haunting. Betsy sued the paper and the story was retracted.

Betsy stayed in Robertson County until 1875, when she finally moved to Panola County, Mississippi to live with her daughter, Eliza. She died in July 1888 at the age of 82 and is buried in Long Branch Grove Cemetery.

She never heard from the Bell Witch again.

DREWRY BELL

As mentioned already, Drewry Bell never married. He lived a bachelor's life and although he acquired a large amount of property, remained secluded and a recluse. He refused to have anything to do with women because he feared that should he fall in love, his engagement might be affected by the witch, as Betsy and Joshua Gardner's had been. The events on his family farm haunted him until the day he died and it was said by his friends that he lived with great foreboding of some dire event concerning the witch in his future. In spite of this, he was adept as business matters and made an initial fortune shipping goods downriver to Natchez and New Orleans with John Jr. and his brother-in-law, Alex Gunn.

He remained a resident of Robertson County his entire life and became a landowner and farmer, living across the Red River from his father's old farm. Drew owned many slaves for that era and went out of his way to care for them very well. In his will, drawn up in 1864, he gave all of his property to his slaves, and gave them their freedom as well. To each of his brothers and sisters, he willed "five dollars and no more", except for Betsy, who received a full twenty-five dollars.

Drew died with only his slaves in attendance on January 1, 1865. His home still stands along the Red River in Adams, Tennessee.

RICHARD WILLIAMS BELL

Richard Bell was a young child when the haunting began but he was the first to break the silence requested by his family about the witch. He wrote the only first hand account about the witch and her effect on the Bell family in 1846. The manuscript was eventually given to his son, who in turn allowed M.V. Ingram to publish it in his own book with the title *Our Family Troubles*. It detailed many of the happenings that Richard could remember clearly and became one of the best records of the case.

Richard settled on a portion of land that he inherited from his father's estate and lived a short but prosperous and contented life. He was the family member who had been most responsible for his father's care during the last year or so of John Bell's life and the experience left a lasting impression upon him.

Richard died in October 1857 at the age of only 46. Remarkably, he had been married three times before his death and produced four children.

JOEL EGBERT BELL

Joel Bell was the youngest of the Bell children was such a small child during the haunting that he had few memories of the terrible events. He became a respected man in Robertson County and was known as being warm and generous and very active in church and community affairs. He married twice in his lifetime and produced 14 children. He lived on a farm a few miles north of Springfield and died there in January 1890 at the age of 77.

Ironically, even though he remembered little of the Bell family troubles, he was likely the family member most responsible for them coming to light. His discussions about the witch with his friend, newspaper publisher Martin Ingram, were almost certainly what motivated Ingram to publish his *Authenticated History* in 1894.

JESSE BELL

As John and Lucy Bell's first son, Jesse spent his early years in North Carolina. As he got older, the circumstances of his family and the outbreak of war allowed him to travel fairly extensively. He was likely the most involved with his family's establishment of the farm in Tennessee and spent his young adulthood establishing good work habits and his own farm near his father's plantation. Jesse and his brother, John Jr., served as volunteers in the infantry of the 2nd Regiment of West Tennessee during the War of 1812. Jesse was elected corporal in his infantry company for service at the Battle of Horseshoe Bend. He later took orders from his younger brother during the Battle of New Orleans.

In 1815, Jesse was teaching school for local students in Robertson County and in 1817, married Martha Lee Gunn and together, they produced nine children. After the death of his father in 1820, Jesse decided to move his family to Panola County, Mississippi. He died of unknown causes in Christian County, Kentucky in October 1843. It is unknown where he is buried.

ESTHER BELL PORTER

Esther was the first daughter of John and Lucy Bell, born in North Carolina. She was just three years-old when her parents moved to Tennessee. Although not much is recorded about her early years, Esther married Alexander Bennett Porter around the time when the witch was first making herself known and also during the time when the church scandals and legal actions were taking their toll on her father.

After the death of John Bell, Esther and her husband moved with her brother, Jesse, to Mississippi. She lived in the Panola and Yalobusha County areas, where Porter farmed, for the rest of her life. They produced 12 children together. She died in May 1859 and is buried in the churchyard of the Union Hill Baptist Church near Oakland, Mississippi.

JOHN BELL JR.

As the namesake of his father, John stayed closer to the original family farm than any of his siblings did and likely for that reason, inherited the bulk of his father's estate. He built a house on the original farm, not far from the old Bell house and acquired a sizable estate through farming and shipping goods downriver with his brother, Drew, and their brother-in-law, Alex Gunn. He married Elizabeth Gunn, the sister of Jesse's wife, in 1828 and they produced eight children.

John became a prosperous farmer and businessman and a politician of good reputation and he rarely ever spoke of the mysterious events that had plagued his family for so long. It would be through his son that the haunting predictions and final appearances of the Bell Witch would become known.

John died in May 1862 and he is buried in the small cemetery that is located near the remains of the old Bell house on the original property.

LUCY BELL

Lucy Bell was married to John Bell in 1782 and together they produced nine children, only one of which did not survive to adulthood. She was described by everyone who knew her as a loving and generous woman and it seems likely that she had a great influence over the lives of her family and over many in the community. She was so loved that even the feared Bell Witch catered to her wishes and praised her constantly.

After the death of her husband, Lucy continued to live with her sons, Richard and Joel, in their original home. She died in January 1837 and is buried beside her husband in the family graveyard, a short distance away from where the horrific events involving the witch took place.

The old Bell farm was located about one mile from what is now Adams, Tennessee, a small village that officially came into existence in 1859 during the building of the Edgefield and Kentucky Railroad. The farm was located along the Red River and the section on which the house was located is still in the Bell family today. It is private property owned by Mr. Carney Bell.

The Bell house was a double log home, which was one-and-a-half stories high. It was weather boarded on the outside and had six large rooms and two halls, making it one of the finest houses in the county during its time. It was located about a half-mile from the river and there was a large orchard in the back. The lawn was covered with pear trees and several outbuildings were also located on the property. During its heyday, it was a comfortable and very functional working farm.

The thriving spot also got its share of visitors, even before the haunting, as it was located on a main, public road. This dirt highway, known as the Brown's Ford and Springfield road, ran about 100 yards from the house. It was said that during the excitement over the witch, it was not uncommon to find a horse hitched to every fence corner of the farm as the house and yard were often filled with people coming to investigate the sensation. Travelers still continued to pass this way for many years, even after the Bell house was abandoned. The site is not accessible by public roads today.

After the death of Lucy Bell, who continued to stay on in the house after her children were gone, no one cared to occupy the place. For some time, the house was used for storing grain and then was torn down. Today, there is little sign that a house once stood on the spot. Only a few stones of the foundation can be seen and the remains of an old well. The land around the house site has since been turned into farming ground, although strangely, the actual location of the house remains untouched.

After the house was abandoned, a number of those who traveled along the old public road began to make reports of strange incidents taking place there. Some claimed to see apparitions wandering about the weed-choked yard and others said that unexplained lights and glowing objects flitted about the fields. Of course, it is possible that these stories can be accounted for as the overactive imaginations of those who knew of the odd stories of this property and who claimed the activities as being the leftover effects of the Bell Witch. But what of the tales which were not so easy to explain?

Some of the weird reports came from travelers with no connections to the immediate area and who knew nothing of the property. A few of the stories also came from reputable residents of the region, like Dr. Gooch, who claimed to see a glowing light emanating from the windows of the Bell house, even though the structure had long been empty and abandoned.

Was it possible that the Bell Witch could have left some sort of lingering atmosphere on the area? I believe it's very possible, along with many other people, and we will discuss this further in a later chapter.

The Bell family cemetery is located about 300 yards north of where the old homestead once stood. It is here where John Bell, Lucy, and their sons Benjamin, Zadok, John Jr. and Richard Williams are buried. According to some, Joel's body is also buried here, but no records remain to say one way or another. There is some confusion as to the exact locations of the graves as well, since the Bell family is joined in death with about 30 of their slaves. The small cemetery is located within a wooded area and is overgrown with weeds and brush.

The old granite markers have long since vanished, having been stolen by souvenir hunters, although narrow flagstones remain to mark the graves of the slaves who are buried here. Unfortunately, many of the graves themselves show signs of being disturbed.

Only one inscribed grave marker remains in the cemetery today and it reads:

JOHN BELL
1750 – 1820
ORIGINAL TOMBSTONE
DISAPPEARED ABOUT 1951
THIS MARKER PLACE 1957
HIS WIFE LUCY WILLIAMS BELL

As with many other things in this region, there is an interesting legend behind the missing tombstone and just how it disappeared around 1951.

It seems that one late evening in 1950 or 1951(or so says the legend), three young men from Nashville went searching for the Bell farm. They had been brought up with the many tales of the witch and decided that a souvenir from the place where the story actually happened would be a great thing to have. So, they drove up to Adams and went poking around on the property where the old house once stood. They were disappointed to find the place was long gone but soon discovered the small family cemetery. When one of the markers there was found to have John Bell's name on it, they realized they had found the perfect keepsake.

The stone was easily removed from the ground and quickly loaded into the trunk of one of the young men's cars. Soon, they were on their way back to Nashville. Unfortunately though, things didn't work out just as they had planned. On the way back to Nashville, the boys were involved in an auto accident and the driver of the car was horribly killed. Over the course of the next two weeks, the other two boys were also involved in accidents.

The wrecked car was taken to the home of the dead boy's parents. His sister was taking a look at the items left in the vehicle when she opened the trunk and found the old tombstone still inside. She too was very familiar with the story of the Bell Witch and she felt a pang of fear when she saw the name on the stone. Could this stolen marker be the reason behind the accidents suffered by the three young men?

Whether it was or not, the girl was determined to return the stone to where it belonged. She loaded it into her own car and carefully drove back to Adams. The problem occurred when she got there and realized that she had no idea where the Bell property had been, nor where the cemetery was located. Unsure of what else to do, she pulled her car over to the side of the road, hoping that she was at least in the general vicinity of the farm, and placed the stone alongside the road.

It is unknown whether this story is true or not, but if so, John Bell's original tombstone is still out there somewhere, perhaps lying in a ditch along some dusty road near Adams, Tennessee.

- CHAPTER SEVEN -
WHO WAS THE BELL WITCH?
WHAT STRANGE FORCES WERE BEHIND AMERICA'S MOST FAMOUS GHOST STORY?

So far no one has ever given any intelligent or comprehensive explanation of the great mystery. Those who came as experts were worse confounded than all others. As I before stated, a few mendacious calumniators were mean enough to charge that it was tricks and inventions of the Bell family to make money and I write for the purpose of branding this version as an infamous falsehood. It was well known in the vicinity and all over the county that every investigation confirmed the fact that the Bell family were the greatest, if not the only sufferers from the visitation, and that no one, or a dozen persons in collusion, could have so long, regularly and persistently practiced such a fraud without detection, nor could they have known the minds and secrets of strangers visiting the place, and detailed events that were then occurring or had just transpired in different localities. Moreover the visitation entailed great sacrifice. As to how long this palavering phenomenon continued in the vicinity...
I am unable to state.
RICHARD WILLIAMS BELL
OUR FAMILY TROUBLES (published in 1894)

There have been many opinions expressed over the years as to what forces were behind the haunting credited to the Bell Witch, to who the witch really was, why she haunted the location and why she had such a hatred for John Bell. Many of these opinions have been clever, some have been educated and others have been downright stupid.

As for my own opinion (which I will share later in the chapter), I can only say that it is a theory and like any other theory, remains for the reader to judge its validity. What I can say in my defense is that I think it may be a new idea, at least in the way that it is expressed in this case, and I hope that you might at least consider it before judging it too harshly in one way or another.

First however, let's take a look at who others believe the Bell Witch may have been, including who the witch herself claimed to be. We should also take a look at who, or what, some of the most popular opinions say the witch really was. These include the idea that the witch was a spirit sent by Kate Batts and the other opinion says that, well - the witch was not a spirit at all!

To start with, let's look at the idea that the entire haunting was a hoax. Of course, this isn't a new idea and has been widely circulated since the days of the case itself. The first suggestions that the strange events were a hoax probably came around 1818, or shortly after the witch first began to speak.

A few people in the neighborhood pointed out that John Bell Jr. and his brother Drew had made a number of trips down river to New Orleans for the purpose of selling goods and cargo from the area. The need for an explanation for the witch gave rise to the speculative idea that John and Drew may have learned ventriloquism, or sleight of hand tricks, while in the city (as there was certainly nowhere to learn such things in Robertson County at the time). When the two young men returned home, it was said they taught those tricks to their sister, Betsy, for the purpose of attracting people to the house and making money.

This story was widely circulated for awhile but it is hard to take it seriously, especially in light of the fact that both John and Drew were absent from home at different times during the haunting and events often occurred outside their presence. The same can also be said for Betsy Bell. While we have already established that much of the activity seemed to center around her, what about the events that happened when she was not present? And in 1828, when the Bell Witch returned, was not even in the same house where phenomena was occurring?

We run into the same problems with the logic of another "explanation" that circulated in the early days. According to this story, the house that the Bell's lived in was allegedly built by a clever man who had constructed it to hide secret passages and hidden hallways in the walls through which a man could easily slip through and hide in. When the Bell's moved into the house and began their own renovations, they discovered the secret passages and devised a plan by which they could bilk gullible people out of money by charging them admission to see their "haunting". Some have also suggested that the haunting was hoaxed by Professor Richard Powell, who knew the secrets of the house. He faked a ghost in order to end the engagement of Betsy and his rival for her affections, Joshua Gardner.

This explanation is as silly as the "ventriloquism theory". For one thing, there are no records to suggest that the Bell house was honeycombed with secret tunnels. If it had been, would the tunnels not have been discovered by the scores of investigators who looked into the case and undoubtedly searched the house looking for clues? It is also rather ridiculous to try and pin the blame for the haunting on Professor Powell. While he had been Betsy's schoolteacher, and may have even been attracted to her when she was a young girl, Powell was married to his first wife throughout most of the haunting. She did not pass away until 1821, then leaving him free to try and court Betsy. He only returns to the story after the death of John Bell and just before the first departure of the witch.

Also, if the case was faked - how do we explain the hundreds of witnesses who came to the farm and saw and heard the witch? Could all of them have been duped? If so, who else was in on the hoax? If John, Drew and Betsy were sometimes absent from the house when the witch was present, who was carrying on the activity at those times? John and Lucy Bell? Was John somehow faking the seizures and attacks that eventually led to his death?

And what of the phenomena itself? If we explain away the voice of Kate as a simple ventriloquist act, how do we then explain the doors and windows that opened by themselves, the items that moved across rooms by their own power, the frequent slaps and beatings suffered by Betsy Bell, the Bell children and others, as well as the sheets and blankets that were literally ripped from the hands of burly men?

The best defense against these accusations rests with the people of the community themselves - the friends, neighbors and men of God who defended and stood by the Bells during their troubles. These good people never questioned the fact that something was occurring that was beyond human explanation. They knew that a hoax was impossible. They also knew that John Bell was not faking his ailments in some shallow scheme to extract money from curiosity-seekers. It has already been stated that Bell charged no admission to the people who came to witness the strange events on his farm. In fact, he was generous with food and lodging for all of them, a great expense that came out of his own pocket. Even if he had charged an admission to come to the farm, he would have most likely have lost more money that he would have gained.

And what of Elizabeth Bell? Was she faking the cruel treatment that she suffered at the hands of the witch? Would the girl have actually slapped herself and pulled her own hair? I ask this because she could not have been pretending to be beaten. There were simply too many reliable witnesses to the reddened cheeks and the mottled skin. And there were too many who saw such marks appear before their very eyes!

And what of Joshua Gardner? Would Betsy Bell have really sabotaged an engagement with a young man whom she had loved since she was a child? And what of all of the others? Could Frank Miles, James Johnston and all of the other good men of the community have gone along with some elaborate charade? For what purpose, I ask you?

Whatever truly happened on the Bell farm, I think that we can rest assured that the case was not a hoax. What else could it have been? Let's explore the other possibilities...

Once the haunting began in earnest, and the witch gained her voice, the investigators (John Bell's committee members) started plying the spirit which questions. Obviously, they wanted to know why the Bell family was bring plagued with strange activity, and second of all, they wanted to know who the witch was and why she haunted the place. We will get to the "why's" in a moment - first let's deal with the "who's".

The witch claimed to be many things during the haunting. One of the first things that she stated (and may have been the only truthful claim) was that she was a spirit whose rest had been disturbed. Pretty vague, isn't it? Apparently, the Bell committee members thought so too, because they continued to pump the witch for more information.

Later, the spirit claimed to be an Indian woman whose body was buried on the Bell farm, then of course, the "traveler" who had buried the fortune in treasure underneath the rock at the spring. You may recall how that turned out. The witch also claimed to be the ghost of John Johnston's step-mother and the spirit of a child, and of a woman, who were said to be buried in North Carolina.

In later years, a legend has sprung up in an attempt to connect the witch's claim of being a woman buried in North Carolina to an incident that supposedly occurred in John Bell's past. As far as I am concerned, the incident is pure fiction (and no evidence of anything like this actually exists), but I present it to complete the record.

As mentioned earlier in this account, the legend alleges that the witch was the spirit of a woman that John Bell had known earlier in life. According to the story, Bell had been engaged to marry a widow woman, before meeting Lucy, while living in North Carolina. He was said to have tried to break off the engagement because of the woman's foul temper and disagreeable personality, but she had refused. One day, the woman had an accident and hit her head. Bell, thinking that she was dead, placed her body in the cool root cellar of the house, then left. It was said that she regained consciousness in the night and called for help. However, there was no one to hear her cries and she died of starvation. The story then goes on to say that this woman's spirit followed Bell to Tennessee, tormented the family and eventually took the life of John Bell.

As you can see, the identity of the witch was a hotly debated topic for many years, and frankly, still is today. The only other real clue that we have (according to contemporary accounts) is the final claim of the spirit herself - that she was the "witch" of Kate Batts.

So, who was Kate Batts?

As we have discussed already, Batts was a local woman whose family had been involved in a bad business deal with John Bell and she made it plain that she disliked the man very much. The events at the Bell household had begun shortly after the business deal. The records show that John Bell sold a slave to Kate Batts' brother-in-law and charged an excessive interest in the matter. This led to not only harsh words between Bell and the Batts' but to legal problems for Bell and excommunication from his church.

As also mentioned, Kate Batts was a rather strange and eccentric woman and counted few friends in the neighborhood. Her husband was an invalid and so she was forced to handle most of their business interests. She had a reputation for being hard to deal with and after the problems with John Bell, she spent a lot of time maligning his character in Robertson County. The dislike and animosity between them was the extent of the problem though. There have been a number of stories to say that Bell murdered Kate Batts but such stories were completely untrue. Kate Batts was not haunting the Bell family because she was alive and well during all of the events and outlived John Bell by some years.

Frederick Batts and his wife, Kate, had three children named Jack, Calvin and Mary. At the time of the haunting, there were actually two Batts families living in the community although they were in no way related. The other family belonged to a man named Jerry Batts, who was a community leader and an acquaintance of John Bell. The other Batts family (about whom we are most interested) was regarded as being as strange as their mother was. A few other Batts children had died years before and they had no other family in the area.

The only family member who managed to shine was Mary, who was described as being beautiful, bright and very popular. Author M.V. Ingram described the two boys as "tall, spindling and gawky, and very droll, and did not take in society". It is not hard to imagine them as being a very stereotypical, backwoods family, like the type you can still sometimes find in many rural areas today.

Frederick Batts was an invalid and was described as being a "helpless cripple". Because of this, Kate assumed control of their farm and business. Regardless, of her strangeness, she was adept at making money and the Batts' were always considered to be quite well off. They had a large, working farm and a impressive number of slaves and if not for their backward personalities, would have been among the leaders of the Robertson County community.

Even though Frederick Batts (because of the times) was avoided in social circles, and his two sons were considered, well, awkward at best, the main reason the family was not well accepted in the community had to do with Kate Batts herself. While nothing of a truly disreputable nature was ever attached to the family, most of the people in the community avoided them, thanks to Mrs. Batts' eccentricities.

So that readers can picture her in their minds, Kate Batts was described as being a large, fleshy woman, weighing well over 200 pounds. It was said that she was very headstrong and very exacting in her business dealings with everyone. She was always quite concerned about her rights, even when she had none to speak of and would not have known what they were if she had. She was always convinced that someone was out to get her, or to cheat her in some way.

Both men and women spoke of Kate Batts' fearful tongue, which she never hesitated to use against anyone who caused her displeasure. Now, most claimed to tolerate this with sympathy, but I would imagine they were more inclined to keep their mouths shut due to the fact that Batts would have surely turned her tongue against them if they spoke up. Thanks to this, and her other odd habits, the ladies in the community were generally afraid of her.

Batts other strange habit was what caused the more superstitious members of the community to regard her as a witch, long before the Bell family spirit ever came along. As mentioned earlier in this volume, it was not uncommon in those days for women who were considered "outside" the community or eccentric, to be branded as witches. In the case of Kate Batts, this conjecture was strengthened by her habit of asking every woman she met to give her a brass pin. Many believed that her possession of these personal items might put the donors under her control. For this reason, many ladies were careful to put their pins out of sight when "Old Kate" came to call. She often traveled throughout the community, sometimes once a week or more, trading and gossiping with the other ladies, and of course, asking each of them to spare a pin. No one dared to question her about this and most simply answered her with a smile and claimed there was not a pin in the place!

Rumors around the area continued about Kate Batts being connected to witchery, especially after one incident that allegedly occurred to Emily Paine. She was churning butter one morning and was in a great hurry to get through with it. She had been at the task for more than two hours and yet the butter still refused to come. Her patience had run out and half-joking, she remarked that old Kate Batts had bewitched the milk and Emily was going to burn her. She set the churn of milk aside and heated an iron poker in the fireplace. When the tool was red-hot, she thrust it down into the churn and left it there. Emily then became determined to see if Kate Batts had been burned. She invented an excuse to call on the woman and, according to her tale, Batts was nursing a sore hand that had been burned that morning.

Of course, the reader is welcome to make whatever they like out of the story, but true or not, it certainly did not add to Kate Batts' standing in the area.

To further add to her dislike among community members, Batts was very conceited, believing that her property entitled her to move in the highest circle of society. She always tended to "put on airs" and used high-sounding, bombastic words for which she most likely did not understand the meanings. Needless to say, this made her the laughing-stock of the settlement and she was subjected to much ridicule - behind her back, of course.

She was also anxious to get her son, Calvin, married off to one of the local girls. Calvin, who was said to resemble "a bean pole" was much too timid to go courting on his own, so Batts took every opportunity to invade the society of young girls in the community. She frequently advertised the young man but not surprisingly, this didn't succeed in winning him much interest. She never bothered to try and marry off her other son, Jack, in this manner. Word had it that he was basically a "lost cause."

In spite of all of her eccentricities, Kate Batts was also regarded as an enthusiastic Christian. She frequently expounded on the scriptures and was quick to assure everyone of the goodness of God. She was also considered to be the most vocal of the hymn singers at the Red River Church and would offer more than her share of rejoicing during the services.

On one occasion, a minister named Reverend Thomas Felts was conducting a revival meeting, which had been in progress for several days. Just as the preacher had finished a rather rousing sermon one evening, Kate Batts arrived at the church. She was a regular attendee for every service, but was habitually late. When Batts arrived, the meeting was in full swing, the church was packed and the congregation was standing and singing. The minister had put forth a call for sinners to come to the front of the church and repent and attention was now focused on a local man named Joe Edwards. Joe was down on all fours at the front altar, praying quite loudly. Apparently, Edwards was a good citizen but a "desperately wicked and undone sinner, and everybody was anxious to have him converted." As he prayed, a number of the other men gathered around him and urged him on.

Just at this moment, Kate Batts entered the church. She elbowed her way to the front and without hesitation, lifted her skirts and sat down on top of Joe Edwards, flattening the man on the floor. Shocked, one of the men standing nearby offered Batts another seat, but she politely declined. After a few moments of this, Edwards began to look a little stressed. His face had turned from a crimson color to one approaching a blue-purple. Once again, several of the men attempted to get Batts to move off Edward's back. Once again, she refused. "But, Sister Batts, the man is suffocating," the deacon pleaded with her.

"Yes, bless Jesus, let him suffocate," Batts replied with a loud exclamation, "he's getting closer to the Lord!"

The situation inside of the church had now gotten serious. Everyone in the place had gotten a glimpse of what was going on and they began to giggle and snicker at the comical scene. Finally, Sister Batts agreed to get up off the poor man and two of the parishioners helped her to her feet. Joe Edwards suddenly jumped up off the ground, shouting in joy at his deliverance, as if some demon had been removed from his back.

Kate Batts clasped her hands together. "Bless the Lord, bless my soul!" she cried, "Jesus is so good to devolve his poor critters from the consternation of Satan's mighty dexterity."

With that, the entire situation had reached its highest comical moment and many in the audience could no longer restrain their laughter. There was a hurried exodus for the fresh air outside - where they could laugh openly. This effectively ended the service and the minister could do little more than dismiss those who were still left inside of the church. Even those who remained inside, however, were suffering as they tried to suppress their own laughter, holding their sides out of respect for the suffering reverend.

The entreaties made to the Bell Witch in an effort to get her to disclose her identity failed miserably until one day when Reverend James Gunn managed to get a strange statement out of the spirit. The witch told him that she would not lie - that she was nothing more nor less that old Kate Batts' witch and she would haunt and torment John Bell as long as he lived.

As mentioned, this statement seemed to satisfy many in the community but most of those involved in the case did not expect the witch to speak the truth anyway, nor did they believe a word of Kate Batts' involvement in the affair. However, the explanation pleased those who already considered Batts to be a witch, or at least very strange. Rumors quickly spread and the stories of the brass pins and the incident with the butter churn began to be told once again.

As the reader can imagine, when word of this development in the case (and the fact that the witch was now being called "Kate") reached the ears of Kate Batts, she was infuriated. It was said that she kept the community spinning for a month trying to find the "corrigendum who dared to splavicate her character with the spirifications of John Bell's witch". Kate vowed that she would show this person the "perspicuity in the constipation of the law."

Needless, to say, Kate Batts never laid her hands on the culprit as the one spreading such rumors was not exactly a person of flesh and blood!

So, was Kate Batts in some way connected to the Bell Witch? It is very, very unlikely but if so, the power manifested at the Bell farm would have had to have been some outward transference of thought that resulted in a telekinetic energy at the house. Could Batts had manifested this unconsciously? Perhaps, but again it seems unlikely, although I would prefer the reader to judge for themselves.

Before reaching your conclusions though, I will leave you with one last tale concerning Kate Batts. As stated previously, Batts passed away long after John Bell did and many years after the haunting at the Bell farm came to an end. On the occasion of her death, the news spread through the community and if was difficult to find any lady to sit the night with the corpse, as was customary in those times.

Finally, a woman named Fanny Sory agreed to do so, but only with the condition that three or four other girls joined her. A group was soon found and after the funeral the following day, all of the girls told how they had been surrounded with black dogs and cats throughout the night. Two of the girls had gone to the well for fresh water during the night and claimed they had to fight off several black dogs to get back to the house. The sounds of barking and snarling were heard coming from the yard all night long and black cats appeared inside of the house. The animals made a nuisance of themselves and kept jumping onto Kate Batts' coffin.

Although some claimed these cats and dogs were merely a joke played on the poor girls by the neighbors ~ many others regarded the animals as an omen. Perhaps, they said, Kate Batts really was a witch after all.

In more recent years, many renowned experts have theorized that the Bell Witch was not a ghost at all and that the haunting experienced at the Bell farm was merely caused by the unconscious effects of Betsy Bell's mind. They believe that all of the activity was caused by Betsy, as she was just the right age for poltergeist-like manifestations of power. They have also surmised that her religious and moral upbringing could have caused her suppressed sexual energies to act out in a manner that would allay her guilty feelings, especially where Joshua Gardner was concerned.

Other researchers have also suggested that Betsy subconsciously caused the phenomena in retaliation for the fact that she had been sexually abused by her father. Of course, there is no evidence of this whatsoever, despite the fact that it has been mentioned in several fictional accounts and even in some serious studies of the case.

The connections between sexual impulses and repressed energy have long been discussed and frankly are quite believable in some cases. The idea that a human agent in a case could be causing the haunting activity is not a new one and such activity has been referred to for many years as "poltergeist-like activity".

Poltergeist activity is probably the most misunderstood form of paranormal activity, at least in conjunction with haunted houses. The word poltergeist actually means "noisy ghost" when translated from German and for many years, researchers believed that noisy ghosts were causing the phenomena reported in these cases. It was assumed that the things that occurred in a house that was "haunted" by a poltergeist were all caused by an outside force, but today, most investigators don't think so.

In a poltergeist case (and its counterpart), there can be a variety of phenomena connected to it. There are reports of knocking and tapping sounds; noises with no visible cause; disturbance of stationary objects like household items and furniture; doors slamming; lights turning on and off; fires breaking out and much more. To early researchers, this type of phenomena represented tangible evidence of ghosts or even "demonic" activity. And while some cases are ghostly in nature, many others are not, although they are certainly paranormal - and unexplained.

The current theory behind this Poltergeist-like phenomena is that the activity is caused by a person in the household, known as the "human agent". The agent is usually an adolescent girl and normally one that is troubled emotionally. It is believed that she unconsciously manipulates physical objects in the house by psychokinesis (PK), the power to move things by energy generated in the brain. This kinetic type of energy remains unexplained, but even some mainstream scientists are starting to explore the idea that it does exist.

It is unknown why this energy seems to appear in females around the age of puberty, but documentation of its existence is starting to appear as more and more case studies have become public in recent years. It seems that when the activity begins to manifest, the girl is usually in the midst of some emotional or sexual turmoil. The presence of the energy is almost always an unconscious one and it is rare when any of the agents actually realize that they are the source of the destruction around them. They do not realize that they are the reason that objects in the home have become displaced and are usually of the impression that a ghost (or some sort of other supernatural entity) is present instead. The bursts of PK come and go and most poltergeist-like cases will peak early and then slowly fade away.

It should be noted that while most cases such as this manifest around young women, it is possible for puberty age boys (and even older adults) to show this same unknowing ability. As with the young women, the vast majority will have no idea that they are causing the activity and will be surprised to find there is even a possibility that strange things are happening because of them.

In the 1940's, a British psychiatrist named Dr. Maxwell Telling first linked poltergeist-like activity to the Bell Witch case, based only on the evidence that Betsy Bell was the right age for the phenomena to have occurred. Unfortunately, he really had no other information that would substantiate this theory but while he was the first to make the connection, he would not be the last.

One of the most acclaimed authorities on the paranormal and the human mind, Nandor Fodor, also connected poltergeist-like phenomena and the Bell Witch haunting in 1951. His opinions on the case were again based on his suppositions that Betsy was the right age for psychic activity to have taken place but he took the situation one step further and has created one of the greatest modern misconceptions of the case.

Fodor called the Bell Witch case, the "greatest American ghost story", but believed the activity reported was generated by Betsy Bell alone. His theory was that Betsy had developed a secondary personality, but this second personality was a mental force that was gifted with both ESP and the ability to move solid objects by thought. The personality could exert physical force, but was not physical in nature. He believed that a deep-seated hatred, even an unconscious one, could create such a personality and that it could be mistaken for an avenging ghost. Fodor based this on the fainting spells that were experienced by Betsy, which he believed were evidence of her mediumistic powers.

Somewhere along the line, Fodor pondered that Betsy, around the onset of puberty, was sexually molested by her father. This incestuous union created a double problem. On one hand, John Bell suffered the torments of his own conscience, creating the physical ailments which plagued, and eventually killed him. On the other hand, Betsy, tortured by shock, betrayal and guilt, created the secondary personality, which became the witch.

Again, it should be noted again that absolutely no evidence exists that says that such molestation took place. Fodor was drawing on his own years of clinical experience and simply took numerous pieces of evidence and placed them into a pattern that he had seen many times before.

The problems with such a theory, however, are many, although I don't wish for the reader to misunderstand my skepticism regarding a theory of this type in the Bell Witch case. I do feel that poltergeist-like activity can, and does, occur in many cases and I also agree that it can be caused by the human mind and that it will center around a human agent in such cases. However, I don't really feel the evidence fits in this case. Even if we ignore the fact that so much of the activity occurred while Betsy Bell was not even present, we are still left with only her age bracket as the compelling evidence that it could have been.

Psychokinesis simply does not explain the events that took place at the Bell farm. The witch not only moved objects about, but she talked as well. The also had a definite character and personality and one which sharply differed from Betsy's. I would agree that the theory of the secondary personality could account for some of the more sensational aspects of the haunting, but once again, we cannot ignore the fact that so many things took place in the house, and in other locations in the community, when

Betsy Bell was not present. What of the many witnesses who attested to the fact that the witch was able to quote verbatim from Sunday services in different locations? Fodor would say that Betsy's other personality could read minds as well. And what of Andrew Jackson's wagon, which refused to move despite the efforts of four draft horses? On this occasion, Fodor would reply that the secondary personality could cause the wagon to halt in its tracks - even though Betsy Bell had no idea that the group of men were even traveling to her home.

Do you see the problem here? If we can simply invent theories to fit the facts then we are left with the absurd! Of course Dr. Telling's reply to that very same suggestion was that "absurd facts require absurd theories".

And perhaps that brings us to our final theory of the Bell Witch.

I live in the woods, in the air and in the water; in houses with people; I live in heaven and in hell; I am all things and anything that I want to be ...
THE BELL WITCH

Throughout this chapter, I have asked that the reader approach the subject matter, and all of the various theories of the witch, with an open mind. Obviously, no one possesses the solution to the mystery of the Bell Witch. As with the enigma of ghosts themselves, the end result is an unexplained one.

However, I do have one other theory of the case for you to consider. It is a favorite of mine and frankly, I feel it just may fit the evidence and the facts of the case - with chilling accuracy. Believe me when I say that I am not sure I understand this any better than you do, but indulge me for a minute as I ask you to ponder this final scenario.

What if I suggested to you that the Bell Witch was not your typical spirit? What if I suggested that the witch did not know anything about the Bells at all? What if I said that I believed the witch had been around for longer than even the Native Americans who had roamed the land before the white men came? What if I asked you to consider the idea that the witch was not a ghost at all - but an entity so strange that it assumed the form of something familiar just so the Bell's could understand it? And what if I told you that there was evidence to suggest all of this in the original accounts?

Would you think I was mad? Bear with me just a little while longer, and remember what I asked you to do - keep an open mind!

Toward the beginning of the case, and just after the witch began to speak, she claimed to be the spirit of an Indian whose grave had been disturbed on the Bell property. This statement brought back a memory from some time before when a burial mound on the Bell farm had been opened up and desecrated by two unknowing boys. What if the witch had been awakened because of the disturbance of the burial mounds? Not because she was the spirit of a Native American who had been laid to rest there, but because she was a spirit who had entered this world through the burial mound? Sound bizarre? Well, it may not be as strange as it sounds - and if this was the case, it might explain some of the weird activity that is still occurring in the area today!

A location such as this disturbed burial mound is referred to as a "portal" and it is the most controversial type of haunting that has been documented to date by paranormal researchers. The idea that this type of activity may actually exist is still mostly theory and conjecture, although evidence is starting to be collected that may actually show these "portals" exist. The problem is that this type of haunting is the least understood and least traditional of all types of spirit activity.

The idea of a "portal" or a "doorway" to another dimension is not a new one. Many researchers believe that there are places all over the world that serve as "doorways" from our world to another. These doorways are thought to provide access for entities to enter our world. They may be the spirits of people who have lived before, or they could be something else altogether. Some researchers even believe that they could be otherworldly beings from some dimension that we cannot even comprehend.

I know that this all sounds far-fetched, but it may not be as strange as it seems. The entities that have been sighted, reported and even photographed around what many believe to be portals could be the spirits of the dead or perhaps something stranger. If locations like this do exist and they are some sort of doorway, it's possible that these spots may have been labeled as being "haunted" over the years by people who saw something near them that they couldn't explain, isn't it? I think it's likely that this has happened many times. In fact, I would even suggest that these places did not "become" haunted as traditional locations do (through death or tragic events), but had been "haunted" for many, many years already.

Some of the most common sites alleged to be portals have been cemeteries. For years, ghost hunters and researchers have collected not only strange stories of haunted cemeteries, but dozens of anomalous photographs from them as well. In many cases, there seems to be no reason why the cemetery might be haunted unless it might somehow provide access for spirits, or entities, to pass from one world to the next.

Of course, some of the cemeteries are haunted in the traditional manner, but it's the ones that aren't that cause such a puzzle. Going back to what was mentioned earlier, it's possible that these sites were "haunted" long before the cemetery was ever located there. Might it be possible that some sort of "psychic draw" to the area was what caused our ancestors to locate a cemetery there in the first place? Perhaps they felt there was something "sacred" or "spiritual" about the place and without realizing why, placed a burial ground on the location and made it a protected spot. According to American Indian lore (and my own discussions with several Native Americans), the early inhabitants of this country chose their burial grounds in a conscious manner, looking for a place to bury the dead that was more closely connected to the next world. Many of these locations, including many disturbed sites, are now considered "haunted" or at least inhabited by spirits.

Cemeteries are not the only places to find these portals. I believe they may exist in other places too, including in places where we would least expect them. These "glitch" areas might be found anywhere, even under a home or building. In fact, these doorways, and the unknown entities that pass through them, might be the explanation for some of the strange sightings that have plagued paranormal research for years. For some time, investigators have attempted to dispel the myths that "ghosts are evil" and that they "hurt people", but what if we are wrong? Or perhaps even partially wrong?

Despite the events in the Bell Witch case, normally, I don't believe that ghosts hurt people. By that I mean that people involved in a haunting are not injured by the discarnate spirits of the dead. There are certainly instances of people being hurt though, but usually because they are struck by an object in a poltergeist outbreak or trip over a shifted piece of furniture. In fact, you are more likely to be hurt running away in terror from ghostly activity than you are by the activity itself!

But what about people who get hurt in other ways? These are the cases that worry everyone and the cases that give rise to the stories of "evil spirits" and dangerous ghosts. In some of these cases, we hear accounts of violent acts, terrifying visions and even strange beings that may have never been human at all! Can we always take such stories seriously? Perhaps not, but they are out there and what if these cases involve entities who are not ghosts at all? Could they be strange spirits who have passed into this world by way of the "portals" that we have been discussing?

This is interesting to think about. If this might be true, such a theory would certainly provide answers for puzzling cases when traditional methods of ghost investigations have not worked. It might also provide a solution as to how stories of "evil spirits" and even "demons" have gotten started.

It might even provide a solution (of sorts) to the events in the Bell Witch haunting. Obviously, this is all conjecture at this point, but consider this for a moment:

I am a spirit... I was once very happy but have been disturbed.
THE BELL WITCH

When Drew and Corban Hall opened up the burial mound on the Bell property, they may have opened some sort of doorway. From this doorway, came the Bell Witch, although not in the incarnation for which she would later become famous.

It is possible that the shapeless entity that came through was very old and had roamed the woods and hollows of the land long before the settlers had arrived. In those days, the creature had moved among the Native Americans and to them, it had been an evil spirit, a monster of myth and legend. In those distant times, it took on the form of a black animal and a large bird, both creatures of ancient American mythology.

When the spirit emerged into the world of 1817, it found that much had changed. It took on the form that it had known before, of the large bird and the black animal, only to find that the people who had once hunted and lived in the region were now gone. They had been replaced by an alien people, an unknown group, who dressed and spoke differently than what the spirit was familiar with. So, the creature began to watch and observe.

As it gained in strength, its animosity for the people grew. The scratching and pounding on the house in which they lived turned into the displacement of objects and violent attacks on the people within. It watched and it learned, of stories and gossip from the area, of hatreds and scandals caused by business deals, and of both good people and bad. Why the attacks began to focus on only two of the individuals is unknown, but perhaps as the spirit watched and waited, it began to develop a personality of its own - a personality based on what it observed in the house and in the community.

Soon, and with much difficulty, the entity began to speak in the voice and in the language of the people that it had been observing. It was not long after that the creature created a world of its own - a world in which it made the laws and handed out the punishments. It was a world that it had learned by watching the petty jealousies and hatreds of man. For what actions did the Bell Witch take which were not mirrored after our own in some way?

When the witch departed from Robertson County, it left using the same doorway that it had once passed through. But what if this doorway to another world has never completely closed? What if this spirit, or other spirits, has managed to pass back and forth between this world and another? What if that energy has caused the area around Adams, Tennessee to become "tainted" in some way - infected by the spirit that came to be known as the Bell Witch.

I should tell you that located on land that was once the Bell farm is a place called the Bell Witch Cave. This passage of stone burrows deep into the bluffs above the Red River. It is a dark and forbidding place and I have referred to it many times as "one of the most haunted locations in America".Would you be interested to learn that the burial mound that was disturbed so many years ago, and from which the spirit of Kate may have come, is located directly above the entrance to the Bell Witch Cave?

You see, there are many people who believe that 1828 did not mark Kate's final visit to Robertson County. Some people believe she has come back to haunt the region...

But what if she never really left at all?

- CHAPTER EIGHT -
THE LEGACY OF THE BELL WITCH
STRANGE HAPPENINGS IN ROBERTSON COUNTY THEN & NOW

No, it's not impossible to explain these related misfortunes as a series of explainable happenings totally unattributable to the Bell Witch. But, on the other hand, what if the Bell Witch has come back?
RICHARD WINER in HAUNTED HOUSES

Located about ten miles northwest of Springfield on Highway 41, and a short distance east of Clarksville, is the small town of Adams, Tennessee. At one time, Adams was an important stop on the Louisville & Nashville railroad line and Highway 41 was the main road connecting Nashville and Hopkinsville, Kentucky. Today however, the town is forgotten. Only a scattering of residents remain, along with a few stores and gas stations. It seems that when Interstate 24 was constructed to the west of Adams several years ago, the town was nearly cut off from the rest of the world.

Adams remains today as a reminder of another time, a place where the adventurous traveler can go and tread the ground where the events of the Bell Witch case actually took place. Spend a little time in Adams and you'll not only pick up pieces of the story of the witch, but you can visit the memorial to the Bell family in nearby Bellwood Cemetery and even drop in at the old Bell School, where on Saturday nights the place comes alive as the Bell Witch Opry treats the crowd to old-time country music. In September, you can return and eat, drink and delve into the ghostly stories of the region at "Kate Fest", an annual festival dedicated to the history of the Bell Witch and the beleaguered family from whence came her name.

And that's not all that you'll find in Adams, or at least that's what the stories say. In addition to remembered anecdotes about the Bell Witch from long ago, you'll also hear tales of the witch that are of a more recent vintage. Some believe that old Kate is still wreaking havoc in Robertson County today.

The stories began not long after the old Bell homestead was abandoned. There were the tales of travelers who passed by the place at night to see strange apparitions, odd sights and the occasional unexplained voice or two. While some of the stories were questionable and likely based on the legends of the old place, it becomes hard to ignore the accounts related by reliable local men, like Dr. Gooch, who claimed to see lights appearing in the long empty house.

And there were other stories as well....

After the death of Lucy Bell, the land was divided and Joel Bell inherited the river plot of the farm, which adjoined with his brother Richard's land on the north. He eventually settled on this land after he was married.

Around 1852, a local medical doctor named Dr. Henry Sugg made a call on Joel Bell's home in regards to a sick child. He recalled later that he traveled out to the home one cold afternoon and arrived at the place to find a comfortable fire burning and the family quite glad to see him. As he walked inside, he placed his medical bag on the floor near the door and seated himself by the fire to get warm.

Suddenly, he heard a rattling of glass inside of the case, which was followed by an explosive sound like the popping of corks and the crashing of glass vials. Dr. Sugg was sure that somehow, every bottle inside of his bag had been smashed and he jumped up to see what had happened. He pulled the valise open and strangely, found nothing out of place inside. All of the bottles and vials were completely undisturbed, although he was sure about what he had heard. Joel had been nearby when the event had occurred and he had also heard the breaking of the glass. However, he also mentioned to the doctor that such things were quite common in the house. He also stated that he never paid much attention to them.

I imagine that such things seemed awfully minor to someone who had grown up in the Bell household!

Another odd event took place on this land around 1861. As time had passed, Joel had sold the property to his brother, Richard, and upon his death, the land went to his son, Allen Bell. Allen had lived on and farmed the land for several years before getting married.

Shortly after the beginning of the Civil War, Allen had returned home from Tennessee after being discharged from the army because of poor health. For some time after his return, he was weak and had trouble taking care of his farm. Many of his friends often came to spend the night with him and help out where they could.

One of these friends was Reynolds Powell, who, after spending one night at Allen's house, had quite a peculiar story to tell. It seems that the two men had been over to Allen's step-mother's house and had returned to Allen's house after dark. They went inside and were sitting and talking, having left the front door open to let in some fresh air to catch the cool breeze from outdoors.

Suddenly, there was a loud barking and howling noise from outside. Allen's dog had begun to bark furiously and then ran into the house, acting very frightened. On the exterior of the house, a scratching and tearing sound could be heard, while inside, the dog continued to snap and growl as though in a battle with something. Both men jumped to their feet to see what was the matter, but could find nothing out of the ordinary. They finally shoved the dog back outside and closed the door. After all of this excitement, they decided to turn in for the night.

All was quiet for the next hour or so and the two men drifted off to sleep. Then, they were suddenly awakened by the quick removal of the bolster (a long pillow) from under their heads! This was followed by the bed sheets being torn out from underneath their bodies!

Needless to say, this got their attention and Allen and Reynolds sprang out of the bed, sure to find some trickster hiding in the house. Their investigation turned up nothing though and so after making sure the front door was bolted, they returned to bed. Allen quickly replaced the sheets and the bolster and then placed a light blanket over them. A few minutes later, the same trick was repeated again and this time, the sheets, the bolster and the additional blanket were all pulled from the bed. They replaced everything and after a few minutes, it happened a third time.

They were prepared if it took place again though. They placed the bolster on the bed and both men lay down on top of it, wrapping their arms around it and holding on to it with all of their strength. There was no way it could be pulled out from under them this time!

Almost immediately after Allen and Reynolds both got solid holds around the bolster, it was snatched away from them and then came down solidly on the backs of their heads! This ended that contest!

Reynolds Powell was killed while serving in the Confederate Army a short time after this incident, but when interviewed much later about it, Allen Bell admitted that it had taken place. He added however, that nothing like that ever happened again while he was living there. Still, he couldn't help but wonder about the similarity of the event to incidents which had taken place at John Bell's house many years before.

Could the Bell Witch still be at her work?

In 1866, another mysterious event was reported on the Bell land, this time by John A. Gunn and A.L. Bartlett, who were both described as "reputable gentlemen" of the area. One afternoon, the two men had occasion to cross the Red River, as they were on there way to visit their best girls. They found the river too swollen to cross, so they left their horses on the south side and crossed over in a canoe.

Later that same day, as they made the return trip, they decided to stop for a moment at the same spring where the witch had, years before, claimed there was treasure hidden. It had been here where Drew Bell and Bennett Porter had worked all day to unearth a large stone as "Old Sugar Mouth" had watched in dismay when no treasure appeared. Gunn and Bartlett paused here for a drink of water and then started back up the hill.

They were just nearing the top of the wooded rise when a startling and clear voice sounded from the area of the spring. The sweet strain of music pierced the air and both men (involuntarily, they reported) sat down on the ground to listen. This eerie and unexplained melody played for close to thirty minutes and both men later referred to it as indescribable and yet unsurpassingly sweet. There was no explanation as to where the music could have come from, other than a supernatural one.

In addition to these two incidents of the middle 1800's, author M.V. Ingram also tells of two incidents that occurred in 1872, just a few miles from the Bell place. He stated that these incidents "were of the same nature and character of the disturbances that annoyed the Bell family so much, and unmistakably emanated from the same source or agency."

When I discovered this notation, I was delighted because here at last might be some solid evidence as to the continuation of the Bell Witch haunting. Unfortunately though, this was not the case.

"These demonstrations," Ingram went on to write, "were witnessed by two young ladies who could not have been mistaken. But, for proper and prudent reasons, they request that the circumstances and details be omitted in this publication, and in deference to their wishes they are not recorded."

And, as far as I have been able to learn, these incidents were not recorded anywhere else either. There was one small glimmer of hope though, as to the belief that the witch continued on!

Ingram wrote further: "However, these incidents are sufficient to enable the author to trace the operations of the agency known as the "Bell Witch" from 1817 to 1872, a period of fifty-five years, and he leaves readers to form their own conclusions as to the nature and authorship of the demonstrations."

Obviously, this author is not the only person to consider the idea that the Bell Witch haunting has had ramifications long after the events of the case came to an end. Another such person was a clever Tennessee defense attorney in 1875 or 1876.

That was the year that a murder took place at a railroad crossing between Cedar Hill and Springfield, a short distance away from Adams. The man who was killed was named Smith and he was murdered by Thomas Clinard and Richard Burgess. All three of the men worked for a local farmer named Fletcher, who had hired Smith after the man had arrived in the county as a stranger. Clinard and Burgess had already been working on the farm for some time.

Smith was definitely an odd one and claimed to be some sort of "wizard". He often boasted of his power to hypnotize people and said that he could lay spells on people and cause them to do his will. He also claimed to have gotten this power from no less than the Bell Witch herself!

The two men were represented after the murder by a Colonel House, who was well-known for being a great lawyer and orator. Now the Colonel never claimed in court that Smith was given powers by the Bell Witch, but he did make a very strong case for self-defense. He stated that Clinard and Burgess were merely defending themselves against the powers that Smith had directed toward them.

House presented overwhelming evidence that Smith had attempted to hypnotize the two men, who were undoubtedly simple drifters with no education and who readily believed whatever Smith told them. The attorney also showed evidence to say the men were completely under Smith's control and that he had made them do a number of foolish things. He also threatened the men with bodily harm and when they tried to avoid him, he threatened more and followed them about warning of impending doom. Under such circumstances, Clinard and Burgess planned Smith's death. They ambushed him and shot him to death, then surrendered themselves to the authorities. They made no effort to deny the fact that they had killed Smith, but insisted that they had done so while trying to protect themselves from the power that he had been given by the Bell Witch. They simply had to kill him, they told the authorities, they had no choice!

The case caught the attention of the entire community and became one of the strangest to ever come before the courts in Robertson County. And yes, the two men were acquitted on a plea of self-defense - all thanks to the Bell Witch.

A few years later, at some point before the turn of the last century, a local man claimed to have an encounter with a spirit that he believed was the Bell Witch. One Sunday night, he had attended church, as he usually did, and this being in the days before automobiles, he had ridden his favorite horse. After the services were finished, he stayed for some time and spoke to several neighbors but as the hour grew late, he decided to start for home. He unhitched the horse, climbed into the saddle and started up the road.

Just moments after he settled himself though, he later reported that he felt someone climb onto the saddle behind him. Looking around to see who it was, he saw no one, even though the pale light of the moon was bright overhead. He shook his head and assumed that he had imagined the whole thing - until he felt a pair of arms slide around his waist and the body of a person press against his back!

The story never goes on to say just how quickly the ride home actually took - or whether or not the fellow rode the horse at a dead run - but it does say that when he reached the barn gate, he quickly dismounted. He trotted a few feet away from the horse and looked again to see if his disembodied passenger had become visible. In the dim light, he still saw that the saddle was empty!

But even as he stood there watching, he heard the leather of the saddle squeak as if someone was dismounting. The creak of the stirrups was followed by the sound of two feet striking the ground. This was enough to terrify him, but then he also heard a woman's voice that followed soon after. "Thank you," he heard the voice murmur and then the words whispered away on the wind.

The man immediately ran for the house!

He only returned outside the next day after the sun was full in the sky. His horse still stood there at the gate, the saddle still across the animal's back. Cautiously, he removed the saddle and the bridle from the horse and let it out into the pasture. It was hard to keep his mind on his work that day, the man recalled some years later, for he often thought of the ghostly passenger that he had brought home with him the night before. He was sure that the specter had been Old Kate and not surprisingly, he was greatly concerned about whether she had walked back to the place where she had come from - or whether she decided to stay around his house! Thankfully, no further incidents of this sort were ever reported by the luckless farmer.

There have been many reports of strange lights on the Bell property. Most of these sightings occurred long after the family had ceased to live in the original house and even after the building was town down. Many of these stories recount mysterious balls of light that are sometimes seen in the fields, woods and along the roadways of the area. These glowing lights have been responsible for scaring many people, intriguing others and it is suggested that they have even been the cause of many close-call auto accidents over the years.

One story of the "ghost lights" is dated back to around the turn of the last century and was recounted by author Charles Edwin Price. He told of a group of young boys who journeyed out to the Bell farm at a time when portions of the house were still standing. The boys arrived around midnight and went inside of the ramshackle old place. Finding nothing of interest, they walked back out into the field. Just then, a glowing ball of blue and white-colored light emerged from the woods where the Bell cemetery is located. The light began moving across the field toward the boys and they froze in their tracks. It bounced along the hills, dipping down now and then as the terrain raised and lowered and then stopped a short distance from where the young men were standing. From nowhere, came the sharp voice of a woman. "Get ye away...ye have no business here", they claimed to hear it say.

That was the last time that any of those boys ever trespassed on the land again!

Another tale is also told about a family who was driving home one night along a country road that passed close to the Bell farm. It was a very dark night, so the man who was driving the car had no problem seeing the headlights that suddenly appeared on the road ahead of him. The two lights seemed to be heading right down the center of the narrow road and coming toward the family's car at a high rate of speed. They neither slowed down, nor moved to one side to let the other car pass.

The driver of the other car began to panic and to look for a place to pull off. There was nowhere to go, other than into the ditch, but as the lights got closer and closer, that was where the driver decided to go! He began to turn the wheel - but before he could swerve to the side, the other car was upon them! The driver cried out to his family and he braced himself for the impact!

Just seconds before the oncoming headlights reached his car though, the lights separated and one passed on each side of the family's automobile, swooshing by at lightning quick speed. There was no car at all, merely two glowing lights with nothing in between them! The driver slammed on the brakes and threw open his car door, climbing out to watch the two lights disappear on down the road.

Other stories say that some people attempt to chase the lights as they travel along the roads and across the open fields. Whatever the source of these bright orbs, they somehow manage to stay just out of reach of those who try and pursue them. The lights will often vanish when approached, only to appear again in another location.

One of the strangest stories of the unexplained lights was recalled by a man who once lived on property near the old Bell place. One evening, he saw an unusually bright light appear at the edge of the field next to the homestead. The light seemed to hover in place for a moment, shining and quivering around the tops of the trees by the field, and then it began to circle in the air directly above the old Bell family cemetery.

The light drifted up above the old graveyard for 15 or 20 minutes and then floated over to the top of a nearby barn. He reported that the object stayed there for some time, giving off a tremendous amount of light. The glow from it was so bright that it lit up a nearby pasture, illuminating all of the cows that had been huddled there in the darkness.

Then, the behavior of the light grew even stranger. While it was suspended at the end of the barn, the light began to grow. A long crooked tail (about four to five feet long) emerged from the ball and trailed along behind it. The light began to move in a circle once more and started to dip and rise as it went around. It began to drift back in the direction that it had come from and when it reached the graveyard again, it slowly began to move in a circle once more, like some sort of weird bird of prey. Eventually, it vanished.

The man who told the story said that he was never surprised by anything that happened on the farm. He said that eventually he had moved away from the place because relatives and company would never come to visit. The visitors who did come claimed to see weird thing and then would leave in a fright. He blamed the weird incidents, not surprisingly, on the Bell Witch.

Strange lights have not been the only unexplained incidents to happen involving cars in the area around Adams.

The Keysburg Road ran north from Adams and crossed the Red River over an old steel bridge for many years. It was finally removed in 1976 and replaced with a concrete bridge that is located about 50 yards down the river.

There were many supernatural incidents reported on the old bridge. Many claimed to encounter a white mist in the form of a person on the bridge after dark. This apparition could only be seen by the headlights of an automobile as it approached. The unnatural mist would then fade away and disappear. It was also said that cars that were running just fine before crossing the bridge, would often die in the middle of the span for no apparent reason. After several minutes of effort by the driver, the motor would then start back up and run as well as before.

There were also stories that dated back to the horse and buggy days and were tales that rang very close to the strange incident of General Andrew Jackson and his wagon. It seems that the carriages would be moving along just fine and then would suddenly freeze up and stop. No matter how loud the driver yelled or how hard he whipped the reins (or how hard the horse pulled), the buggy would simply refuse to move. After several minutes, the carriage would suddenly start to roll again, as if nothing had ever happened!

A similar incident was said to have happened to a local man many years ago, but after the days when buggies were being used for transportation. In those days, there was a sawmill that operated on part of the old Bell farm, just a short distance from the family cemetery. The mentioned gentleman was driving himself and several other men to work in a Model T Ford.

They were within a few hundred yards of the sawmill when the car came to a sudden halt. The motor was still running and everything seemed be operable, but the car refused to move. Several of the men got out to push, but were unable to budge it from the spot. The wheels would even spin and churn up the earth, but it was as if something was holding it there!

Finally, the driver suggested that they simply walk to work and then see if they could get the Ford moving again later in the day. They walked up the road to the sawmill and later on, after finishing work, walked back to the car. They had no idea if they could get it moving again, but they were determined to try. They had discussed the situation all day long and several of the men suggested possible ways to get the Ford back in motion.

Fearing a repeat of the morning, the driver climbed behind the wheel and one of the other men cranked the motor. To their surprise, the engine fired up and when put into gear, the Ford easily rolled away!

There are other auto-related tales connected to the old steel bridge that used to span the Red River. According to a number of witnesses, strange sounds were often heard on the bridge and on the "S" curve that led into the bridge crossing.

Stories told by former residents of a house near the bridge attest to the fact that this short stretch of Highway 41 was the scene of many automobile and truck accidents, and that several people were killed along this hazardous stretch of road over the years. It is true that this section of highway, with its curves and narrow bridge, was very dangerous, but these dangers do not explain what was heard there over the years.

On a number of occasions, witnesses claimed to hear the sound of screeching tires and locked brakes, followed by what sounded like an automobile crashing into a solid wall, tree or another car. When the nearby residents would go to investigate these sounds, they would find no wrecked cars, nor anything else to explain the horrible things they had just heard. The reports almost always came after dark and sometimes late into the night.

Then, in 1968, came the most eerie auto-related story to ever be told around

Adams. As with anything else that smacks of the paranormal in the region, it was blamed on the spirit of old Kate. Bell Witch or not though, this story will send a chill up your spine!

A soldier from Fort Campbell (near Clarksville) picked up his girlfriend in Cedar Hill and then took her back to Clarksville to see a movie. The route the soldier chose to take his girl home afterward caused them to pass through Adams on Highway 76 and then the plan was to take Highway 41 the short distance to Cedar Hill.

They were running a bit late coming home and the soldier was driving at a pretty good rate of speed along the dark and twisting roads. Just on the outskirts of Adams, the young man saw a child walk out onto the road ahead! He immediately went for his brakes and tried his best to stop! He was moving at a high rate of speed however and there was no chance of missing the little girl. The couple felt a sickening thud against the front of the car as they struck the child – and could hear a rattle from beneath the vehicle as her tiny body was pulled under it and dragged along the highway.

The soldier continued to mash the brake pedal to the floor and finally the car came to a shuddering halt. He threw open his door and jumped out to find the child. He followed his skid marks up the highway, looking for the small body, but she was nowhere to be found. He called to his girlfriend and she got out, weeping over the events that had just taken place, and ran to the young man. Together, the two of them began searching the roadway for the child, then searched through the weeds and brush at the side of the road. They searched frantically, their stomachs knotted with fear over the horrific scene they were sure to find when they discovered the body.

After spending nearly 30 minutes looking for the child, the soldier thought it best to call the authorities. He drove his girlfriend to Cedar Hill and from her house, called the sheriff in Springfield. He explained what had happened and told the dispatcher that he had been unable to find the little girl. He told them that he would meet them at the scene and show them where the accident had occurred. The sheriff's office contacted the local paramedics and all of them met the soldier back on the highway outside of Adams.

He showed the authorities where he had felt the car strike the child and the place where he had finally been able to stop. The paramedics, a number of police officers and the young man began to search the roadside and the ditches once again. After that, they expanded the search to include areas away from the road and into the edge of the woods. They believed that perhaps the child had been struck and then had somehow crawled out of sight in the darkness. The search continued with flashlights until dawn and then, joined by local people, it went on for several more hours.

The girl was never found and no one from Adams ever reported a missing child. It was as if the child had never existed at all – and perhaps she didn't. In fact, the officers (and perhaps even the young man himself) would have been willing to dismiss the whole incident as a vivid hallucination, except for one thing....

When the young soldier went to show a sheriff's deputy just where the car had struck the girl, they saw something that chilled their blood! They walked around to the front end of the automobile and there, imprinted in the dust on the front bumper of the car, was the print of a small hand and some fingers!

Every few years, new stories come along to revive the story of the Bell Witch in the public mind, especially in Tennessee. One such story appeared in a November 1965 newspaper article in which a Nashville newspaper asked the question, "Does the Bell Witch - 150 year old goblin, who in 1817 terrorized Robertson County - still make her presence known today?"

The article then goes on to tell the story of a Mrs. Adams, who owned a small antique shop about eight miles from the old Bell farm. She was talking with some customers in her shop one day when two strangers came in and asked to buy a rocking chair that was behind the desk. Mrs. Adams had purchased it recently at auction from the estate of Charlie Willett, a local attorney and a descendant of the Bell family (Note: The reader might remember the name Charles Willett as being the man who had secretly courted a member of the Gardner family but never married her). Mrs. Adams had decided to keep the chair and not sell it.

The two strangers were a couple, a middle-aged man and woman, and while they were disappointed about not being able to buy the chair, the woman asked if she could sit down in it. Mrs. Adams told her that it was fine and went back to helping her other customers. After she rocked in the chair for about 30 minutes, the lady got up and they left the store.

Mrs. Adams had completely forgotten about this incident until about two weeks later, when a visitor appeared at her home. She had been making dinner for some guests when a knock came at the front door. She answered it to find a young woman standing there.

"Are you the lady who showed my mother a chair that once belonged to a Charlie Willett?" she asked Mrs. Adams. "It was about two weeks ago."

The older woman suddenly recalled the odd incident with the couple and replied that she had. Mrs. Adams asked the young woman to come in and then the girl explained that the older couple had been her parents. She said that her husband had been skeptical about what had happened when her parents had left Mrs. Adams' antique store.

"What happened?" asked Mrs. Adams.

The girl then went on to tell her story to Mrs. Adams and a number of the guests who were present for dinner. "After my mother sat in the chair and meditated," the visitor explained, "they drove to the Bell cemetery. My father stayed in the car while my mother got out and went all around the lot. She was sitting down near the tallest monument when she heard a voice - it was the Bell Witch talking to her.

" The voice told her to stand up and look around and she would find something of value."

The young woman went on to say that instead of looking around, her mother had hurried back to the car and climbed inside, frightened by the strange voice.

"My father tried to get the car started," she continued on, "but it would only cough and sputter. Finally, they were able to get it started and they began to drive back toward Springfield.

"Soon after they left the cemetery, they both heard the witch say to stop the car and look around," the young woman said.

The woman's father quickly stopped the car and this time, he joined his wife outside. They got out of the car and walked out into a nearby field. About halfway across the field, the girl's mother saw a black iron kettle that was turned upside down. When she turned the kettle over, she found a pearl buckle lying in the grass. She took them both and put them in the car. The next day, the woman took the buckle to a jeweler, who examined it and estimated its age at 150-200 years old. He remarked that it was quite valuable.

When the woman finished her story, she asked Mrs. Adams if she too might be able to go down to the shop and meditate in the chair. "The witch told my mother several things about me," she said, "and maybe I can find out more."

Although perplexed, Mrs. Adams asked her son-in-law to accompany the woman down to the store and he agreed. He returned a little while later and said that the young woman had rocked in the chair for several minutes, thanked him and left. His only comment when returning to the house was that it was all "real weird" - two words that perfectly sum up the entire story!

As the reader has seen, there are many events in the area that are blamed on, or connected to, the Bell Witch. While many of these stories seem rather chilling, it is difficult to make the connection to the witch with some of them unless you try very hard.

However, these are some incidents - and in this case some people - who are more closely tied to the return of the Bell Witch than others. Take, for instance, the information recounted by author Susy Smith in the late 1960's, which could well indicate that certain descendants of John Bell continued to fall under the curse of the Bell Witch, long after the witch was said to have departed.

Smith wrote of an interview she conducted with Robert Borden Adam, the son of Ann Bell Adam. His mother had been the daughter of John Elijah Bell II of Tennessee. During Smith's interview, which took place in 1969, Adam told about how he had been sent home on emergency leave from Navy basic training in 1968 after his two sisters and his father burned to death in the family home. Although fire investigators did not rule out arson, Adam was convinced the fire had been started by the Bell Witch.

Several months later, his mother committed suicide by taking an overdose of sleeping pills.

And this wasn't all - he also told Smith how his great-grandfather, John Elijah Bell, had come to a sudden and violent end after being struck by a speeding ambulance in Memphis. Then, in 1969, his grandmother, the widow of John Elijah Bell's son, became afflicted with a mysterious illness like the one that had plagued John Bell. According to doctors, it was a strange nerve disorder that caused her throat and mouth to become stiff and swollen and made it hard for her to swallow and talk. Her death came suddenly and quite unexpectedly.

A fateful coincidence or real evidence of the return of the witch? Most would not be too quick to accept the presence of the supernatural in this story, preferring to believe that the cruel hand of fate had more to do with the strange deaths in the family that the witch did. It should be remembered that the Bell family had scores of descendants and the majority of them lived normal, happy lives - despite the stories that have plagued the family for generations. Even today, some members of the Bell family still refuse to discuss the events that took place between 1817 and 1821. Do they believe that to speak of the "family troubles" might be to incur the wrath of the witch once more? It's likely that most of them do not, but in some cases, a few family members are hard to convince that the curse of the witch is not still preying on those who followed after John Bell.

"I couldn't say whether it has caused all that has happened so far," Robert Borden Adam told Susy Smith, "but I do believe it has returned and I'll probably believe it until the day I die."

- CHAPTER NINE -
THE BELL WITCH CAVE
THE TALES OF BILL EDEN

The Bell Witch has Returned. It has remanifested itself on Bill Eden's farm, which was once land belonging to John Bell. Eden, his family and even visitors to the farm have encountered the Bell Witch. As of this writing, the Witch stalks Bill Eden's land.
RICHARD WINER in HAUNTED HOUSES

Near the Red River, on the former Bell farm, is a cave that has been called the "Bell Witch Cave". Thanks to local legend and lore, many people have come to believe that when the spirit of the witch departed from the torment of the Bell family, she went into this cave. Others (myself included) believe that the cave marks the entrance to a doorway through which Kate came into the world, departed, and perhaps even returns today. Who knows? But I can tell you that with the large number of bizarre incidents reported in and around the cave in modern times, notions of the witch returning may not be as odd as you might think.

While the cave had become quite famous in recent years, there is little mention of it in contemporary accounts of the haunting. It is believed that the cave might have been used for the cool storage of food in those days, thanks to the fact that it remains a constant 56 degrees. It was also mentioned in some accounts that Kate's voice was often heard nearby and one day, Betsy Bell and several of her friends had a close encounter with the witch inside of the cave.

The cave itself is located in the center of a large bluff that overlooks the river. The mouth of the cave opens widely but entrance to the cavern itself must be gained through a fairly long tunnel. The cave is not large compared to most commercial caves, however its true length is unknown because of narrow passages that go beyond the 500 or so feet accessible to visitors. Although geologically, this is a dry cave that has been carved from limestone, in wet weather, a stream gushes from the mouth of the cavern and tumbles over a cliff into the river below. This make the cave nearly impossible to navigate and even shouted conversations become inaudible over the roar of the water.

In dry times, the cave has proven to be quite an attraction to curiosity-seekers and ghost hunters. Once you pass through the entrance passage, the visitor enters a large room that opens into yet another tunnel and an overhead passageway. Another large room can be found at the rear of the explored portion of the cave, but from that point on the tunnels become smaller, narrower and much more dangerous.

Betsy Bell recalled many explorations of the cave that she and her friends took part in when she was growing up on the farm. There was sufficient room at the mouth of the cave for the young folks to picnic and the river below offered a fishing hole that was often enjoyed by the group. "None of us ever knew of the cave being occupied by the spirit," she later remembered, "but on our pleasure trips we always heard its voice on the river or in the cave."

One day, Betsy Bell and some of her friends were exploring the cave, using candles as a source of light. There was a number of beautiful formations in the cavern that could be seen and Betsy and her friends often went back to a room that she described as being "some thirty feet high, with a kind of upstairs to it." Beyond this room, the passage got smaller.

One of the boys came to a place in the passageway where he had to get down on his hands and knees to get through. He inched along the corridor and then suddenly went into what Betsy called a "quicksand deposit" and got stuck. He was soon so jammed in that he was unable to get out. He twisted around trying to get free and in his panic, dropped his candle and it was snuffed out. He called for help and while his friends could hear him, could not find him in the total blackness of the cave.

Suddenly, the boy heard the voice of the witch coming out of the darkness behind him. "I'll get you out," Kate assured him and the boy began to feel his legs being pulled as if twin vices had been cinched around his ankles. He was dragged through the muddy cave all of the way back to the entrance and was deposited there in small pool of water. He was a bit worse for wear, but at least he was alive.

"We all agreed not to tell our parents of this nearly fatal accident", said Betsy, "but that night when the spirit arrived at the usual neighborhood gathering at our home, it asked the parents of the boy if they had gotten the mud out of the boy's ears. Then, it told them of his predicament in the cave and advised them to put a halter on him the next time so his companions could pull him out if he got stuck again!"

The Bell Witch Cave became an attraction thanks largely to a man named Bill Eden, who owned the property for a number of years (although interestingly, Betsy Bell referred to the place as the "Bell Witch Cave" in Charles Bailey Bell's 1934 book on the haunting - leading many to wonder just how old this name might be for the place). Eden was a wealth of information about the cave and about the fact that strange occurrences were continuing to take place on the land that once belonged to John Bell. Although he was mainly a farmer, Eden did make some early improvements to the cave by adding electrical lights, but that was about all.

Despite being undeveloped though, the cave managed to attract hundreds of visitors every year who wanted to be shown through it. Bill always obliged although was always puzzled about how they found the place. There were no signs to point the way at that time but somehow people found it and they always asked to hear the stories of the witch, and the stories that Eden spun from his own weird experiences at the place.

Eden bought the farm where the cave is located in 1964, and owned the place for 17 years. However, he had lived on various parts of the Bell farm for more than four decades. He and his wife, Frances, had resided in various farmhouses around the property and both could recall a number of strange incidents that had occurred in them. It seemed that every house had come with knocking noises, apparitions or other unexplained oddities.

Eventually, Bill grew tired of living in old, haunted farmhouses so he tore down an old Bell family house and built a modern, one-story brick home (that still stands today) in its place. This however, did not bring an end to the strange events there, as the current owners can tell you!

But perhaps it is the property, and not the house, that is haunted! Years before Eden lived there, while the other house was still standing, a section of woods had run from the house all of the way to Adams, which is about a mile to the south. Those who traveled from the immediate vicinity into Adams at that time would take a well worn path that provided a short cut into town.

The stories said that sometimes, just as darkness was falling, a figure would walk down the path and out of the woods and into a low place in the yard. This figure would never stop walking and would go down toward a big oak tree and then vanish from sight. This would happen only periodically and there seemed to be no set pattern as to when this figure might appear. There was one strange thing about this person though - it seems that he, or she, had no head!

Another tale about the land where Eden built the new brick house stated that for many years, a bright light was seen there almost every night. This mysterious globe looked much like a lantern, although no earthly hand could be seen carrying it. The light would rise from just below the top of the bluff and float high into the air before coming to rest in a large oak tree in front of the original house.

One night, the man of the house decided that he was going to shoot that light out of the tree. He went into the house and got his rifle. Then, taking careful aim, he fired. As the rifle cracked, the light tumbled down through the branches of the tree and vanished into the grass and brush beneath it.

Everyone who had gathered to watch ran over to see where the light had gone and just what the strange object had been. Despite a careful search though, they found nothing. Whatever it had been, the family believed that the days of watching the light were over, and they were - but only for about three nights. As inexplicable as it had always been, the light was back, although for how long it stayed is unknown.

"Do you believe the Bell Witch exists?" author Richard Winer asked Bill Eden during a 1978 interview. Winer and his co-author, Nancy Osborn, had traveled to Tennessee to visit the Bell Witch Cave and to see the land where John Bell and his family had been haunted.

"Yes, sir!" Bill Eden replied. "There are too many things which happen around here that you can't explain."

One night a number of years before, Eden had been keeping some dairy cows in an old barn a short distance from the house. After a long day of farming, he ate his dinner and then headed up to the barn to do the milking. It was fairly late and quite dark. The barn was located just east of Eden's house, along a section of the old dirt road that used to connect Nashville to Clarksville in the early 1800's. After awhile, Eden finished his chores and started back to the house. He was about halfway along the old road, and coming up a small hill, when he felt someone take a hold of his arm. It was a light, but rather firm, squeeze of his upper arm and then it was gone.

"I thought it was one of my boys hiding beside the road trying to scare me," he recalled. "I lit my cigarette lighter and there was nobody on the road but me. I couldn't hear no sound and I couldn't see nothing. There wasn't anything there that you could see at all."

Eden went on to describe some of the other incidents that had taken place on the property, including the sounds of footsteps that seemed to continuously plague the new house that he built. The same incessant pacing had also been heard in the home that had once stood on the spot, but had been torn down. Apparently, the change in structures had not bothered the unexplainable sounds. He also reported hearing knocking on the front door and walking up and down the hallway at all hours of the night.

Another eerie event involving phantom footsteps inside of the residence occurred one day when Eden came home and entered the house through the basement door, right next to where he parked his truck. Just moments after he got to the bottom of the stairs, he heard the sound of someone walking across the floor above his head. After that occasion, these same sounds were heard from the basement on many occasions. In fact, it happened so often that Eden and his family always knew where the sounds would stop and start. They would begin in the same place, move down the hallway and enter the same bedroom, where they would halt. No explanation was ever discovered for the source of the sounds.

" A few weeks ago," he added, "my wife was fixing dinner and she heard someone in the basement like they were dragging an old straight-backed chair around. She went down there twice, but she still couldn't find anything."

Eden also described the peculiar actions of the cabinet doors in the kitchen. Apparently, when the doors were left partially open, something would come along and close them, as if hitting them with an open hand, and they would slam shut. On other occasions, the cabinets would be closed and then would fly open under their own power.

One winter, a very strange event took place at the house. It was the middle of January and the ground was covered with snow and ice. Around two o'clock in the morning, a knocking came on the front door of the house. It was incessant beating that woke Eden from a sound sleep. He jumped out of bed and hurried to the front door, peering out through the living room curtains to see who was there. He saw no one standing on the porch.

Now, odd things like this had happened in the past, but Eden decided that if a human culprit was at work, he would catch them in the act. "So instead of going to bed, I went into the bathroom and there I lit myself up a cigar and sat on the commode and smoked," Eden explained. "In a few minutes, the knock came again and knocked about three times, so I sneaked back in there to the living room to look."

Eden looked carefully out the front window again and this time, saw a person walking back up the front walk. Whoever it was, they were wearing a long black coat, which almost dragged the ground, with the collar turned up high around the ears. He couldn't tell if it was a man or a woman. At the end of the walk, the person turned and went down the hill.

"I didn't see a car out there, and I was wondering where the car was," Eden said. "It went behind a big tree but didn't come out the other side. So I called my wife and woke her up. She came to the living room and said, 'What in the world are you doing in here?'"

At this point, Eden instructed his wife to watch behind the tree and make sure that no one came out from behind it. He was sure that whoever the trespasser was, they were hiding out there for some reason. In the meantime, Eden quickly got dressed and fetched his gun. He was still thinking that someone had tried, or was still trying, to break into the house.

"So I got dressed and went down through the basement with my shotgun and light and sneaked a way around and came all the way behind it," he continued. "I kept peeping and looking and walked clear around that tree. I looked down for the tracks in the snow - but there was only my tracks. And I looked over that walkway, and there wasn't a single track on my walkway. And so, it's such things that make me believe in ghosts."

Eden also spoke of working outside sometimes and hearing what sounded like a woman's voice calling his name. When this happened at first, he would turn all around to see where it was coming from. After awhile, he stopped looking.

The same thing often happened to Bill's wife, who had her own share of encounters in the house. One day, she was fixing lunch and heard a noise like someone had come through the front door, dragging a chain behind them. "They came in and dragged it all the way through the living room, into the dining room and right into the kitchen where she was standing by the cook stove," Eden reported. "It was like they was dragging a log chain- but she couldn't see a thing."

Frances also reported hearing the sound of a woman's scream and it would often come from the kitchen. It was a loud, shrill cry and one that Bill recalled hearing inside of the cave on occasion. He would often follow it but was never able to catch up to whoever was causing the sound. He said that it sounded like a woman in misery.

And there were many other stories to tell in regards to the Bell Witch Cave! Many of the strange experiences actually happened to Bill Eden himself, while others involved visitors to the cave. For instance, a woman came to visit one day and asked to go down and see the cave. She had brought a group of friends along and in all, about fifteen people followed Eden down the rather treacherous path to the cave's entrance. All at once, the woman in charge of the group abruptly sat down in the middle of the path. One of the people who was with her asked why she was sitting there, and she answered that she wasn't! She claimed that a heavy weight, which felt like a ton of lead, was pressing her down to the ground and she couldn't get up. Several members of the group managed to get the lady to her feet and half carried her back up the hill to her car.

Bill Eden could also recount a number of encounters he had on his own in the cave. "You can hear footsteps in there all the time and I saw one thing," he said in the interview with Winer. "Lots of people come out here expecting to see a ghost or a witch of whatever you want to call it. I just call it a spirit - and it looked like a person with its back turned to you. Looked like it was built out of real white-looking heavy fog or snow, or something real solid white. But you couldn't see through it. It had the complete figure of a person till it got down to about its ankles. It wasn't touching the floor at all. It was just drifting - bouncing along."

On another occasion, Eden was leading a man, his wife and grown son on a tour of the cave. They were all walking along through the cave and Eden was pointing out some of the rock formations in the cavern, along with telling tales of the witch. The group was standing in the back room of the cave (as far back as the tour goes) when the woman happened to look up over some rock formations. Suddenly, she began to scream! "Look at that woman!" she screamed at Eden and her family. "She's not walking! She's floating through the air!"

The men looked to where she pointed and then looked at each other. None of them saw anything! Eden looked over at the woman again and by this time, her knees had buckled and she had fallen to the floor of the cave. They quickly helped her up and started walking her toward the front of the cave.

When they made it to the front room, another strange occurrence took place. Close by the entrance to the passage that connects the two large rooms, there is a limestone outcropping that comes out from the wall. As they got close to this limestone section, they heard what sounded like loud, raspy breathing coming (it seemed) from the rock itself! Eden would later say that it was like the hard and labored breathing of a person, which became more labored until it was finally the struggling breath of someone dying. Of course, no matter what it sounded like, it was quite frightening in the dark recesses of the cave!

The woman almost collapsed again and she began to weep. She turned to Eden, quite angry, and stated that he ought to be arrested for rigging the cave in that way! "You're going to kill somebody if you don't stop!" she declared.

Eden replied that he had no idea what she had seen, or what that breathing sound could had been, but he assured her that he had done nothing to rig things up. Her husband came to Bill's defense and insisted that he had seen no wires or anything else to indicate that Eden had rigged things to happen in the cave.

The lady slowly became convinced, although I imagine this was the last time that she visited the Bell Witch Cave!

As Eden mentioned in his interview with Richard Winer, a lot of people came to the cave hoping to see, or experience, a ghost. While many of them went away disappointed, some got a little more than they bargained for.

Eden had taken a group of young people into the cave one evening for a tour. They had been inside for about an hour and had stopped in the back room where they talked for awhile and Bill told of his experiences in the area. As they were starting to leave, one of the girls in the group started to make some remarks about the authenticity of the place, whether or not it was really haunted, and about how disappointed she was that nothing had appeared or had happened. She continued this monologue into the passage connecting the two rooms, which is quite narrow. Everyone else in the group seemed to be having a good time and Eden was used to the squeals, giggles and laughter that often accompanied young people on tours of the cave. The girl who was complaining was walking directly in front of Eden at this point.

She was walking along and then all of the sudden, stumbled backwards as if she had been pushed. She took a couple of step back and then sat down hard on the floor of the cave. "Somebody slapped me!" the girl yelled.

Eden shook his head. "You must have bumped your head," he told her and explained that the ceiling is pretty low in spots and sometimes people had to duck down to avoid being injured.

"No," the girl insisted. "I didn't bump my head, whatever it was hit me on the jaw."

Eden helped the girl to her feet, still skeptical, and they all moved to the front room of the cave. Once there, he shined his light on her face to see how badly she had been hurt. He looked at her cheek and was surprised to see a red welt - and the prints of fingers that were still visible where she had been struck! He certainly had no explanation for how bumping her head on a low ceiling could have accomplished that!

Another young woman came to the cave one day, also in hopes of catching a glimpse of the resident spirit. According to Eden, she had visited the cave several times before and returned one after with a group of friends who wanted to try and conduct a seance to get in touch with Kate.

The group arranged themselves in the position that they wanted to be in and then asked Eden if he would mind shutting off all of the lights in the cave. Amused, Bill decided to go along with their experiment and so he shut them all out. The light switch was located just inside of the gate at the front entrance to the cave and when Eden turned the lights off, he stayed nearby, waiting to switch them back on again when needed. A few moments after the lights went out, he heard the group of young people begin calling for the spirit to appear.

It was only a few minutes later before one of the members of the group inside began calling for Bill to turn the lights back on - and to do so in a hurry! Eden said that he could tell by the sound of the young man's voice, and by all of the hollering coming from the cave, that something had happened. Turning on all of the lights, he started down the passage to see what was wrong and ran into two boys who were carrying the girl who had so badly wanted to arrange the seance and to see Kate. They were holding her under her arms and were simply dragging her out of the cave. The girl had fainted and was now completely unconscious. They took her outside and Bill splashed some cave water on her face to bring her around.

When she came to and was able to talk, she told Eden about seeing a figure in the darkness. Apparently, their summoning had worked! Not surprisingly, the girl's description of the apparition matched closely with others who claimed to see a ghost in the cave. The figure was said to float just off the floor and to be made up of a misty white form - strangely though, the girl also said that she appeared to be young and pretty, with dark hair hanging down her back.

Could the unusual sighting have been merely her imagination at work - or did she really see a ghost on that afternoon in the cave? Although hallucinations can certainly have a strange effect on people, it seems possible that the fainting spell can be accepted as evidence that the girl saw *something* that day. What it may have been though, could still be anyone's guess!

It's likely that the incident just described was what caused Eden to become reluctant about getting involved in any such experiments in the future. He had no desire to "call Kate out", having already had enough strange encounters with what he perceived to be the spirit already. However, one afternoon, another group of young people visited the cave with the intentions of trying to see the ghost. They hoped to make some sort of contact with the spirit but had no idea how to go about it. Thinking that Eden would know what to do, they asked him to help.

He explained to the group that he had never tried to get Kate to make an appearance and wasn't sure that he could do so. In truth, he really had no desire to do so either. After some amount of convincing though, Bill hesitantly agreed to try. He turned out all of the lights and he and the group walked cautiously into the cave.

The young people all assembled around Eden in the first large room in the cave and he began asking Kate to come out, all the while secretly hoping that she wouldn't. A few moments after he began to speak, Eden claimed that he felt a very familiar hand grip his arm. It was the exact same grip that he had felt one evening as he was walking from the house to the barn and he knew that it was Kate herself who was coming to call. The pressure of the phantom hand spooked Eden so badly that he blurted out, "Oh, no! Not me! They're the ones that wanted you!" Seconds after he cried out, the grip on his arm vanished.

Almost as soon as the hand let go, one of the boys who was nearby began yelling that someone had snatched the hat off his head. He demanded that it be given back but the other confused voices in the dark room denied having taken it. When the boy asked Eden to turn the lights on so that he could find it, Bill let out a sigh of relief to have the lights back on in the cave again. He could not recall a time when he was as unnerved in the cave as he was that day.

Eden quickly walked up and turned on the lights and then returned to the room. The boy was searching for his hat and Bill handed he and his friends a flashlight to help them to look. The cap was nowhere to be found - and simply nowhere that it could have disappeared to without some assistance!

After they searched for a little while and were ready to give up, someone aimed a light up toward a passageway that exits off from the ceiling. To everyone's amazement, they saw the hat - it was hanging from a projecting rock about 20 feet from the cave floor!

In the early summer of 1977, several soldiers from Fort Campbell came over to visit the cave. Eden took the young men on a tour and ended up in the back room, where all of them sat around talking and Eden told his stories of the odd events on the farm.

One of the men politely expressed some doubts about the validity of the story. He had been to many places that were supposedly haunted and nothing out of the ordinary had ever occurred to him. Eden laughed and shrugged his shoulders. The man could believe whatever he wanted to, but as for Bill, well, he had seen enough things on the farm to know that something unexplainable was going on. "If something happened, you probably wouldn't ever come back here again," Bill added with a grin.

The group sat and talked for a short while longer and then they all got up to leave - all except for the young man who had spoke up about his disbelief in ghosts. "Mr. Eden! Come here and help me," the soldier said. "I can't get up."

Eden and the man's friends all assumed that he was joking and they all began to laugh. It wasn't until Bill took a good look at the man that he realized that something really was wrong. The young man was now begging for help and his face was drenched so badly with sweat that it looked like someone had poured a bucket of water over him. When Eden took hold of his hand to help him up, he could feel the man's hand was cold and clammy as if he were going into shock.

The man continued to call for help and claimed that he could feel strong arms wrapped around his chest. They were squeezing him tightly, he said, and he was unable to breathe. Eden and the other men helped their friend to his feet and while the soldiers supported him, Bill wiped his face off with some run-off water from the cave. When the soldier got to feeling better, they took him outside of the cave. By the time they were ready to leave, the young man had completely recovered and was suffering no ill effects from his harrowing experience.

As he was heading to his car, he stopped and shook Bill Eden's hand. "Well, you were right about one thing, Mr. Eden," the young soldier said. "I won't ever be back here again."

The winter rains in Tennessee wreak havoc on the Bell Witch Cave, which is why Bill Eden (and the current owners) usually only opened the cave during the summer and early autumn months. Each spring, Bill always had a lot of work to do on the floor of the cave where the rushing water had carved out small holes and ditches.

One Sunday morning, Eden had taken his shovel and rake and was working back some distance in the cave, trying to level out the more damaged portions of the floor. He was chopping at and smoothing over the gravel when he heard a noise that he was not making himself. He spun around because he realized that it was coming from behind him, from the further recesses of the cave.

In the darkness, he could hear the distinct sound of someone walking down the passage, their feet crunching in the gravel on the floor. The sounds kept coming, moving toward him, until they stopped a few feet away. Eden strained his eyes to peer into the shadows, but he could see no one there.

"Something I can do for you?" he called out, but he got no answer. He called again, but still no answer came.

Although he most likely would have hated to admit it, I imagine this incident raised the hairs on the back of Bill's neck. He decided that he would probably get more work done near the entrance of the cave - where it was much lighter - so he picked up his tools and headed in that direction. He walked up front and as he passed through the first room, he noticed his dog sleeping on the little ledge over on the left side of the room.

For the next thirty minutes or so, Eden worked on the floor between the iron gate at the mouth of the cave and the first room. He had just stopped for a moment to rest when he heard the familiar footsteps, tracking through the gravel once more. They were once again coming from the back of the cave and quickly approached the first room, where Bill's dog was sleeping.

Suddenly, the animal's ears pricked up and he jumped to his feet. The hackles raised on the back of his neck and Bill saw his lips curl back to reveal the dog's rather intimidating set of teeth. The animal didn't move though. He just stood there, looking directly at the spot where the footsteps had last been heard. The gravel began crunching again and moved forward, in the direction of where Bill was standing. As the sounds moved past the dog, he stared ahead, as though watching someone that Eden was unable to see. The footsteps came directly toward Bill, passed by him, and then continued to the outside of the cave.

Immediately after, both Bill and the dog hurried outside into the sunlight. He admitted later that he did not have the nerve to go back inside right away, nor for several days afterward. From that time on, that particular dog never entered the main part of the cave again. He would follow people to the steel gate, which is about 30 feet inside, but then he would either wait there or return outside.

Whatever he had seen that day had frightened him away for good!

And those were not likely the end of the stories told by Bill Eden about the farm and about the Bell Witch Cave. There were many other incidents that took place that were never recorded as Eden never got tired of telling the tales to just about anyone who would listen.

"They call me William, they call me W.M., they call me Bill, they call me Judd, and they call me the 'Bell Witch Man'". This was the way that Bill Eden introduced himself to Richard Winer in 1978. A few short years later, Bill Eden passed away and sadly, his death closed a fascinating chapter in the history of the Bell Witch saga.

There is no doubt about it, Mr. Eden was a true American character and the impression that he left on the place, like the impression left by Kate herself, will always remain.

- CHAPTER TEN -
THE BELL WITCH CAVE
THE HAUNTING CONTINUES!

There are few places that I have visited which are more haunted than the famous Bell Witch Cave in Tennessee. There is just something about the place... just after you stare into that inky blackness behind the steel gate... that can give you a case of the cold shivers.
You have to wonder, in the back of your mind, if that gate is there to keep people out... or to keep something else in!
From THE HAUNTING OF AMERICA

Just about anyone who visits the Bell Witch Cave, and who brings along a camera, wants to snap a photograph of the entrance to the cave.

This is a shadowy and forbidding spot, but on the other hand, quite beautiful. As you walk down the gravel path from the top of the bluff and cross the last wooden walkway, you find yourself standing just outside of the gaping mouth of the cave itself. The overhanging rock succeeds in cutting off a great portion of the overhead sky and a damp chill filters out from the cave, provoking goose pimples on your exposed skin. Behind you, over the edge of the bluff, you can hear the dull roar of the Red River and you can't help but ponder the distance to the water below.

If you have brought a camera along, this would be the perfect opportunity to use it. By standing back toward the spot where the bluff comes to a sudden end, you should be able to take a photo of the cave entrance and the rocks overhead.

The reader may have noticed that I have written that you *should* be able to take such a photograph - the problem is that few are ever able to do so! Believe me, hundreds have tried and failed. For some reason, there is a spot outside the cave where not only cameras fail, but sometimes flashlights and batteries refuse to work. In 1997, I was present at the

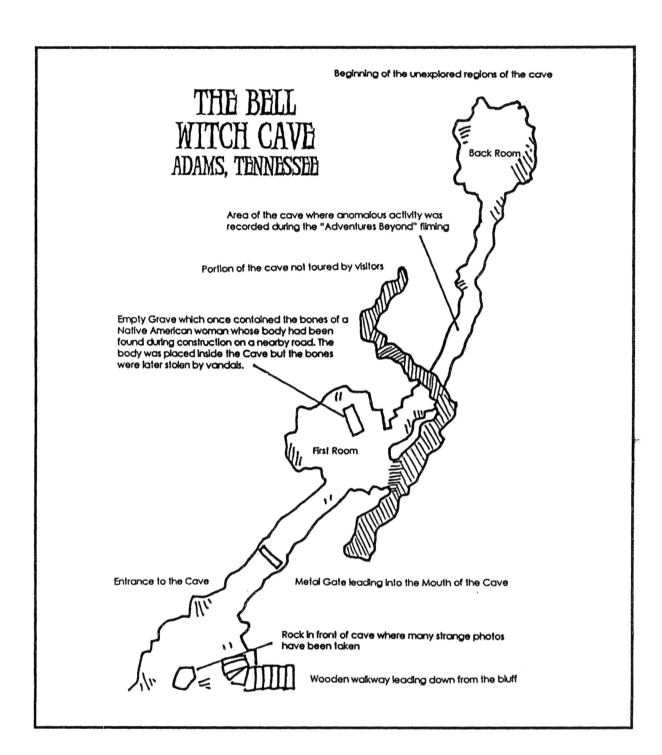

THE BELL WITCH CAVE
ADAMS, TENNESSEE

Beginning of the unexplored regions of the cave

Back Room

Area of the cave where anomalous activity was recorded during the "Adventures Beyond" filming

Portion of the cave not toured by visitors

Empty Grave which once contained the bones of a Native American woman whose body had been found during construction on a nearby road. The body was placed inside the Cave but the bones were later stolen by vandals.

First Room

Entrance to the Cave

Metal Gate leading into the Mouth of the Cave

Rock in front of cave where many strange photos have been taken

Wooden walkway leading down from the bluff

cave when an entire computer system that had been set up to monitor activity in the area refused to work properly. Thanks to whatever anomaly exists here, there are very few photographs in existence of the entrance to the cave. According to the current owners, I have been lucky and have managed to take several good shots of the outside of the cave, but I am one of the few.

Even in Bill Eden's time, the cave entrance was hard to photograph. One day, after finishing a tour of the cave, a man was standing and talking to Bill and he asked one of his sons to pose for a picture in front of the cave. The boy took his dog and stood near a large rock in front of the cave. It would be a perfect shot. The man was using a brand new Polaroid camera and he had taken a number of very nice photos inside of the cave. He asked Bill to hold onto the developed shots while he took another one. The man then aimed the camera at the boy and snapped the photo.

After the photo developed, the gentleman noticed something strange about the picture - something that he had not noticed when the photo was being taken. The photo showed the dog and the lower part of the boy's body, but the boy's head and shoulders were missing. It looked as though someone had stretched a white, cloudy sheet from one side of the cave to the other, completely covering the boy's face.

A young woman named Leslie Seay had a similar experience at the entrance to the cave in 1989. A friend of hers was visiting from up north and wanted to see the sights of middle Tennessee. Since Leslie lived in Clarksville at the time, she decided to take her to the Bell Witch Cave. As this was between the time when Bill Eden owned the cave and before the current owners had taken over the property, no tours were being offer of the place. However, Leslie and her friend did convince the caretakers to allow them to go down and take a look at the cave, but promised not to go inside. They hiked down the trail and ended up in front of the cave entrance.

There is a large rock that rests directly in front of the entrance and Leslie's friend decided that she wanted her photo taken while sitting on it. Leslie obliged and snapped the picture and then the two of them walked back up the bluff and let the owners know that they had returned safely.

"About two weeks later, I sent the film to be developed," Leslie told me. "When I picked up the pictures, the girl told me that one of the photos did not process correctly and that I did not have to pay for it. I didn't look at the pictures until I got to my mother's house and as we were going through them, my mother said that the one in her hand looked rather odd."

She handed the photograph to her daughter and Leslie felt a chill go down her spine. The photo that her mother handed her was the one that she had taken of her friend on the rock outside of the Bell Witch Cave. The photograph was perfectly ordinary - except for the fact that a large white mist was looming over her friend's head!

"It looked almost like a death shroud", Leslie remembered. "Growing up, I had always heard stories about Kate, but we always considered them to be ghost stories to be told while roasting marshmallows around the campfire. Not until that photo was taken did I ever believe them!"

The current owners have a scrap book of strange photos they have taken, along with photos that are sent to them in the mail by people who have visited the cave. They receive dozens of them every year, some showing strange balls of light, misty shapes and fogs and then there are the really weird photos - photos that simply have no explanation at all! Many of these have been taken outside the entrance to the cave.

One such photo shows a girl seated outside of the cave on a large rock. The photo also shows the apparition of a boy who seems to be looming directly behind her. Despite the odd configuration of the images in the photo, it does not at all appear to be a double-exposure.

And this isn't the strangest one! Another photo was taken of two Girl Scouts during a trip to the cave. In the photo, one of the girls is visible, but the other is only partially present and she appears in the photo turned at an impossible angle! Worse yet, is the completely unexplainable image of a two-headed snake that is slithering up the leg of the first girl. Obviously, this was not there when the photo was taken and how it could have appeared in the photograph is totally without explanation.

The present-day owners of the Bell Witch Cave, and the piece of the old Bell farm made so famous by Bill Eden, are Chris and Walter Kirby. Walter is a tobacco farmer and Chris manages to stay busy managing the upkeep and tours of the cave. In the summer months, this task is more than a full-time job. Luckily, she also has her daughter, Candi, to help out.

The Kirby's purchased the land in April 1993. The place had been empty for several years, after the death of Bill Eden, but by that summer, the cave was open again for business. Over the course of the next year or so, they made a number of improvements to the cave, which included new lights, a new electrical system, an improved path to the cave, wooden walkways to cross the most treacherous areas of the trail, and a number of other things. These improvements continue today.

It wasn't long after the Kirby's moved to the farm, and began conducting tours in the cave, before they realized things were not quite right on the property. They began to notice first that there were strange noises that didn't have an easy explanation. "We've heard them in the cave and we've heard them in the house," Chris has said on occasion. "I feel like if there's anyplace that could be haunted, it's this place here. First of all, it's got the legend of being haunted. There's an Indian burial mound right above the mouth of the cave on the bluff. And the previous owner of the cave died in our bedroom."

Shortly after moving onto the farm, Chris was photographing parts of the property and one of the photos on the developed roll of film managed to capture something pretty amazing. She saw nothing when she took the photo and yet, on the developed print, was a misty shape that hovered above a sinkhole leading down into the cave. The photo continues to defy explanation and was even submitted to Kodak in 1997 for analysis. They stated that there appeared to be nothing wrong with the film or with the developing of the photograph. They also added that there appeared to have been no manipulation with the print and that it was not a double exposure. In short, none of the technicians who examined the film had any explanation for what they saw in the photograph. These were almost identical replies to queries that I would make a year later concerning photos that I had taken myself at the cave!

I first met Chris Kirby in the Spring of 1997. I had long been interested in the Bell Witch case and knew that there was a cave located on the property that was purported to be haunted. My wife and I were on a trip down south at the time and decided to take a side trip over to Adams. After seeing the Bellwood Cemetery and the old Bell School, we headed for the cave. In a town the size of Adams, it's not hard to find but it can easily be reached by turning off Highway 41, right next to the Bell School. You can't miss the sign for the cave alongside the roadway and a right turn takes you onto a curving gravel road and up to a small brick house, which was built by Bill Eden. There is a sign here that reads "Bell Cave Parking."

Over to the right of the parking lot is a large, wooded area that contains the sinkhole near where Chris took the photograph of the strange mist. Behind the house is the trail that leads down to the cave. As we walked back along that way, we crossed an abandoned road that is really not much more than a depression in the earth now. Later, I would have the chance to walk some distance on this old road and I would learn more about the historical footsteps that I was following. It had been this road that Andrew Jackson had traveled on when he came to visit the Bell farm. It once linked up with an old trace, a last remaining piece of the old Nashville to Clarksville road that now serves as nothing more than a lane for farm equipment. It was along this stretch of road that Jackson's wagon became mysteriously stuck on his way to the Bell farm and it was also here that Bill Eden encountered the strange hand on his arm many years later.

My own journey along this road would later take me back to the site of the Bell home and the cemetery where the bones of John Bell, several family members and some 30 slaves were laid to rest. It is an eerie roadway in some places and even on a bright and sunny afternoon, you can often understand why locals refer to some of the woods back here as being "haunted". I found one of the most unnerving places on the old Bell property to be the family cemetery. I can't really explain what bothered me about it so much, for it was not because it was a burial ground. There is just something about the forest on that part of the old farm that will leave you with little doubt that the stories of the Bell Witch are true! I was not surprised to learn that others who have come to this place have felt much the same that I did and still others claims to have encountered ghostly apparitions, and cold chills and have heard voices and sounds that cannot be explained.

After walking past the house and across the old road, we started down the gloomy pathway that would take us to the Bell Witch Cave. As mentioned earlier, the entrance to the cave is closed off by a locked, heavy steel gate. It is supposed to stop unauthorized visitors from entering the cave, which can be very dangerous, especially in the darkness. There are many sections of the cave that remain unexplored and this fact, along with the ghost stories, proves to be a real magnet for teenagers and curiosity seekers. Chris stated they always worry that someone will be hurt in there because the gate does not always stop the trespassers. They even had two break-ins within a few weeks of buying the property. In fact, the trespassing becomes so bad at certain times of year that the Kirby's have been forced to prosecute anyone caught inside of the cave at night.

And as it has been suggested that perhaps the gate is not always there to keep people out, but to keep something else inside? On afternoon in the late fall of 1977 (during Bill Eden's ownership of the cave), a group of people drove up from Nashville hoping to take a tour of the place. When they arrived on the property, they found that Eden was not home. Disappointed after having driven so far to get there, they decided that they would at least go down the bluff to have a look at the cave entrance before going home. The visitors hiked down the trail and then entered the mouth of the cave, walking back just far enough to peer into the shadows beyond the gate. As they stood there, one of the group commented that he could almost feel someone watching them from the darkness. Perhaps he was right, for a few moments later, the clear sound of a woman singing could be heard from inside of the cave! They later described it as a high pitched keening noise that was certainly an attempt at singing, although they could not distinguish the words. The group quickly left and climbed to the top of the bluff in about half the time that it took for them to come down!

Although I have since traveled the path a number of times over the years, I still remember my first descent down the bluff - and my first look at the cave entrance that I had heard so much about. I could imagine Betsy Bell and her friends having their picnics on the spot where I was now standing and I hoped that if I listened closely, I might hear the voice of the witch singing as the "cave explorers" of Betsy's day, and the trespassers of 1977, so eerily did. While I heard no supernatural sounds emanating from the cave that day, I was introduced to the strange incidents that Chris Kirby and her family had experienced since purchasing the property a few years before. The oddities had been weird and frightening enough that Chris told us that she had never been into the cave by herself - nor did she ever intend to come here alone!

One day, Chris and her dog were leading a tour of the cave for a group of visitors. She was just opening the steel gate that leads inside when she heard a strange sound - the same sort of sound described by Bill Eden and one of his tour groups years before. "It sounded like real raspy breathing sounds," she said, "like someone couldn't get their breath. It only lasted for a minute and then it was gone." Chris looked back to her tour group, but they were quietly talking amongst themselves and hadn't heard a thing.

The tour continued through the first room, down the narrow passage and into the second room. Here, as is the tradition in Bell Witch Cave Tours, Chris began telling stories of the witch, the haunting and strange incidents on the farm. As she was talking, the dog suddenly reacted to something that no one else could see. The hair on the animal's back stood up and she began showing her teeth and growling. The tour group asked what was wrong with the dog, but Chris had no idea. She was finally able to calm the dog down, but then the animal began whining and tucked her tail between her legs. She cowered back against Chris and at that same moment, the flashlight in Chris' hand suddenly went out!

" I guessed that it was just the battery at first," Chris remembered, "but then a lady's video camera stopped working too. We were all standing there in the dark and I'll tell you, I was ready to get out of there and everyone else was too!"

Chris also told us about the strange apparitions that she and visitors to the cave have reported. Some of these shapes are misty and fog-like, sometimes appearing in different parts of the cave, only to vanish when approached. She also recalled another type of image they had seen. "It looked like heat waves that come up over the highway in the summer time," she explained. "You can see them out of the corner of your eye and then they're gone."

One of the ongoing traditions (or legends, if you will) of the Bell Witch Cave involves the removal of any sort of artifact from the premises, be it rocks or anything else found inside of the cave. Some believe that perhaps the energy of the area is imbedded in some way within the actual makeup of the place and by removing a portion of the cave, you are inviting the phenomena that occurs here to travel with you. Others are not so scientific - they believe that the spirit of the witch will follow anyone who removes something from the cave!

It's likely that this tradition got started a number of years ago when the remains of a young Native American woman were discovered by men doing construction work on one of the local roads. Because it is well known that the former Bell farm contains a burial mound, it was requested that the bones of the Indian woman be entombed within the Bell Witch Cave. The remains were laid out in the first room of the cave in a shallow indention that was then lined with limestone slabs. Unfortunately, they did not remain there for long.

A short time later, trespassers into the cave made off with the bones, but according to local lore - not without a price! Gossip in the community has it that each of the persons who removed one of the relics suffered a series of misfortunes, accidents and injuries within days of the theft. For this reason, it has come to be believed that it is bad luck to remove anything at all from the cave. Over the last several years, I have received a number of accounts from people who claim to have taken away stones from the Bell Witch Cave, only to then experience not only bad luck, but strange happenings in their previous un-haunted homes! Chris Kirby has assured me that she has received a number of packages in the mail over the years that have contained rocks and stones that were removed from the cave. After getting them home, the folks who removed them began to suffer all sorts of problems and weird events. They believe that by mailing them back to the cave, they might alleviate their problems.

Even the Kirby's themselves have not been immune to the strange happenings! Candi Kirby can recall the time that she was exploring the cave one day and found a small and unusual looking rock, which she proceeded to slip into her pocket and take home. She knew that there was a story about bad luck occurring to anyone who removed something from the cave, but she didn't take it seriously. Just one week later though, the family's tobacco barn collapsed without warning, ruining a portion of their crop and doing expensive damage. Just a coincidence? Candi didn't think so and has taken no further chances by removing anything else from the cave.

I also spoke to a woman named Tara Kane, who visited the Bell Witch Cave back in 2000. She and her boyfriend, although warned about doing so, decided to take home a rock from the site during their visit. When they arrived home, they placed the rock on a shelf in their kitchen and thought little more about it until about a week later. On a Monday afternoon, Tara received a telephone call at work from her neighbor, insisting that she come home right away. When she arrived, she was greeted by the sight of fire trucks and emergency vehicles, as a small fire had broken out - in her kitchen! Luckily for her, the damage was minimal but strangely, the cause of the fire was never determined. She did, however, return the rock that she had taken from the cave on the next trip that she made to the area.

But not all of the peculiar events that have occurred involve accidents and mishaps. Some of the events are even stranger! Nancy Napier and her daughter Tammy visited the Bell Witch Cave and took with them the young daughter of a relative. While Nancy was touring the cave with Chris Kirby, Tammy and the little girl decided to stay outside until she returned. Tammy was sitting down and happened to look up and notice the child stuffing her pockets with rocks from around the mouth of the cave. Being well aware of the stories of bad luck being associated with objects being removed from the site, Tammy immediately turned the girl's pockets inside-out and not only dumped the rocks, but attempted to clean out all of the dust from her pockets as well. But was that enough?

After leaving the cave, Nancy and Tammy planned to drive back to their relative's house and spend the night. Even though they had just taken the same route to get to the Adams, they got lost trying to go back. They were willing to write this off to coincidence though and tried not to worry about the rocks. Then, while still in the car, Tammy's cellular phone rang with bad new from her boyfriend. The doctors had diagnosed him with a debilitating disease and had just made the pronouncement that they never expected his condition to improve. He wanted to call and tell Tammy the tragic news as soon as he heard it. Although it was expected, it still came as quite a shock to the Napier's now they had started to wonder if perhaps there was not more going on than just happenstance. But even after that, they did not really believe that unusual events were occurring until later that evening...

In the middle of the night, as both of them were sleeping and sharing a bed at their relative's home, the bed literally collapsed with no warning and for absolutely no reason! It simply fell, slamming to the floor and jarring both of them awake. When their relative came running in to see if everything all right, he couldn't explain what had happened either. There was nothing wrong with the bed and nothing was broken - it had just fallen to the floor.

Thankfully though, that was the last of the weird happenings for the Napier's. As Nancy told me later, "We left all of the rocks and the dust in Tennessee," she said, "and we certainly didn't want anything to follow us home!"

Since the late 1970's, the Bell Witch Cave has a destination point for ghost hunters, curiosity seekers and paranormal enthusiasts. In recent years, there have been a number of investigators who have attempted to document the supernatural events at the Bell Witch Cave but I don't think that any of them have done so with the same enthusiasm, or with the same chilling results, as Bob Schott. In 1997, Schott, a film and television producer with a company called Global Media Productions, became interested in the story of the Bell Witch and the hauntings at the old Bell farm. He contacted me about the stories and in perhaps working with him on a (now sadly defunct) series called *Adventures Beyond*, which specialized in intense paranormal phenomena. As it turned out, the Bell Witch Cave was featured on one of the only installments of the series, an episode called *America's Most Haunted*.

The format of Schott's series was different that most seen on television in that it was not a documentary with historical re-enactments but rather about paranormal investigations using the most advanced types of equipment and techniques available. For this particular installment, Schott and the investigative team (which I was lucky enough to be a member of) were equipped with high-tech temperature monitoring equipment, electro-magnetic field fluctuation detectors, military quality night vision equipment, infrared cameras, and a computer system that was capable of detecting any type of change in several different energy fields. As mentioned earlier, the computer system failed completely while it was set up at the mouth of the cave - something that had never happened before and has not happened since!

"I was looking for a place that was really haunted, really active," Schott reported. "I was familiar, of course, with the story of the Bell Witch and when Troy told me about the phenomena still be encountered on the property today - I knew this was the place."

During the investigation, we spent several days on the Kirby farm, exploring the cave, the sinkhole where Chris had photographed the strange energy, and even the cemetery where John Bell is buried. Our best results came during our late-night forays into the cave itself.

At one point, using two different infrared temperature probes, we picked up a sudden drop in the temperature of the cave. It was as if something very cold moved past us and then continued on through the cave passage. A photograph taken at that same moment was developed and revealed a glowing ball of light. The energy inside of the globe is so intense that it appears to be giving off light. Examinations by independent photography labs, including Kodak, revealed that the image in the photo was not a reflection, nor was it any artificial or natural part of the cave. They could offer no explanation for what it might have been.

In addition, we also had some interesting (and rather chilling) results using a video camera that had been fitted with a Generation III Night Vision lens, which was reportedly 5 times more sensitive than the equipment used by the U.S. Military during the Gulf War. The lens was so advanced that it had not been available on the civilian market until a short time before the investigation. It had been loaned to Schott by the manufacturer, a company that deals specifically with sensitive government and military contracts.

During the investigation, the camera and lens picked up what can only be described as a "doorway effect" that appears in the long passage between the first room and the second room in the cave. This "doorway" appears to be an array of light that crosses from one side of the passage to the other, lasting only a few seconds, and then vanishes. What is especially eerie about the effect is when it is watched frame by frame. As the light moves across and then back, two very distinct faces emerge from the "doorway", remain for a second or two, and then retreat back into the light array again!

I have never been able to explain what this "doorway" could be, nor what the images are in the light, other than faces of unknown origin. Not only have I been stumped, but so were the manufacturers of the night vision equipment, as well as independent labs and analysts.

One of Bob Schott's aggressive investigative techniques was to present whatever evidence he obtained to a skeptical, but fair, laboratory for analysis. "We knew that we had good evidence," Bob said, "but it really proves nothing unless we can stump the experts with it."

This is what he did with the film footage from the passageway. The company that made the equipment took a look at a copy of the film and were puzzled by what they saw. They, along with other film experts, ran the clip over and over and put it through all sorts of tests to determine if it had been hoaxed, or merely an accident of light that had created the "doorway effect" and the faces. In their final report on the footage, they stated that they had no explanation for the strange anomalies and that these images could only be paranormal in origin.

"This is some of the best evidence ever obtained for the existence of the supernatural," stated Schott. "We came to the Bell Witch Cave because we heard that it was haunted - I think that after this investigation, I can say with a lot of certainty that it is!"

- AFTERWORD -

No one in this day and age actually believes in ghosts, right?

Isn't that what makes this story so appealing? We are fascinated by the story of the Bell Witch because such things couldn't really happen, could they?

Of course, I write this final section to the book and pose questions like these to the reader in an attempt to leave something with you to think about after you close the book and place it upon your book shelf. A story such as this one could not be true, could it? In truth, I believe that many of the events that have appeared in these pages actually did occur, as the reader may have already discerned. I confess though that I have a hard time believing all of it. I think that too much time has passed and the original story has passed through too many hands for some of the details to have emerged from the passage of time unscathed.

But I do believe that *something* took place on the John Bell farm between 1817 and 1821 and I also believe that it was supernatural in origin. I also believe (and can tell you first hand) that strange things continue to happen on this land today. Can I say with absolute conviction that all of them are handiwork of the Bell Witch? Perhaps not, but trust me when I say that the supernatural is alive and flourishing in Robertson County, Tennessee!

But what about those readers who remain unconvinced?

There are many readers who do believe that ghosts are real and who have had their own strange experiences over the years. Like many of us, they have tried to explain them away, but cannot. These folks are quick to accept the possibility that ghosts, and perhaps even the Bell Witch, exist but many readers are not so open-minded.

Those who do not believe in ghosts say that spirits are merely the figments of our imagination. Ghost stories, these readers insist, are the creations of fools, drunkards and folklorists. Such a reader will most likely finish this book and will still be unable to consider the idea that ghosts might exist. In that case, I can only hope to entertain this person with the history and horrific tale of the infamous Bell Witch.

If you are such a person though, I hope that you will not be too quick to assume that you have all of the answers. Can you really say for sure that ghosts aren't real? Can you know for a fact that the Bell Witch never plagued the people of Robertson County, Tennessee? These are questions that you should ask yourself, but not from the comfort of your home, but perhaps while standing at the mouth of the Bell Witch Cave? Or perhaps from the ghostly woods near the grave that marks the resting place of old John Bell?

Is that moaning wail that you hear really just the wind whispering in your ear, or could it be the voices of old Kate, still crying out from another time?

Is that merely a patch of fog that you see rising up from the river bottoms, or could it be one of the apparitions that are often reported around the mouth of the cave?

Are those lights in the distance merely the reflection of passing cars on the distant highway, or are they the mysterious ghost lights that have been reported for decades?

Is that rustling in the leaves really just a passing breeze, or is it the ominous sound of footsteps coming up behind you?

If you suddenly turn to look, then you might realize that, despite the fact that there is no living person around you, you just might not be alone! Perhaps you are not as sure as you thought you were about the existence of ghosts. Perhaps the Bell Witch is not simply a part of the fanciful lore of the region after all. Perhaps no one person among us has all of the answers....

Remember that there are stranger things, to paraphrase the poet, than are dreamt of in our philosophies. Some of these strange things are lurking just around the corner, in the dark shadows of a little town in Tennessee.

Sleep well and of course, pleasant dreams.

Tammy Napier and the child who collected the "cursed" rocks peer down the path towards the Bell Witch Cave. A sign warns them to "Enter at Own Risk"!

- SELECT BIBLIOGRAPHY & RECOMMENDED READING -

Bell, Charles Bailey ~ A Mysterious Spirit: The Bell Witch of Tennessee (1934)

Bell, Richard Williams ~ Our Family Troubles (Published 1894)
This title, which can be found inside of Martin Ingram's History on the Bell Witch is the only real first hand account of the case, aside from interviews with Betsy Bell in the book by her descendant, Charles Bailey Bell. It is a must read book if you can find a copy.

Bingham, Joan & Dolores Riccio ~ More Haunted Houses (1991)
Brehm, H.C. ~ Echoes of the Bell Witch in the Twentieth Century (1979)
This is an odd little booklet that must have been privately printed in 1979. I don't have much information about it but it is a great resource for history and lore about the Bill Eden days at the Bell Witch Cave.

Carrington, Hereward & Nandor Fodor ~ Haunted People (1951)
Clarke, Ida Clyde ~ Men Who Wouldn't Stay Dead (1945)
Coleman, Christopher ~ Strange Tales of the Dark & Bloody Ground (1998)
Cook, Jack ~ *Spirit of the Red River* (Unpublished 1992)
I hope that this author manages to get his writings about the Witch published at some point! This is an indispensable internet document about the history of the Bell family. The author has done some tireless research into the old records and his work will make an amazing book someday!

Fitzhugh, Pat ~ Bell Witch Haunting (1999)
I am including Pat's book as "recommended reading" for anyone with an interest in the case. In truth, I did not read his book until after I had completed the new edition that you hold in your hands because I wanted to be sure that I was not influenced by it in any way. After reading it, I encourage you to hunt down a copy! In addition to his writing and unflagging interest in the case, Pat also runs the Bell Witch Historical Society, the Bell Witch website (www.bellwitch.org) and organizes the annual Kate Fest celebration in Adams each September.

Gay, William ~ *Queen of the Haunted Dell* (*Oxford* Magazine - October 2000)
Ghosts of the Prairie Magazine & Website (www.prairieghosts.com)
Goodspeed's History of Tennessee (1886)

Guiley, Rosemary Ellen - Encyclopedia of Ghosts & Spirits (2000)
Hauck, Dennis William - Haunted Places: National Directory (1996)
Ingram, M.V. - An Authenticated History of the Famous Bell Witch (1894)
Miller, Harriet Parks - The Bell Witch of Middle Tennessee (1930)
Price, Charles Edwin- Haunted Tennessee (1995)
Price, Charles Edwin - Infamous Bell Witch of Tennessee (1994)
Smith, Susy - Ghosts Around the House (1970)
Smith, Susy - Prominent American Ghosts (1967)
Somerlott, Robert - Here, Mr. Splitfoot: Exploration into Modern Occultism (1972)
Schott, Bob (Global Media Productions) America's Most Haunted (1998)
Steiger, Brad - Strange Guests (1966)
Tackaberry, Andrew- Famous Ghosts, Phantoms and Poltergeists for the Millions (1967)
Wilson, Colin - Mammoth Book of the Supernatural (1991)

Winer, Richard & Nancy Osborn - Haunted Houses (1979)
This book is a classic and is sadly out of print. It provided not only one of my earliest accounts of the Bell Witch but also introduced me to the Bell Witch Cave for the first time. The images that were presented in the book never stopped haunting me and eventually convinced me to put my own ideas about the story onto paper.

Personal Interviews and Correspondence

- ABOUT THE AUTHOR -

Troy Taylor is the author of 23 previous books about ghosts and hauntings in America, including HAUNTED ILLINOIS, SPIRITS OF THE CIVIL WAR, THE GHOST HUNTER'S GUIDEBOOK. He is also the editor of GHOSTS OF THE PRAIRIE Magazine, a travel guide to haunted places in America. A number of his articles have been published here and in other ghost-related publications.

Taylor is the president of the "American Ghost Society", a network of ghost hunters, which boasts more than 450 active members in the United States and Canada. The group collects stories of ghost sightings and haunted houses and uses investigative techniques to track down evidence of the supernatural. In addition, he also hosts a National Conference each year in conjunction with the group which usually attracts several hundred ghost enthusiasts from around the country.

Along with writing about ghosts, Taylor is also a public speaker on the subject and has spoken to well over 300 private and public groups on a variety of paranormal subjects. He has appeared in literally dozens of newspaper and magazine articles about ghosts and hauntings. He has also been fortunate enough to be interviewed over 300 times for radio and television broadcasts about the supernatural. He has also appeared in a number of documentary films like AMERICA'S MOST HAUNTED, BEYOND HUMAN SENSES, GHOST WATERS, NIGHT VISITORS and in one feature film, THE ST. FRANCISVILLE EXPERIMENT.

Born and raised in Illinois, Taylor has long had an affinity for "things that go bump in the night" and published his first book HAUNTED DECATUR in 1995. For six years, he was also the host of the popular, and award-winning, "Haunted Decatur" ghost tours of the city for which he sometimes still appears as a guest host. He also hosts the "History & Hauntings Tours" of Alton, Illinois and St. Charles, Missouri.

In 1996, Taylor married Amy Van Lear, the Managing Director of Whitechapel Press, and they currently reside in a restored 1850's bakery in Alton. In 2002, their daughter Margaret Opal was born and joined her siblings, Orrin and Anastasia.

ABOUT WHITECHAPEL PRODUCTIONS PRESS

Whitechapel Productions Press is a small press publisher, specializing in books about ghosts and hauntings. Since 1993, the company has been one of America's leading publishers of supernatural books. Located in Alton, Illinois, they also produce the "Ghosts of the Prairie" internet web page.

In addition to publishing books on history and hauntings, they also host and distribute the Haunted America Catalog, which features over 500 different books about ghosts and hauntings from authors all over the United States. A complete selection of these books can be browsed in person at the "History & Hauntings Book Co." Store in Alton.

Visit Whitechapel Productions Press on the internet and browse through our selection of over ghostly titles, plus information on ghosts and hauntings; haunted history; spirit photographs; information on ghost hunting and much more. Visit the internet web page at:

www.prairieghosts.com

Or visit the Haunted Book Co. in Person at:

515 East Third Street
Alton, Illinois t2002
(618)-456-1086

Printed in the United States
63043LVS00003B/59-86